This anthology contains a total of seventy-eight prose and poetry contributions from members of either FAW in Hobart or its branch, FAWNW (Fellowship of Australian Writers North West).

FAWNW has been operating for almost sixty years and its members are spread widely along the North West Coast of Tasmania and occasionally further afield.

Meetings are held monthly. Visitors are always welcome. See https://fawtasnorthwest.blogspot.com/

Contact: fawtas@y7mail.com for more details.

Published by:
FAWNW
c/o Allan Jamieson
P.O. Box 608
Burnie
Tasmania
Australia 7320

Cover design: Germancreative at Fiverr website

Ideas Are Like Rabbits

Collated and edited by Allan Jamieson

The 2021 anthology of FAWNW
(Federation of Australian Writers – North West branch)

"Ideas Are Like Rabbits. You get a couple and learn how to handle them and pretty soon, you have a dozen." - John Steinbeck

Table of Contents

Jack and Jill – What Really Happened
Ant Dry

Jack and Jill went up the hill to fetch a pail of water.

Well actually, only Jack went. He and Jill had had a huge fight over the pigs and who was supposed to clean out the sty. Jack had said that the pig didn't care how dirty he was. Jill said her mother didn't like pigs and since she was coming to visit, Jack had better bloody clean out the sty or else.

Jack muttered as he clomped up the hill.

'Hey diddle diddle', he thought to himself, 'always trouble at home.'

Today it was the pig sty, yesterday had been the cow. He'd been up in the hayloft practicing his fiddle. He was to play a solo in the Christmas pageant. The only soul in sight had been Ratty the cat, who had sat round eyed and suspicious as he had tried to wring some melody out of the old instrument.

Unbeknownst to Jack and the cat, the cow had escaped from the field and had snuck into the barn underneath them and had proceeded to gnaw away at a bag of corn Jill was specially keeping aside for her mother's visit.

Jill had stormed into the barn to tell Jack to 'shut up for Christ's sake, that bloody noise is killing me', when she saw the cow munching her corn.

She had absolutely flipped her lid.

She'd taken a break from her cooking to come and yell at Jack, and was still holding a dish of cake mixture and a spoon. In fury she had thrown both at the cow. The dish, being full of cake mix, was heavy and landed with a wet thump between the cow's eyes, spilling the mixture over its face, blinding it.

The spoon's leather strap became entangled with the cow's horn, and as the cow twitched its head up in surprise, the spoon swung around and clanged into the dish.

In sheer terror the cow had kicked and jumped and bucked and run around in circles until it broke through the door and sped away. As Jack and the cat stood, mouths agape, Jack with fiddle in hand, they watched as the cow disappeared into the distance, still bucking and jumping as the dish and spoon sounded out their rage and just as the moon started to put in its appearance on the horizon between the legs of the fleeing cow.

Somewhere in the middle of its rampage, the cow had trodden on Jill's little dog's foot, and the dog sat up and howled and hiccupped in pain.

Yes, yesterday had been quite a day.

Ah, well, better get the water.

Jack trudged up the hill to the well which was at the top. He'd never understood why they had put the well on the top of the hill and the house at the bottom. It seemed daft especially as the well was so deep. Maybe it had something to do with his old uncle who, when he had been the grand old duke of York had been fond of meaningless labour. Jack remembered tales of how his uncle had marched his troops all the way to the top of the hill and all the way down again, just for fun. He supposed the well was part of the same thinking.

As he arrived at the top of the hill, he heard his wife shouting again. Wearily he turned towards the noise. As usual, he couldn't hear a word. No matter where he was she always talked or shouted as if he were within earshot. He shrugged his shoulders and cupped his ears to indicate that he couldn't hear and turned back to the well.

One thing at a time.

He lowered the bucket bit by bit, looking over the edge to make sure there was nothing in the way. Slowly, slowly does it.

'What the hell are you up to, you lazy lout!'

Jack nearly jumped out of his skin, Jill had arrived, and she was steaming.

'I'm getting water…'

'I called you. I need you at the house.' She yelled, taking a swipe at him.

Jack ducked, fell down and smashed his head on the base of the well. Jill, not expecting him to have ducked, missed, overbalanced and fell over. In slow motion at first, but speeding up quickly, they tumbled down the hill together.

At the bottom, Jack jumped up, and in an attempt to escape his enraged wife, ran towards the house as fast as he could caper.

He ran inside, slammed the door, climbed under the kitchen table and sat there quivering.

There was a deathly silence for a long while.

Eventually, Jack crept to the window and peeped out. He saw Jill limping towards the house in tears.

'Jack' she called, 'I'm sorry.'

He opened the door and went out to help her. She fell into his arms sobbing.

They didn't have a lot of medical equipment, so later after he had wrapped up her swollen ankle in their one spare towel, Jill, in an attempt to stanch the blood, wrapped up his still bleeding head in vinegar and brown paper.

Where Magic Happens
Meg McLaren

Cassandra embodies the old order
        buried deep in folklore,
        where magic happens.
Where Faeries change into wind-tossed butterflies
        and an eagle soars with a prince in armour
        safe upon its great back.

Chromosomes, flow like patchwork,
stir up feelings from the Unknown.
A shadowy place filled with the ghosts
of those who came and went,
long before her journey to the planet.
Brave warriors of Erin,
lighting their fires on the Hill of Tara.
Fierce Highland soldiers
from across the broad, rough sea
that washes the trackless shores of Scotland.

In the frenzied, swirling storm,
        she remains fixed and steady,
        like a figure in a snow dome.
Within a tabernacle of light,
        her candle burns
        at the threshold of a sacred well.

This child of my heart draws comfort
from the wisdom of her kinfolk;
those distant people of the northern lights.
They will lead her through the labyrinth
to the rain-washed glens of Tomintoul,
to lie beneath a Michaelmas moon
alongside the 'black cattle' with far-reaching horns.
Hidden beneath craggy uplands clothed in purple
she will come to understand
that nothing is ever lost or forgotten.

Ode to a Stomach Bug
Brenda Slavoff

You're one of Nature's humblest forms,
And the lowest form of life!
A protozoan, microscopic
Gut pain like a knife;
The uninvited, uninviting
Thrill I'd do without,
I did not see you enter and
I cannot kick you out.

When did we meet, amoebic friend,
Was it that time I yawned?
Did you sneak in my breakfast,
On my cornflakes were you spawned?
I can't believe it was a kiss
So loaded up with germs -
(Suppose I should be grateful
That at least it wasn't worms?)

Your past is rich, you've travelled far,
You mighty, big Bacteria!
You've sat upon the backs of fleas,
And brought great armies to their knees,
You've walked with high
And stooped with low,
You've flown through sky
And slept in snow,
You've lived like kings, and yet you know
Your host rejoices when you go.

And now you've worn your welcome out
And worn me out as well,
I'll send you without blessing on
To someone else's hell!

Talk and Walk: You'll Live Longer
Allan Jamieson

It's funny how things turn out.

'Jim Johnston is my name and Jim Johnston is my game.'

A nonsensical sentence, yet talking out loud as I walked along, this was the sentence I most often heard myself saying.

You see, six months ago, I was convinced that something had to be done. I was overweight then – 85 kg – when, for all my adult life, I had rarely weighed anything over 75 kg. At 56 years of age, the extra 10 kg was bad news.

'Walk briskly for 30 minutes three times a week,' he had said. He was one of those fit young bastards who could do one-arm push-ups while us clapped-out old wrinklies stood, watched and lost count. 'And talk! How else will you know how hard to walk? You should just be on the point of being breathless when you talk and walk.'

Walking had always been a pleasurable pastime for me, but talking and walking was something new. What to talk about?

'Left, right, left, right'? 'One, two, three, four, …'?

After my first 30 minute talk and walk, I was reduced to babbling inanities. And so, 'Jim Johnston is my name and Jim Johnston is my game' became the recurring theme. I walked alone. Not surprising, given my new habit of talking meaningless drivel. Yet, it was important that I talk while walking; that fit young bloke had said so!

Short sentences! I was quickly breathless when I started to talk and walk. In one sense, things didn't get better, because I found myself walking faster or longer as I got fitter, thereby maintaining the breathless state.

I'd come to Melbourne for the Christmas holidays. Out of the house I was renting in an eastern suburb, I would walk along Murray Street, then turn up Wattle Avenue, along Bentleigh Grove then down Thomas Street. Along Murray Street again and so back home – around the block. Three kilometres in thirty minutes was my walking rate; after a meal and in the cool of the evening.

Three days ago, I was coming down Thomas Street for the fourth time in a bit over a week when I thought of the house up ahead, number 34. On my previous walk, two days before, I had caught a glimpse of a skeleton seated at a table. Would it still be there?

There was a high, thick cedar hedge at front. Just past the end of the hedge, a large pine tree stood. On the lawn behind the tree was a garden swing-seat. You know, one of those things with a canvas awning over a canvas bench seat which was suspended on bearings so you could sit and rock backwards and forwards under the shade of the awning. Anyway, this device blocked a view of the window and the only spot from which I could see in the window was at the very end of the hedge. A step either way and the hedge or the tree hid the window. On Tuesday, it was through this narrow gap that I had glanced into the room. Intent on my talk and walk then, I hadn't retraced my step for a second look.

I slowed now as I neared the spot again. Yes, the skeleton was still there, sitting with arm bones resting on the table, staring straight ahead. I wanted a better look. The front gate was open, inviting. I walked through and onto the lawn. The house was old; brick with a verandah and old-style sash windows. There were no curtains. If there was a blind, it was right up at the top of the window.

I stepped onto the verandah and stopped just at the side of the window. I peeped in. The finger bones were plain to see.

A hand grabbed my shoulder.

'WAAAHWAAH!!' I let out a wail.

'Don't look around! Look straight ahead.' A man spoke behind me. I stood still or, rather, my feet didn't move. I was shaking. The hand grip was firm. I dared to glance down and back towards my shoulder. Bones! It was the hand of a skeleton.

'Walk!' I was pushed towards the front door, which I saw was open.

'What's that smell? Oh, you've shat yourself. You're the first one that's done that. Messy!'

My trousers felt wet. Had I pissed myself as well? Half walking, half stumbling, I was steered inside the house by the Hand. I had to turn left and enter the room. The room was almost bare, save for a large, oblong dining table. Three skeletons sat at the table. There was one empty chair, at the remaining unoccupied side of the table and I was made to sit on the chair.

'Put your arms on the table.'

All the skeletons had their arms on the table.

The Hand was still on my shoulder. There was no mirror in the room but a painting hung on the wall opposite. It had a glass cover. I saw a white square, the reflection in the glass of the window behind me. I saw one dark shape – me – and a larger dark shape – the owner of the Hand. This shape was solid. This wasn't the reflection of a skeleton! I dared to take another glance at my shoulder. Ah hah – the Hand wore a black glove and white bones were painted on the fingers of the glove.

'What's going on here?' I asked, coming to my senses.

'Shut up. I ask the questions.' A bag came down over my head and body. I could see nothing. The weight of the Hand was lifted, but a rope or something came around my body, pinning my upper arms to my sides and pulling me against the back of the chair.

'I've got another one', I heard the Hand say from somewhere behind me. 'A full house, just like at our last place.'

A phone rang. 'Get that, Gina.' I heard footsteps walk past in front of me. The ringing stopped.

'Hullo', a female voice said.

'YEEIOOUWWYEEIOOUWW', I screamed.

The voice said, 'Oh, that – I just trod on the cat's tail. No, we don't want to give our opinions on anything.' I heard the phone being put down. 'Bloody opinion surveys! You would think the world had more important things to do. I'll get the axe.'

'No rush,' said the Hand from somewhere behind me. 'He ain't going anywhere. It's great that we got another one just now. I was beginning to get worried that time would run out.' And then, from just beside my ear, the Hand said, 'Ok, Jim Johnston, what is your game?'

This was my second moment of truth. I had fluffed the first, when I shat myself instead of breaking free and running out the gate. Would I fluff this one too? What to say? That my name wasn't Jim Johnston? That Jim and Johnston were just two words that had a rhythm about them, like name and game? That I had no 'game'? That I was alone in Melbourne and it would be at least a week before anyone made an inquiry about my whereabouts? Why say anything? Nothing in my head seemed to lead to an advantage for me. Far better stay silent.

'Come on. I heard you talking to yourself. "Jim Johnston is my name and Jim Johnston is my game".' The Hand followed up by giving me a cuff behind the ear. Might I not be better off talking? Another cuff behind the ear – harder! My ear throbbed. It might be bleeding. Yes, I was sure it was bleeding.

'I am a film producer. Making videos and films is my game. I'm on my way to do a scene now.'

'Is that so? What kind of movie is it?' The Hand sounded interested.

'Yes, it's a crime movie. We're going to shoot a scene tonight.'

'I don't believe you. A gangster movie? You? Scared shitless you are!'

'You've noticed.' Another cuff on the head.

The Hand's tone changed. 'No jokes either. I make the jokes and I ask the questions. How many persons in this scene of yours?'

'Just three actors, but it takes fifteen people to shoot the scene.'

'Whereabouts?'

'Murray Street.'

'What number?'

'It's on the street; a street scene.'

'Did you hear all that Gina? Go and check it out.' The door sounded shut behind and to my right. For a while there was silence then the Hand spoke.

'I've never heard of you. You're walking to the scene? I thought movie producers rode in Cadillacs and smoked cigars. I don't believe you. Soon Gina will come back to prove me right.'

He was right. And then a scaly, cold thing slithered over my left wrist and over my right arm. A snake! Petrified, I broke out in profuse sweat but I dared not flinch. Any arm movement might cause the snake to bite. I would have pissed myself, but I already had.

Fish! I smelled a fish smell. Could it be that the Hand was playing a joke, dragging a fish over my bare skin, to make me think it was a snake?

'Don't be fooled by stereotypes.' Somehow I got the words out in a hoarse whisper. 'Making movies is my business.' Another few moments of bluff, I thought.

No response. Silence. Then a patter, patter, scratch sound. What was that? A dog walking on the vinyl floor? A slobbering, licking, sniffing sound. Breathing at my ear. A big dog. A bloody big Doberman, I guessed. I am frightened of dogs – all dogs. I shouted 'Get away.' A low growl rolled around the room and through my head. There was a tug at the cloth covering my head. I tried to scream but no sound came out.

'Sit,' said the Hand from somewhere in front of me. A steady panting sound dominated the room. 'You'll get your fresh meat soon.'

The door opened. Gina had returned.

'There's a scene on Murray Street all right with cameras and people shouting instructions.'

The Hand spoke. For the first time, I detected a note of uncertainty. 'Johnston? They wouldn't shoot the scene without you. What's going on?'

Whatever Gina had seen, I had to run with it. It occurred to me that the Murray Street scene might have been a road accident. The cameras would have belonged to TV crews.

'Yes and no. We had worked out the scene, so the crew would be doing a few shots while they wait for me. I'll look at the tapes later and something good might come of it. You know, only about one percent of all the material we record ever gets in the final film, but you cannot predict which parts until everything has been recorded and viewed.'

I was warming to my game; 'We have to see the rushes, as we say. We –'

'Shut up.' Gina had spoken. 'I'm worried. We might have another Anita Daley on our hands. We had to move here because of her. It's a bloody miracle we weren't caught then and we've done another three in since then too. We can't afford to have the whole street turned upside down while they look for this bloke here. If two people disappear in the Bentleigh Grove area, the cops will do a house to house search this time, mark – my – word! Why'd you grab him? He doesn't look down and out. You might have guessed he was important.'

'Oh, you shut up too,' shouted the Hand. 'You're always wise after the event. You wanted the dog, remember? It's your dog. You feed it.   Johnston talks to himself – almost as if he was delirious – and he walks. His sandshoes have seen better days and he obviously doesn't buy new clothes for himself. He seemed worthless to me.'

Anita Daley. I dimly recalled how she had gone missing about six months ago and how, after a lot of searching, the police concluded she was last seen in Bentleigh Grove, but they found no sign of her.

'Don't shout at me,' Gina said with a raised pitch. 'All right, he's my dog but you were the one who hit on the idea of cheap meat. "We won't have to pay a cent", you said. Didn't you?'

'Well, it's worked so far and it's still working. And this is the better house of the two to be in. That old tramp sitting at the end of the table has done his bit. He fed the dog and now he has lured Johnston here.'

'I say you've picked the wrong body this time and we can't risk feeding him to the dog.'

The dog growled in my ear. Would it take things into its own control while its masters were squabbling?

'Then, get your dog off me!'

'Shit, we can't sort this out in front of Johnston,' said Gina. 'We'll have to make his death seem like an accident. And he can't be found near here.'

'But we don't have a car. How the hell do we get him away from here? If we cut him up so we can carry him it won't be an accident any longer when he's found.'

Gina said in a steady voice, 'Let's think about this. His body has to be found someplace else.'

The Hand must have come to my chair because he bent down, mouth near my ear and said 'All right, Mr Whizzbang Producer, invent a scenario that we can use to dispose of you "by an accident."'

Here was the moment of truth. Could I dream up a plot that took Gina and the Hand in and yet still allowed me to escape? For the first time since I walked through the open gate, my prospects had improved! They wouldn't kill me now until they knew and accepted my plan.

Someone turned on a TV in the house. I jumped at the sound. 'Turn off that TV! I can't think if there's a noise about. And I might have to ask you some questions for a change, if I'm to do what you want.' To my relief the TV was turned off. At least, Gina's mistake, in thinking she saw my scene being shot, wasn't going to be revealed on a newsbreak before I'd had a chance to think up a plan.

'And get the bloody dog out of this room, too.' Scratching and patter, patter sounds told me I was being listened to. Things had changed for the better! 'And, if there's a snake in this room then move it too.' No comment. I still didn't know if it was a snake or a fish. Then, from the next room, (the kitchen perhaps) I heard a faint voice, Gina's! 'What's he on about?' No answer. Well, that seemed to make clear it was a fish. That eliminates one option. Dying from snakebite was a plausible 'accident'. Right time of year too, with the warm weather bringing snakes out and about. Yet, I imagined snake poison was not too pleasant and hardly a nice way to go.

I really had to learn more about Gina and the Hand. There was an unusual dynamic between them. They must have a source of money, though the Hand's choice of dog food suggested otherwise. Did he do this to spite Gina? I would have to delve further into the mental side of my captors, though my physical predicament was taking precedence. The stale sweat from my brisk walk was one thing; the pong from my loose bowels was another thing altogether. I stank! I was miserable. So, first things first, I needed a bath and some clean clothes.

Gina spoke. 'You're awfully quiet. You can't sit here forever you know. You've got a job to do for us.' I had not heard her enter the room. Was she barefoot? Did this signify a person keen to keep her house clean? If so, the goings on here must have troubled her a great deal – time to test the water.

'I'm sorry, but I need a bath and a change of clothes,' I said. To justify this, I told her the story of the Czechoslovakian Foreign Minister who apparently fell from a window to his death in 1948, but who was quickly deemed to have been pushed out, murdered, after a trace of faeces was found on the windowsill.

'If I'm to die naturally, so to speak, it won't do for me to be soaking in my own shit', I observed.

Footsteps. 'I heard that,' said the Hand.

'Well, then, untie me and let me use your bathroom.'

Hands worked busily around me. Suddenly, my upper arms were free. I moved to take off the bag, but the Hand quickly stopped me. 'Not so fast. Stand up and move where I push you.'

After 10 or 15 paces, I was in another room. It was cooler and had a different smell to it. In one moment, the bag was lifted and a door shut behind me. It was dark. Had night fallen already? I groped and found a wall, then a switch. I was in the bathroom: Actually a combination bathroom and toilet, with only a very small window high up above the toilet. The only way out – alive – would be back through the door!

I took a long time. My ear still throbbed but it wasn't bleeding. If I say it myself, I smelled like a rose when I'd finished. I looked around the room, neat and clean – the hand of a woman. No clean clothes. I wrapped the towel around my midriff and opened the door. A light down the hallway showed the direction. I turned the corner, back into the room where I had spent an agonising hour. One chair was vacant. Was it the same one? It looked clean. Had Gina been at work while I was in the other room?

Speak of the devil! In she came. A blond, not too bad looking, about 30, I guessed. In came the dog too – a Doberman, in seconds, it had me bailed up in a corner. Gina spoke. 'Alex, come here now.' The dog backed off. She motioned to me. 'Sit down again.' Gina walked around the table. She had another bag. Should I have resisted? What would Alex have done then? I was cocooned again.

'You might as well burn my old clothes, but I would like some new trousers.'

'One thing at a time.' The Hand was standing behind me again. 'Your solution comes first.'

Yes, I thought, the solution to how I was to die *naturally*!

'So, let me get this straight! You've been feeding the dog on bodies of hapless tramps that have been enticed to enter your house and then killed. The dog is getting hungry again and I was to be his next tin of Pal, except, you now realise I will be missed – in fact, I will already have been missed – and suspicion will fall on this Bentleigh Grove area. As soon as the cops are notified, they'll be round here looking for a possible serial killer. So, I'm to be killed all right – no option given what I know – but it must not appear like a murder and my body must be found away from Bentleigh Grove. Unfortunately, you don't trust me enough to let me walk out of here and shoot myself and you don't have a car in which to transport me. I'm sure you have been through my pockets, so you know I'm skint! Finally, you've no idea how to solve this problem of yours and I am to be the brains trust for the deal.'

The Hand gave a soft laugh and said, 'You've been reading my mail.'

'You mystify me,' I said. 'Why string up bones into skeletons seated at tables? Why not let the dog have the bones? Why don't you have enough money for dog food? And what do you and Gina eat anyway? Why did ...'

'Too many questions. I told you before, I ask the questions here. You know too much already.'

'But knowing a bit more won't hurt and it might help me to understand how the three of us will work together – as surely we must. For instance, could you get a car? Can one of you drive? Would you allow me to drive?'

In a quiet voice, Gina said, 'John has a station wagon, but he can't know why we need it to go someplace.'

The Hand demanded, 'Who's John?'

Gina replied with an edge in her voice, 'John's my bloody brother!'

The Hand replied, 'Shut up! Alright, your brother is called John, but thousands of men are called John. Where do we take Johnston?'

Did I see a glimmer of hope? I wasn't born in Melbourne, but I'd spent some years here, off and on. I'd had an aunt – I assume she's dead by now – who had a beach house at Mt. Eliza, with a boatshed. I'd been there once, not long after I'd finished university. I know there's a section of coast down there called Canadian Bay. That might suffice. Mt. Eliza is a place of escape for wealthy Melbournians; I reckon my captors would be clueless of that area.

'If I'm to die, I'd like it to be at a nice place, not some rubbish tip or car wrecker's yard. Do you know the Mt. Eliza area by any chance?'

'What's so special? It's a long way from here!'

The Hand's voice had changed; was he excited by my potential value – implied when I mentioned Mt Eliza?

'Don't forget, we film producers get around and I know that area. I'm going to die, right, but you could at least arrange for me to die where the location will fit my character.'

'Maybe, but how do we get from here to there without a car chase and screaming sirens?'

'Do you have the money to pay for an Uber? Their drivers often go under the radar, if you know what I mean – no questions asked – safer than a taxi in this instance. You can explain that we're all friends; that I am about to be married and you're giving me the first taste of what life will be like from now on when I am no longer a free man. And, the place we're going to belongs to Gina's aunt.'

Silence! Was my scenario a bit too much to absorb all at once? It didn't surprise me that Gina was first to react. 'I'll need an address', she said. 'Just say it's near the end of Canadian Bay Road'. Was there such a road? I hoped so.

The Hand started to get his thoughts sorted out. 'What's to stop you telling the driver to go to the nearest police station?'

'Nothing – you'll have to trust me, but you can always laugh and tell the driver to ignore me. Mt Eliza is a good fare – he won't want to cut his drive short. And you can explain to me that the cops won't act to get me out of married life – so get used to it.'

'And, how am I to kill you?'

'That's your territory. You figure it out.'

Gina came to my aid. 'Yes, just get him away from here. We'll figure out a way when we get there.'

That agreed, the bag was lifted off my head. The Hand was not a very inspiring specimen of a male; unshaven and with long hair, he looked like he relied on his size not his brain. It has always puzzled me why seemingly intelligent women end up with dumb men. I was given a shirt and trousers that were a bit too large for me, but that was better than their being too small.

After the very harrowing time I'd spent in the room, the Uber ride was quite uneventful. The driver showed no interest in us; I preferred to go the whole way to the beach, where I had a plan I hoped would work, than take a chance and end up who knows where in a part of the city I didn't know; and there was a Canadian

Bay Road! Were the stars aligning for me? I thought I would help Gina. 'You said it was the last house on the left, didn't you?' Alert, Gina said, 'Yes, just stop there, driver.'

We left the Uber. The Hand and Gina each had hold of an arm of mine as we walked along the footpath in silence. It was dark, no moon, with only a distant street light for illumination. A walking track led towards the beach from where the road ended and I headed along this. The sound of the waves was close-by and we soon descended to the sand – all alone and in near enough to pitch darkness.

I turned deliberately to walk south along the beach, as if heading for a particular spot. I was no longer in their territory and their silence implied they were uncertain what to do next, waiting for a sign from me. 'Pity you're about to kill me; a night time swim would have been nice, eh!'

I wrenched my arms free and ran as fast as I could. The tide was on the way out, so the sand was flat and compact. I dove headfirst into the water and swam away from the beach, diving under the surface as soon as I could to avoid the sound of my arms breaking the water. I turned to the north and kept swimming in the hope of confusing my captors. The months spent talking and walking had paid off in terms of my fitness! Cautiously, I let my head break the surface.

'I can't swim, I told you. Let go of me!' It was Gina. What was the Hand doing? 'Shut up and help me. He's gone in this direction.'

I went underwater again and headed further out to sea, breaking the surface as quietly as I could to regain my breath, before diving again. After several more underwater exertions, I resurfaced and listened. It was hard to judge how far I had come, but it was quiet – no voices.

I swam leisurely and quietly, parallel to the beach and towards the north. I guessed I had to get around the next headland and well along the next beach, at least, before I might be able to go ashore safely. There was a structure on the headland – hard to see in detail in the darkness (a yacht club, perhaps). I don't know how much further I swam, 400~500 metres perhaps, then I turned towards the shore. No sign or sound of anyone. There were some moderately tall trees behind the beach, so I headed among these to spend the night.

Dawn! I was very hungry, with no money, but I was still alive. Getting back to my rental house would probably take all day. I walked away from the beach until I reached a main road heading north and started thumbing for a lift into Melbourne. I chose not to talk and walk – that had got me into heaps of trouble!

===//===

'And that's what I can recall, Inspector. I'll sign under the statement once you have typed it up.'

The Amazing Anniversary of Lieutenant Arthur Long

Lesley Podmore

We've lately had a 'versary
A hundred year one too,
For a brave and gallant airman,
Who across Bass Strait he flew.

The first world war had finished,
And by boat he brought his plane,
All placed in packing cases,
To assemble here again.

Childhood was spent near Hobart Town,
In a farming community,
But this famous flight of his began
From far north-west --- Stanley.

December 16 was the date,
The year 1919,
When intrepid Arthur
Prepared his small machine.

None had made this flight before.
Bass Strait was rough and wide,
But Arthur knew he was the one
To first reach the other side.

Now word had got about
In this locality,
And many people came
The hero for to see.

They marveled at the wooden plane
About to take to air,
And saw that Arthur was
Innovative, debonair,

Was dressed in many layers
With goggles, mitts, thick socks,
And had a gallant friend
To pull away the chocks.

He'd had a willing local lad
To sleep beneath the plane
To keep away the nosey ones,
E'en though 'twas pouring rain.

Now Arthur knew this plane quite well,
He knew its need for oil.
He'd tied the extra can he'd need
On seat with thick rope coil.

The weather cleared around the dawn.
He checked his petrol --- on!
With propeller swung by trusty friend
He soon would be long gone.

But wait!! Across the paddock came
A man with special gift –
A lifebuoy for young Arthur
In case he needed it.

At last the plane began to move;
The engine was quite loud.
The plane was up and heading off.
A cheer came from the crowd.

Arthur Long was flying now
Away from Tassie's shore.
He knew he'd reach his target
In several hours or more.

He flew quite near King Island.
No doubt gave them a wave,
Then veered right for Victoria
To avoid a watery grave.

He flew near Airey's Inlet
Upon Victoria's shore.
Put down upon a grassy field
With engine all a-roar.

He'd tried to top the oil up
While flying in the air.
But the rope had snapped!!
Oh dear! – Oh drat!! – beyond repair!!!

Thank goodness that he'd reached the shore.
His oil was all but gone.
He filled it up with engine on,
And then flew further on.

At last he sighted Melbourne.
Did circles all around.
And landed near the city's port,
Firm on solid ground.

No-one expected Arthur,
He'd snuck up like a ghost.
He was just glad he'd made it.
He'd flown from coast to coast!!

Young Arthur liked the place he saw.
He had an uncle here,
And made his home Victoria,
For many a long year.

****

And so a century has passed,
And gathered on that hill,
A crowd viewed model plane and plaque,
Wrought by some locals' skill.

We listened to some speeches
From parliamentarian and mayor,
A lad from Stanley school as well,
And Arthur's son was there.

People came from far and near.
Arthur now has acclaim.
We lauded him, and clapped and cheered,
And we're all glad he came.

Our museum has this story now,
To help us all remember
Brave Arthur Long, some others too,
2019 in December.

As a Bird Sees It
Dawn Meredith

Do it! The voice in my head said. Go on. This is your moment.
You've always wanted to do this!

Did I really?

My heart was pounding painfully, my breathing shallow.
Crouched on a seat in a small plane, wearing a jumpsuit, the roar of
the single engine making conversation impossible. This is what I
had always wanted?

Be daring. Totally mad! The voice continued eagerly. Just
think how surprised the family will be – the looks on their faces –
priceless! They think they know you, but show them who you
really are. An adventurer.

Even at my age? What if something goes horribly wrong?
My stomach lurched at the thought. I looked across at my
instructor; twenty-something Josh, who sat calmly texting, his legs
apart. Big sturdy boots, broad shoulders, khaki trousers, tee shirt,
cropped hair – Army?

I pictured my mangled corpse from above – a jumbled
inhuman creature sprawled on a green meadow, cows lumbering
over to inspect this strange new being.

Movement caught my eye. Josh was giving me the thumbs
up and grinning. Then suddenly, the door slid back and there was
nothing but blue. No buildings, no safe, groundy stuff. Just blue
nothingness. So wide…

I gulped down my fear.

You can do this! You've always wanted to do this. Harry
would be so proud.

Would he really?

An image of my husband flashed into my mind – his white,
white face resting on the satin pillow, eyes closed. Fifty-two years.
He was like my arm or leg. Or my heart. A part of me ripped
away, gone. I had spent five years trying to grow back another
heart.

Then another image flashed. Tilly, my favourite
granddaughter, (although you shouldn't have favourites, of course).
In what kind of world was she growing up? Would she be inspired
by her grandmother's reckless act?

It's time. Let's go, dammit!

That damn voice was bossy. My body moved numbly, disconnectedly towards the open door. I felt Josh behind me, clipping me to the harness on his broad chest. I stared at the blue nothingness in front of me and shivered violently. The wind rushed by the open door like the WHOOSH after a hurtling freight train. We inched forward.

That's it. Nearly there. This is going to be so fantastic! Enjoy it. It'll be over so quickly.

My hands clutched the door frame. Old, speckled hands with bright red nails. How did I get this old? Josh gently took them, gave a squeeze then placed them crossed over my chest. He hoisted me up until my feet dangled. The cold air shoved at my face, like a bad-breathed stranger, repelling me.

And then we fell out.

My scream sounded like a rusty tap as the wind invaded my mouth. I screwed my eyes shut, tasting only dread.

We were falling.

FALLING!

Whose stupid idea was this?

Hang on, I thought angrily. It wasn't me who dreamt of this, to prove the family wrong. It was bloody Harry!

My tears squeezed out and my chest heaved with a sob. Behind me, like a giant Siamese twin, Josh's body was warm and strong, enveloping my frail old-lady-ness.

Stupid! That's what you are, I told myself. Ridiculous. Foolish! Look at what you're doing, woman!

A rough jerk and we were yanked upwards. The wind softened. We were floating.

I opened my eyes.

And saw my world as a bird sees it. Soaring over the domed Earth, green and brown and golden below, white tufts all around me in the delicious blue. My arms flew from my sides and my chest filled with it.

Absolute joy.

Maybe it was my dream after all.

Was Lydia Dead?
Lesley Podmore

Lydia had started the day early, as usual every Tuesday, and taken her grandson to school. She had been very tired of late, and decided to sit on the park bench by the duck pond on the way home.

Her old bones ached, and she must have drifted off for a while.

When she came to, she stretched herself, easily this time. The sun had taken on a gentler hue. The water seemed golden, and there, just across the pond, was a beautiful white summerhouse. Funny she'd never noticed it before. 'I'll go and investigate,' she thought.

The walk was easy. Nearing her car she noticed her son and a policeman peering in, scratching their heads, and wondering about spare keys. 'That's odd,' she thought; 'they just have to ask me - but I'll go to the summerhouse first.'

A few more steps along the path she was greeted by her beloved dog Jasper. He came running with delight to greet her. 'Oh you wonderful boy. The last time I saw you, you were old and arthritic. Look at you now!! Come on, let's have a look up here.'

Lydia began to feel a wonderful warmth imbuing her body. She was happy. 'Well here is the summerhouse, Jasper.'

Beaming smiles and loving arms greeted her: her father and little sister.

'Oh! Where have you been for so long?' she cried. Lydia couldn't remember how long ago it was that they had all been together. This was nice.

'You've come to join us,' they said. 'It's wonderful here.'

The Conversation at the Bar
Ant Dry

The two men sat facing each other at the bar in Frankfurt airport.

'You enjoyed yourself last night,' started the white man.

The black man smiled.

'Eesh, Smith, those women……'

Smith smiled tightly.

The black man reached into the pocket of his jacket and pulled out a bill. It had 'Five Roses Nightclub' written on it and the value of Euro 100 printed in the corner.

'I didn't use it all, my friend. I'll keep this for next time.'

'Right. Next time. So what happens now?' asked the white man.

The black man shrugged.

Smith persevered. 'We found him. He confirmed everything. His lawyers confirmed everything. "You know we weren't lying. We know we didn't lose your money. Fidelis did."'

The black man blew on the froth on his beer and sighed heavily.

'You worry too much, Smith. Eesh. Those women last night. Did you see what she did with that beer bottle? Did you see that one with the red scarf on? Ow, but they were very beautiful. Too beautiful to waste on these stupid Germans.' And he laughed, his huge belly wobbling, loosening his shirt so that Smith was treated to a glimpse of a hairy belly button.

Smith sipped his beer.

'Mr. Makadza, what happens now?'

'It is not for me to decide.'

'We found him. He acknowledged he'd lost your money.'

Makadza tipped his head back in in three gulps, finished his beer.

'I'll have another.'

Smith called the barman over and paid for the drink.

'I need to buy some things for my wife.'

'How much?'

'Two hundred should be enough.'

Smith handed over the cash.

Three more swallows and Makadza waddled away. He was back in twenty minutes, panting from exertion, his bag bulging with cigars, the big fat Cuban ones.

'I'll have another.'

Smith pulled out his wallet and called over the barman.

'Mr. Makadza, I need to know what is the next step here. I have people who need to know. We have decisions to make.'

'I shall report to the Minister.'

'What will you tell him?'

Makadza gulped his beer and belched loudly. He laughed.

'What was the name of that woman, the one with the red scarf?'

'Mr. Makadza, I don't remember any of their names. They were just girls at the night club.'

'Aaah, but she was a beautiful one. Big breasts.' He held out his hands as if grasping oversized beasts, and he laughed. 'Yes, she was a beautiful woman.'

Smith ordered himself a Scotch. The beer wasn't working.

'Mr. Makadza. You made the payment to Fidelis direct. You chose to do that. If you had paid us as we suggested, we would have held the money until we had the vehicles. You paid him directly. We have been to see him and we have seen his lawyers. Fidelis has taken your money and he has gone broke. It's not our fault. It's Fidelis's fault.'

Makadza looked at Smith.

'You worry too much.'

'I don't think so. We're talking about Euro 700,000. You were there with me when the Minster told me I was personally responsible for the full amount. Me. Personally. It's a lot of money. I don't have anything like that sort of money. The company doesn't have anything like that. I need to know what you are going to tell the Minister.'

The hostess behind the desk announced that their plane was starting to board. 'First class passengers please go to the front,' She purred.

Makadza looked at the hostess in admiration.

'She is also very beautiful. These German women are all beautiful. I must go. We shall talk when we get to Harare. You coming?'

He stood to queue with the First Class passengers.

Smith remained seated. 'No, not now. I'll see you later. Economy always boards later.'

Free speech
Anne Layton-Bennett

choose your words with care,
speak them with caution
simplicity is best
so no-one can misconstrue
their meaning
or baste them
in deception -
blacken them
and roast them in the
conceited ovens of
your regime

© 2020 Anne Layton-Bennett

Not For Sale
Meg McLaren

After Alice died, he never went out on the river again. Never scrambled down steep banks, covered in bracken, to board the small boat sheltered in a calm inlet where the water rested. It was a grand little boat. Big enough for two and a couple of rods, some bait and an ancient tobacco tin filled with lures. 'Don't forget me!' Champ seemed to say as he barked sharply, squeezing in between the tangle. They would cast off at dawn and drift through the shadows watching as the sun kissed the cold earth.

'I must say I enjoy life,' she said once, while placidly sipping from a flask of tea. 'For instance, what could be nicer than this?' Champ, with his paw on her leg, stared from one to the other with a warm, loving look. 'We shouldn't think of unpleasant things.'

She was from Corfu. Her great dark eyes and olive skin bringing to mind thoughts of two wineglasses and an empty bottle of Moselle, a plate with crumbs of Feta and some uneaten olives. And he felt that even if he gazed at her all day he could not love her more.

That Saturday the wind came up from the night-black river. Red gums groaning and creaking, weaving in a wild dance. He thought she should have been home by now. Then he saw her driving down the bumpy, uncomfortable, pathway to the house, waving. She didn't know she would never again stretch against tossed pillows, turning to hold his face to hers. Never again pull on that cobalt blouse that enriched the colour of her eyes or drop onto the sofa, kicking off her shoes. He heard the branch crack. It was loud, louder than the wind. Champ moaned and they stood helpless looking out of the window at all the things of autumn.

The room is now washed in white, the walls displaying paintings of the rugged landscape that surrounds him. A coffee table and brightly upholstered sofa nestles in front of the fireplace. There is a box by the fire of dried applewood, gathered when the orchard trees were pruned. A car slows to a halt on the windswept road. Strapped to its roof he can see a fishing rod. A man, ruddy faced, grey beanie pulled down over his ears, looks out at the boat, shrugs his shoulders and moves on.

He sits at the window, stroking Champ's head, a light and frothing Boags in his hand. The sunshine feels cold. He can see the boat standing high on a wooden frame near a bank covered with a forest of plants. The beam of the sun lights up a notice, painted in white, on a square piece of timber - NOT FOR SALE. He remembers those vanished days, his mind circling like the memory rings on a red gum, and he sighs.

'Why? Why? Why?'

Bovine Insomnia
Pete Stratford

Straggling out of their tour coach, the visitors were greeted by a sun bronzed fellow to guide them around the dairy on a large property in North-West Tasmania.

Almost immediately some began clicking away, capturing any object or creature that moved or moo-ed, to enthral those back home when they returned to tell of their travels.

Beginning his spiel, their guide explained the operating procedure of a large automated dairy to those who listened, while others were distracted by the 'lovely baby calves and haven't they got beautiful eyelashes?' Click-click-click, to ensure those back home get to see the beautiful eyelashes.

Then moving on into the automated milking area where cows appear oblivious of the people as they randomly amble in through electronically controlled gates to placidly stand on a platform while robotic machinery washes their teats, applies the milking cups, then removes them once all the milk has been extracted. Meanwhile another device has read the collar tag and has provided each animal with a nutritious snack commensurate to the amount of milk it has produced. This all fascinated some of the visitors though a few thought it was 'un-natural' however it's a safe bet they will continue to purchase milk, yoghurt, cheese, etc. from their local shop giving no thought to where it came from originally.

Noticing that unlike the calves, all of the cows were missing the long hairy swishy portion off their tails, someone asks why this is so.

'Well' says the guide 'it's all to do with this Daylight Saving Time and the effect that has on pasture growth. Any gardeners amongst you will know how the sunshine creates growth in plants and pasture growth is also given a boost by that extra hour of sunshine. That new growth tends to be softer and juicier than the rest and the cows really like it so eat more of it, but unfortunately this has an adverse effect on their digestive system and causes their ... er ... excrement to be rather fluid, shall we say? I've always thought it to be a design fault but you may notice that a cow's tail hangs immediately in front of their ... ah ... ah ... orifice from which that is ejected. Because of the tail's placement there, it gets frequently coated with that by-product which dries quickly in the sun, layer upon layer gradually producing a huge ball of sh ... ah ... excrement. This, of course, becomes very heavy indeed until eventually that weight on their tail pulls tightly on the skin along the cows back. In severe cases this tension on the skin goes all along the backbone up the neck and on down the forehead pulling the top eyelids up until the poor animal is unable to shut its eyes to sleep at night.

We call this condition Bovine Insomnia, which naturally is a cause of considerable discomfort to the cow and also impacts on the profitability of the farm. As you will appreciate, if a cow has no sleep then it has less inclination to feed which in turn equals less milk production.

So we dock their tails as a preventative measure against this terrible condition of Bovine Insomnia. Thank you for asking that question, as I'm sure that many people are quite unaware of our great concern for the comfort and welfare of our animals.

You ask why haven't the bulls had their tails docked? Well, the truth is that they're so exhausted each night that they're able to sleep with their eyes open!'

Gate (West Coast, Tasmania)
Graeme Hetherington

Perched on our rusting iron gate
Strung side to side with wire, I'd play,
In combination with the wind,

Tunes on it with my heels and wait
For granddad who lived close to us
To pause on his way home from work

To lift me higher, give a hug
My parents never ever did.
He'd put me back to sit astride

And win the Melbourne Cup or use
It as a stage, preparing to
Orate like him at Lodge, become

Prime Minister one day because
John Curtin was his god. Though it
Was strong enough to take my weight,

It dragged and bumped, and I if caught
Performing there by my turncoat,
Working-class, Menzies-obsessed dad

Who loathed pop's politics and said,
Cutting his ear while barbering,
That now he'd be deaf to such rot,

Risked bed without tea, gatings, all,
With hindsight, worth it on behalf
Of serving an apprenticeship

With poetry through music made
In otherwise unhappy times,
Enthroned and looking out for love.

Mr Twigg
(A picture book text)
Dawn Meredith

In Tulip street, at number four, lives Mr Twigg.
His tiny, red brick house is nestled among bright flowers.
Mr Twigg has short wavy hair and a springy step.
Each day he walks to the corner shop with his little black dog called Velvet.
Before he sets off he brings in the bottle of milk left at the doorstep by the milkman.
Mr Twigg clips on Velvet's lead and off they go
to buy bread and a newspaper.
Mr Twigg sometimes buys cheese too, because that's Velvet's favourite.

On his way to the shop Mr Twigg passes number eight,
where Mr and Mrs Buckle live.
They like to read a lot.
They sit in the sun and read. Hello!
They read the newspaper, they read the TV guide, they read books,
They read letters and they read labels.
There's always a lot to read and it's fun.

Mr Twigg passes number sixteen, where Mary Beetlestone lives.
Mary likes to play tennis, but she's getting a bit old.
She sets off down the street in her white tennis outfit and racquet.
Mary lives with her two Red Setter dogs, Charlie and Wolfie.
Sometimes she plays with them in her front garden.
Sometimes Charlie and Wolfie dig a hole to bury something.
And sometimes they dig a hole to escape the garden and wander the street happily.

Mr Twigg passes number twenty.
Mrs Box has a lolly shop here and lives upstairs in a little flat with Mr Box.
Mr Box is ill and Mrs Box looks after him.
In her shop Mrs Box sells lollies of all colours and shapes. Yum!

But Mrs Box gets angry when children try to steal lollies from her shop.
She chases them out with a broom.

Mr Twigg passes number twenty three, where the Geer family live.
The Geers have a special cat called Buttons.
Buttons loves to chew off buttons, from coats, shirts, dresses and blouses.
Naughty Buttons!
He chews and chews until the button drops off and then he finds the next one to chew.
Mr Geer is always sitting on the front porch sewing them on again.

Mr Twigg passes number twenty six, where Mr Hadfield lives.
He came to visit his daughter, Emily, and never went home again.
Mr Hadfield grows lots of tomatoes in the back garden.
He is a nice man and gives away all the extra tomatoes to his neighbours.
He likes to be helpful.
He also has a rooster called Morris, who crows at anyone walking past the garden.
Mr Twigg waves to Mr Hadfield. And he waves to Morris too.

Mr Twigg passes number twenty seven, where Mr Barnes lives.
Mr Barnes has lots of pear trees.
But Mr Barnes doesn't give any of his extra pears away.
He's grumpy! He shouts at the birds for pecking at his fruit.
He shouts at the children walking past on their way to school.
And he shakes his fist whenever the train toots coming into the local station.
Mr Barnes isn't very happy at all.

Mr Twigg passes number thirty one, where Julia lives with her family.
Her brother, Malcolm, likes motorbikes.
Her mother is a hairdresser and her father is a tailor.
Sometimes Julia plays with her best friend, Shirley, in the back yard.
And she likes to dress up her ginger cat, Topsy, in doll's clothes.
Julia likes to swing on the gate and watch people walk past.
Mr Twigg and Velvet always stop for a chat.

Mr Twigg passes the wool shop, the post office, run by Mr Buggs,
Then the laundromat and the iron mongers.
And the hairdressers where Julia's mother works.
He waves to the ladies getting their hair done.
The bell above the door rings as he enters the corner shop.
He greets Mrs Thompson, buys his newspaper and bread.
And of course, a treat for Velvet.
Then Mr Twigg sets off home again.

Tulip Street is a quiet road, with hardly any cars or traffic.
There are lots of beautiful gardens to admire
And people to chat to.
Mr Twigg arrives back home, puts the kettle on to boil
And makes the tea, then settles down to read the paper.
And Velvet rushes to his basket with his treat.

Mountain Rescue
Graeme Bourke

It was around lunchtime when a car came down our driveway, it was a police car. Father and I watched the four-wheel drive plough through the unblemished snow in the driveway, its uniformity and the gently sloping whiteness marred by deep furrows and tinges of red as the mud splattered up on the snow, defacing it, and destroying its purity. We knew who it was, Constable Ryan from Bothwell. Father went out to meet him.

I heard the car stop, and the sound of their voices. They didn't talk for long when I heard the car start up and father returned to the warmth of the kitchen.

'It seems two hunters are missing on the other side of Ouse River. The constable wants us to give them a hand to try and find them. He is going to meet us at the road where the Ouse and the canal meet.'

There was never any question if we would go, or who would go, at times like this when someone was in trouble, we knew what we had to do. It was sheer luck that we had the float and the four-wheel drive. We would be able to take the horses with us.

At eighteen I had trapped, hunted and fished in the central highlands since I was old enough to walk, I knew the country, knew how to handle the conditions. Father and I had been out searching for lost walkers, hunters and fishermen many times before.

'How long have they been missing?' I asked.

'They were supposed to return last night. Their families called the police this morning and informed them that they hadn't arrived home. Luckily, they knew which area they were hunting in, so that will help narrow the search,' said Father, slipping on his hooded parka.

'If they managed to survive last night's snow storm they won't see through another night if they are out in the open.'

'That's why we need to take the horses, the river will probably be flooded and we can cover a lot more ground than if we were walking. I'll get the horses loaded up while you gather up some warm clothes and some food and drink. Might pay to grab a couple of blankets off the spare beds, we might need them.'

Nothing more was said as I busied myself gathering what we needed while Mother made up two thermos bottles of hot coffee and some sandwiches. She came to the barn helping me to carry everything and stow it in the back seat. Father had hooked the float on and loaded the horses. The engine was running, and a stream of hot-misty air was blowing from the tailpipe.

'You two be careful now, no heroics,' she said as she hugged me and gave me a kiss on the cheek. She gave father a hug.

'Don't worry about us,' said Father, 'we'll be alright, but we might be late getting back as we will search until dark.'

Mother stayed in the yard watching us leave. She waved to us and never moved until eventually she disappeared behind a wall of snow that was driving itself over the land once again.

It was a slow drive around the southern end of the lake as the road was quite slippery, we were running in four-wheel drive Hi as the weight of the float had been pushing us around when we were in two-wheel drive. There was a risk that it might have rammed us off the road which would have done no one any good. We left the cover of the forest and felt the buffeting wind as we drove out into the open moor of heath, rock, and snow. There was no protection here from the wind, it had swept across miles of barren plain, unheeded and unimpaired as it gathered to unleash the full force of the cold air that had been driven up from Antarctica. I hoped that the hunters were experienced enough to find some sort of shelter, any shelter.

After crossing the canal which was full of rushing, dark-blue water, we turned left off the main road leaving behind the small cluster of green-painted iron sheds known as Liawenee. These huts were where the fisheries people stayed when they were in the highlands. We followed the channels in the snow made by the police vehicle that had gone on ahead of us. The snow was by now almost eight or ten inches deep on the road.

The road wound its way along beside the canal. The speeding ice-blue water was a magnet to my eyes as we drove along. The snow had stopped falling and through the milk-white clouds I saw patches of bright-indigo blue that could be a sign that the snowstorm was losing its strength, fading away to nothing, as it sometimes did. But this was no guarantee as the weather here in the highlands was confusing, fickle, and seemed to have a mind of its own at times.

We had reached the top of the hill where the road dipped rather steeply. Below we could see the police vehicle parked beside the canal with another vehicle, a cream-coloured station wagon. Father stopped the four-wheel drive at the top of the hill.

'I'll get you take the horses out here, Leif. The road is going to be slippery and we don't want to end up in the canal.'

'Okay,' I replied, understanding his concern as I peered down the hill at the wild, cascading water as it funnelled from the dam into the canal. A white hovering mist hung over the turbulent waters of blue and white. I slipped on my gloves and balaclava and jumped out of the vehicle instantly hearing and feeling the frozen snow crunch beneath my feet. I undid the bolts on the door of the float and lowered the door down to the ground. I could smell the musky odour of the horses as I slipped between them, I could also feel the warmth of their bodies as I spoke to them softly, urging them to back out of the float. Once they were out and the door lifted back into place, I yelled out to father to let him know that he could move off. I watched, somewhat apprehensively, as he crept down the hill. The most dangerous section was at the bottom of the hill where the sharp bend met the bridge; if the vehicle failed to turn on the ice it could keep going right in to the canal, into the foaming, violent raging water.

I had no reason to worry as the vehicle turned easily and crossed the bridge, although it might have been different with the weight of the horses in the float. Constable Ryan and a second constable named, Roberson, met us with gloved hands and fur-lined coats. The plan was for father and I to go out further into the wilderness while the two policemen searched the first ridge on the other side of the river.

'There is a hut over on McDowall Ridge, we'll check that first,' said Father as he tightened the saddle on Trigger. I would be riding Shadow. We divided up the sandwiches and had a thermos each that went into the saddle bags. And we took a couple of blankets as well, for if we found the hunters, they would more than likely be feeling the cold. For the moment the snow had stopped falling and the puffy white clouds were racing at breakneck speed across the patchy-blue sky.

'The river is too high for us to walk across,' said Constable Ryan. 'You will have to give us a lift.'

'Have either of you crossed a river on a horse before?' Father asked.

'No,' was the nervous reply from Constable Ryan.

'There are two simple rules; don't under any circumstances panic, the horse might feel as though they are struggling, but they know how to cross a river, and second, hang on firmly. Leif, you go first and take Constable Roberson.'

I helped Roberson up onto the horse behind me and headed down towards the river where the water was twisting and turning around the scattered drab-grey boulders. I studied the path before me and chose what I thought was the best section, where there weren't too many large boulders, and the water was not as broken and violent as the rest of the river.

'Have you done this before?' asked Roberson.

'Yes,' I replied, studying the water ahead of me as I urged Shadow into the river. The depth of the water slowly rose up under Shadow's flanks. We had to lift our feet up to keep them from getting wet. I was pretty sure that it wouldn't get any deeper. I could see the rocky bottom in the translucent water. Roberson had his arms around me rather tightly. I understood his fear, for I had felt that same fear the first time I crossed a river on a horse, but now, it was second nature to me. We arrived safely on the other side and unloaded our passengers.

'We have only about three to four hours of daylight left,' said Constable Ryan, checking his watch beneath the thick woolen glove. 'We can meet back here at five thirty.'

Father and I rode together, past the first lot of decaying rustic huts on the flat and on to the trail that led toward the ridge and the old shepherd's hut.

'If they hunted this area frequently, they must know of the hut,' I said as we rode along at a casual pace.

'Yes, you would think so,' replied Father.

'I have a feeling that something has happened to them, an accident of some sort.'

Father urged the horse on at a quicker pace. 'You might be right, Leif.'

It didn't take us long to reach the snow-covered hut. It was a rough wooden-planked hovel with a rusted galvanised-iron roof that no ordinary person would live in today, but here in the wilderness of the highlands it would be a virtual paradise in this weather. Our worst fears were realised as we opened the door. Cups and eating utensils lay undisturbed on the table. Canned food was piled at the rear of the bare wooden table, in the fireplace a blackened kettle sat to one side. Father knelt down and put his fingers in the ash remains of the fire.

'Cold, stone motherless cold, they haven't been here for some time.'

'I think it would better if we split up, we can cover more ground.'

Father stood up and looked at me, he knew what I was saying was right, even though he probably didn't like the idea of me going off on my own.

'I'll go around the ridge and follow it on the western side, you take the eastern side. No heroics, like your mother said, when it's time to turn back, turn back,' he said with a sharpness in his voice.

I mounted the horse, waved farewell to Father, and headed down the hill to where the rusted wires and the thin rotted posts of an old fence line were just visible from out of the top of the snow that was about two-feet deep. But it didn't bother Shadow; he seemed to be enjoying this outing as his hooves kicked at the snow and flung waves of white powder into the air. I cast my eyes over an alabaster of barren land, there was nothing to see, no sign of life of any kind.

I stopped every now and then and called out, there were no echoes here; my shouts were instantly cut off, muffled by the snow. The forest ended and there was a saddle, a crossing over the ridge. I rode to the top of the saddle and peered out over the flat, undulating country to the west, nothing moved except for the occasional whipping of the snow into the air by the wind. I saw father off to my right. He was scouring the ridge looking for sign. I was glad to be on the sheltered side of the hill away from the biting wind. I turned and went back down behind the hill to where the forest started again.

I kept checking my watch. Time was running out, soon I would have to turn back if I was to be at the river by the appointed time. But I thought of the men trapped out here somewhere, they would be hoping, praying that someone would find them. If we didn't find them, they might not survive another night in the freezing temperatures. When the time came to turn back, I decided that I couldn't give up, not just yet anyway, another half an hour I told myself. Pulling the gloves from my hands I rubbed some warmth back into my cold fingers and then put the gloves back on. I moved my toes in the thick-leather boots, pleased that I could still feel them in the cold.

Every five minutes I called out, stopping each time to listen, but there was nothing, only the roaring sound of the wind in the trees. The half hour was up, but I chose to go on for another ten minutes. Finally, I stopped, and gave what would be my last call. No reply came back, no familiar sound or voices. I wanted to go on, to continue searching, but it was hopeless, soon it would be dark and the chances of finding anybody out here would be impossible. I pulled at the reins and turned for home, the only hope I had was that Father or one of the policemen had found them.

Then I heard a sound. I stopped and removed the balaclava so I could hear properly. At first, I thought it was my imagination, I yelled out at the top of my voice, and then heard it again. It was the barking of a dog! No one had mentioned that the men had a dog with them, but then, what hunter wouldn't have a dog out here. They were essential to rouse the kangaroo out of their hiding places beneath the low-lying scrub.

'Come on, Shadow,' I said, kicking my heels into his flanks. 'I think we've found them.'

I followed the sound of the barking to a small cliff and found a black kelpie dog with a white patch on his head at the base of the cliff, guarding what looked like some kind of lean-to made of brush and gum boughs. I climbed from the horse and walked over and moved some of the brush aside, the two men were lying on the ground huddled up together. One of them opened up his tired looking eyes and stared at me.

'Am I dreaming?' he asked.

'This is no dream. I'm here to get you out of here.'

'We thought we were goners,' he said as he prodded his partner to wake him up.

I went back to the horse and retrieved the thermos and sandwiches from the saddle bags. When I returned the second man was awake; his eyes mirrored his pain. 'What happened?' I asked.

'Geoff here was standing on a rock on the edge of the cliff taking a shot at a kangaroo when a couple more came out of the scrub. I jumped up on the rock and the bloody thing moved; next thing we knew were going over the edge. Geoff has a broken right leg, and I think I've cracked a rib or two.'

'My name is Leif O'Connor,' I said, putting out my hand.

'Paul Johnson, and this here is Geoff Wiseman,' he said, shaking my hand. Geoff shook my hand as well.

'How are you going to get us out of here, Mr O'Connor?' asked Geoff.

'Call me Leif. I have a horse, so you two will be going out in style,' I said, pouring a cup of hot coffee out for them. They shared the cup. Then I tipped out what was left from the thermos. I took a sip myself and then gave them the rest. I let them have all the sandwiches as well. They wolfed them down pretty quickly.

'Can you walk?' I asked Paul.

'Yes, but I can't take a deep breath, the pain is too great.'

'Where's your leg broken, Geoff?'

'Below the knee.'

'Well, at least you will be able to sit on the horse, but it isn't going to be easy.'

'I don't want to spend another night out here,' he replied.

I helped Paul to stand, he stamped his feet to try and get some circulation back into his legs. He grimaced in pain as tried to breathe as shallowly as possible. Both of us took hold of Geoff, he yelled out in pain as the weight of his broken leg strained against the broken bones. There were tears in his eyes. We managed to get Geoff into the saddle, lord knows how, but we did. Paul climbed up behind Geoff. I gave them a blanket each from the saddle bags. I took hold of the reins and we began the long trek back.

Darkness was already creeping over the land, I was late, and father would be worrying about me. At first, I walked easily and we made good time, but as we went lower into the valley the snow became deeper and the going much harder. I found myself having to stop for a breather. Paul offered to give me a spell but I knew that it would be impossible for him as the hard labour of walking in the snow would cause him too much pain. I thanked him, and declined his offer.

Although I knew this country very well, the pitch-black darkness was causing me some concern. I knew I was heading in the right direction and that we would eventually come to the river, but it would be far easier if we could find the old fence line which would give us a clear run down the middle of the valley. Eventually we found it, or should I say Shadow found it, he stopped when we came to the fence. I hadn't been able to see it until then. It was only a matter of following the stunted posts to where they stopped, turn right onto the trail and follow the path through the forest and then down to the river.

Each time we stopped, Patch, I had since found out his name, although it should have been obvious, stood with his tail wagging and barked at us. I'm sure he was urging us on, urging us to keep going. Each time we started off he stopped barking and trotted along beside us as if happy that we were moving again. Even with his four legs, Patch was having just as much difficulty as I was in the snow that was now up to my knees.

One of the most difficult things I had to do was to keep talking to Paul and Geoff. I had to keep their spirits up. I had to keep them awake. For I knew if they dozed off, they might fall off the horse and it would be extremely difficult for me to get them back up, if at all.

It wasn't just cold any more, it was absolutely freezing. There was no wind now, just the eerie silence of a cold-black night. Even though all of us had gloves, hats or balaclavas on, and were dressed well for the conditions, the icy chill eventually permeated through our outer clothing. No amount of clothing would keep this cold out, I thought to myself as I lifted my unfeeling feet out of the snow. My hands were just the same. I twisted the reins around my right hand so I wouldn't lose my hold on the horse.

We were two thirds of the way back. It would take us another hour at least to reach the river. I continued talking to Paul and Geoff, we talked about hunting and about family. We talked about the bloody weather, we even laughed sometimes.

By now I was becoming tired, it took all my strength to lift my feet out of the snow, we stopped more and more frequently. I had no energy left to talk. One hour stretched into two, I wasn't sure where we were going anymore, my eyes were becoming blurred and I felt dizzy. I fell over several times and it was only by the good grace of Shadow who pulled on the reins that I was able to get back onto my feet. I don't recall coming to the river, but Patch started barking, and I heard voices. We had made it.

'I thought I told you no bloody heroics.'

I heard Father's voice before I saw him. He was climbing down off the other horse and he reached out and literally pried my fingers from the reins.

'I'm afraid we got caught in traffic,' I mumbled with a forced grin on my face.

'Always the joker, Leif, always the bloody joker.'

I think he was glad to see me.

Buttons – a poem
Ant Dry

Buttons is a bunny and a very fine one too
He lives in my old wood pile; and of kids he has a few
There's Mora and there's Flora and there's funny little Tim
All of whom spend their time trying to keep me trim
As every time I see them, I fly into a rage
I grab my gun and fly around as if I'm on the stage
For all those little bastards, every single sodding one
Likes to eat my cabbages and have a bit of fun.
I've chased them round the ground and I've chased them to the sea,
But every time I look around, they're looking back at me.
So now I find myself at war and cunning I must be
Coz Buttons and his fellow thieves are always breaking free
They dodge me and they bait me with a jaunty wag of tail
When all I want to do is to lock them safely in my jail
Genghis Khan knew a thing or two of war and hardened battle
He'd never have swallowed the rabbit's bird and allowed him so to rattle
So off I sailed to Caltex and obtained a pint or two,
And threw it on the wood heap, to feed the ants on rabbit stew.

Political manipulation
Anne Layton-Bennett

i'm done with the lies
and promises that are never kept
i'm done with the sleaze
the fake news
the greed
the profligacy
and determined avoidance
of accountability and
responsibility

i'm done with how your side
disparage dissent
accuse your critics
blame the poor
and
trample the struggling
further into the gutter

i'm done with your smirk
your self-righteous intolerance
and your carefully constructed
mask of serenity
that's finally, finally showing signs
of cracking

pass me the sanitiser
because
i'm done with your brand
i want a refund
and a transition
to a kinder, gentler
place

© 2021 Anne Layton-Bennett

My Friends The Mountains
(Rosebery, West Coast, Tasmania)
Graeme Hetherington

My father thought I was a 'nance'
For singing in a church choir dressed
In cassock, surplice, lizard frill,
My mother chased me with his belt

And screamed 'you little bugger' as
We went. My brother was my foe,
And when my sister's coming turned
My love, forbidden, into hate,

Mount Black, so close our lawn was dark
And wet all year, confirmed my need
To hug shadows, see on nearby
Sombrely grey, deceptively,

Sometimes-sunlit, Mount Murchison,
A face resembling mine, to which
I felt welcomed to give my lone,
Unforgiving, cold-hardened heart.

'Welcome to Russia'
Allan Jamieson

When I set out to plan a visit to Russia in 1980, I was partly influenced by my experience eleven years previously, when I made my first visit there. That visit turned out to be of enormous help in 1980.

In 1964, I had immigrated to Canada and in 1969 I decided to pay my first visit "back home" to Australia. In 1969, a major decision point was approaching also in the company where I had worked the past five years. The company, CIL, sold chemicals to pulp and paper mills in Canada, but did not operate a mill of its own. In 1967, the General Manager of CIL's Chemical Division, who I will call Rhys, had met the Research Manager of the large Swedish pulp company known as MoDo and had learned of MoDo's strong research position with a dramatic new pulp bleaching process using oxygen gas. CIL did not sell oxygen, nor was it likely to do so, but the use of oxygen (if adopted by the pulp industry) could diminish or eliminate sales of CIL's main chemical, chlorine. A fellow researcher and I were commissioned by Rhys to learn what we could about oxygen bleaching. We quickly made two discoveries and obtained patents for both. One of our inventions seemed to ensure an on-going demand for chlorine and Rhys was keen to move these ideas out of the laboratory and to a pilot plant evaluation.

MoDo's own 100 tonne per day pilot plant was soon to begin operation at its Husum pulp mill in northern Sweden. Should CIL pool its patents and join forces with MoDo? Rhys asked me to go to Sweden and spend two weeks evaluating if MoDo's plant could be used, or easily modified, to test CIL's own technology. He would meet me at an airport near Husum – on my own – so that I could give him my conclusion before he met MoDo's management.

This I could do, if I returned to Canada from Australia via Sweden. A direct route would be through India and Russia. I decided to spend one day in Moscow and three in Leningrad. I would fly to Moscow from Delhi on an Air India plane, from Moscow to Leningrad by Aeroflot and from Leningrad to Sweden (via Helsinki) with Finnair.

While in Australia, I went to the Russian Embassy in Canberra to obtain a visa. My travel plan was clearly defined – stopovers in Moscow and Leningrad – but, the Embassy could not tell me the names of my hotels; I would only get this information from Intourist on arrival at Moscow airport. The clerk at the Embassy waxed enthusiastically about Siberia, but I wasn't intending to go there! I received my passport with a visa paper pinned at the back and the clerk gave me a shopping bag full of literature. Back in central Canberra, while waiting for the airport bus, I looked at what was in the bag. Six books on Siberia: nothing, not even one page, on Moscow or Leningrad. I left the whole lot at the bus station.

This glimpse of the Russian system seemed amusing then. Little did I realise how immovable and all-pervasive the system was in Russia.

My flight over Russia started in magnificent style with glorious weather. I had a window seat on the right side. The Himalayas were not "*down* there"; rather, they were "*out* there", seemingly on the same level as the plane. We overflew Kabul, Afghanistan, before passing over the Aral Sea; spectacular country!

The plane was a Boeing 707; one aisle. My fellow passengers – Indians all – were apparently immigrating to England, the ultimate destination of the plane. Every family had its belongings wrapped in large hessian bags, overflowing the solitary aisle. By some near-Herculean effort the crew actually supplied a meal (lunch) to each of us during the seven hour flight.

In early afternoon, we landed at Moscow and stopped a long way from the terminal. Only Moscow-destined passengers were to get off. Transit passengers were to stay on board. This rule didn't sink in to the 130-odd passengers, all of whom stood up and totally blocked the aisle for a good 20 minutes until the crew's endlessly repeated requests led to only a half dozen of us remaining on our feet. I made my way gradually to the front door, where I looked down the steep ladder to the ground. An Indian woman in a sari had reached the concrete carrying an infant and one bag. She was now attempting to get back up the ladder, but she wasn't moving because the way was blocked by a young (early 20's?) soldier resplendent in a bottle-green uniform with bright red and yellow trim and wearing the very characteristic, very wide, brimmed hat. It was his semi-automatic rifle, however, that said it all. 'Nyet.' Nobody was getting on this plane!

After much wailing from the woman and gun-waving by the Russian, a stewardess picked up one large hessian bag, fully a metre in diameter, and carried the bag down to the second last step, held the bag out with a horizontal arm and dropped it the last 20 centimetres to the ground. She hadn't touched Russian soil and was allowed to go back up the stairs.

The Indian lady collected her bag; the rest of us deplaned without incident, and rode a bus to the terminal building.

'Welcome to Russia', I thought to myself. Nobody ever says that in Russia, because Russia doesn't want anyone to ever go there.

At the terminal, I collected my suitcase, underwent a minutely detailed customs search and then found the Intourist desk. I was to stay at the Hotel Metropole and an Intourist car transported me into Moscow. These days Google Maps describes the Metropole as; 'a Posh hotel with fine dining and bar'. That maybe, but when I stayed there in 1969, it didn't have any plugs for the basin or bath and the toilet paper comprised highly glazed and totally non-absorbent brown squares of wrapping paper.

The Metropole was an easy walk from Red Square, with the Kremlin's bleak, high walls on one side overshadowing Lenin's Mausoleum, the onion-domes of St Basil's Cathedral at one end and the huge department store (GUM) on the other side. I bought a fur hat at GUM. As with any and every purchase made by anybody in Russia, I had to stand in three queues. First, I waited in line until a shopgirl assisted me to choose what I wanted to buy. She gave me an invoice that I had to take to a solitary cashier at the end of another *long* queue. Having paid, I was given a receipt to take back to the original counter and wait my turn until "served" again. At least, the system keeps everybody occupied, I thought.

That evening, I tried to get a meal at the Metropole restaurant. After being studiously ignored for a good 30 minutes, I stuck my foot out in the aisle in front of the waiter. He saw me, at last! 'You bastard', I thought. The menu was in Russian only, but I had spent some months in the early 1960's in Melbourne studying scientific Russian and so could decipher the Cyrillic script. I ordered Borscht. Eventually it came; a creamy white soup with purplish tinges slowly diffusing out from floating pieces of beetroot. It was cold. So ended Day One!

I thought Moscow a provincial, country town – more Asian than European – and too close to Soviet power. No culture whatsoever. I longed to get to Leningrad, a goal of mine since 1962 when I had read the totally absorbing autobiography of a young Russian girl (*Tomorrow Will Come*, by E. Almedingen), describing her time in the city during the first turbulent twenty years of the 20th Century, culminating with the frightening turmoil of the Russian Revolution, from which she eventually escaped to England. Despite the trauma of those events, her love of the city shone through. I immediately felt it too, when I was driven across Nevsky Prospekt to my hotel, the Astoria.

Leningrad, or St. Petersburg to give the city its original name (and its current name), was designed for Peter the Great by Italian architects. They established a fine principle: no building could be taller than the street it was on was wide. Eminently sensible for a city as far north as Leningrad (60°N) where the sun is low to the horizon for many months each year; the principle also provided grand, nicely proportioned vistas and wide streets in all directions; a truly magnificent city.

I bought a very, very good pocket guide of the city and explored as much as I could. There was much to see. I gazed at the majestic Neva River and marvelled at the white nights in late June. Never had I experienced sunlight so late into the night.

The Astoria was a grand old hotel, built in 1917, but the first night there exhausted my interest in its ability to entertain me. On the second evening, I met an American, who said he was a Congressman from California. He suggested a walk to another hotel, Europa, on Nevsky Prospekt. The Europa had a bar where we could actually get served a drink and there was a guitarist who provided continuous music, including the Russian melody *Moscow nights,* that was on all the Western Hit Parades at the time.

At around 11 pm, we left the Europa. We saw three girls walking in the same direction on the other side of the street. We crossed the street. They were well dressed – significant, as most Russians only have ill-fitting, drab clothes – and they were happy. They smiled. They were the only people in Russia who smiled! One spoke good English and she said that they were nurses. Eventually, we reached the corner where we would turn off to go to the Astoria. The girls waved and headed off in another direction. The American said; *'Nice girls can't afford to be seen near a hotel where foreigners stay.'* His remark made me recall the hordes of middle-aged men who spent all their time standing, singly and silently, in and near the hotel lobbies. What were they paid to do? Spy on everyone who came and went, I guessed.

And so, I stepped on board my Finnair plane and left Russia. The Finnair stewardess was strikingly beautiful, pleasant and smiling, smiling, smiling. It was so great to be out of Russia and in the West again. I concluded that I could only put up with the Russian system for maybe three days, but what of the poor Russians who had to live there?

I went on to Sweden, examined MoDo's pilot plant plans and recommended to Rhys that CIL join forces with MoDo. Ten months later, I was in Sweden to represent CIL's interests in the pilot plant trials that occupied the next two years. The trials were very successful and marketing of oxygen bleaching began worldwide. In 1972, I joined MoDo, as I felt that I could learn far more about the pulp and paper industry by working in the industry than as a supplier to the industry. In 1975, I moved to Tokyo on a two-year contract to help MoDo's agent in Japan, Ebara Corporation, to market several Swedish technologies including oxygen bleaching. Within three months, an Ebara manager – playing the traditional role of "go-between" – had introduced me to Kuniko, who soon became my wife.

In 1978, I was in Leningrad again. The Swedish and Russian governments were keen to show goodwill to each other and a delegation of Swedish forest industry people were sponsored to make a technical visit to Leningrad University. Oxygen bleaching was one topic and this was fitting because the first-ever publication on the use of oxygen for bleaching pulp (in *Bumazhnaya Promyslennost*, 1964) was by Prof. Nikitin and Dr Gary Akim of that university. This had been the spark that set MoDo (and later CIL) down the road to commercial use of oxygen. I met Dr Akim in 1978 when we visited the University.

There were about eight of us in the delegation, three being from MoDo. A Swedish man, resident in Leningrad, made all the arrangements, which helped enormously. We stayed at a new skyscraper hotel located on a canal beside the cruiser *Aurora*, whose canon had fired in 1917 to signal the start of the communist grab for power.

On the second night, the University hosted a dinner. There were about twenty of us seated at one long table. A Russian sat opposite each foreigner. Between each pair was a bottle of vodka. It was obvious that nobody would be allowed to leave until each person had made a speech and every bottle was empty. I tried to go slow but my host, who spoke no English (or Swedish) showed annoyance by grunting and jabbing his finger at my glass until I emptied it, whereupon he filled it up again.

Eventually, it was my turn to speak. I stood up and started by pointing out that I was Australian, not Swedish, and that I was especially proud to be in Russia. This was an unexpected opening statement; what would I say next? After a suitable pause for the translation to be made and "sink in", I continued; *we Australians are very impressed by the fact that the first-ever school of Australian Literature established anywhere in the world was at Moscow University.'* I could now sit down and finish my vodka.

Around midnight, the party ended and we went back to our hotel. Three of us had arranged to take a taxi to the Czar's Summer Palace at Petrodvorets the next morning. I awoke, surprised at how well (relatively!) I felt. If you're going to drink all night, drink vodka only is my recommendation.

The taxi arrived and we sped off at high speed through the streets of Leningrad. We were all still hung over or it would have been even more frightening. Then, after about 20 minutes of this break-neck careering, we reached the countryside and immediately the driver slowed to a very sedate and non-varying 30 km/hr speed for the next hour until we reached our destination. We found the palace and its grounds fascinating. The return journey was a repeat – in reverse. We crawled along at 30 km/hr until we entered the streets of Leningrad, when the speedometer climbed instantly to 90 km/hr and stayed there as we "ran the gauntlet" of streets, traffic, trams and traffic lights all the way to the hotel. This was a feature of the Russian system that surprised all of us and which, to this day, remains unexplained.

The next day, we left early for the airport. It was raining and our taxi had no heater and no windshield wipers. Through a fogged and watery windscreen, our driver steered the car at up to 90 km/hr along streets until we reached the airport. We were overjoyed to see the terminal building! What _is_ it about Russian road laws?

That was the sum total of my experience of Russia when I contemplated a visit in 1980, the Moscow Olympics year; surely Russia would put on a good face for visitors in 1980! I decided to limit the stay to three days, but I did want to show Leningrad to Kuniko.

In late June, I was invited to speak at a symposium in Helsinki. I arranged for Kuniko and me to take a train from Helsinki to Leningrad and back to Helsinki. On the fateful day, I gave my talk at a resort hotel some way out of Helsinki and we had just enough time to take a taxi to the Helsinki station before the train departed. It was 1 pm. There was no food on the train! No lunch! Little did we know what that was going to mean.

It was a Russian train, running on their ultra-wide (1.5 m gauge) rail line. Our carriage had compartments accessible from a corridor down one side of the carriage. There was space for six people but, apart from Kuniko and myself (we sat at the windows), there was only one other person in our compartment, an elderly lady who sat near the door nursing a large bouquet of flowers.

We moved through the Finnish countryside for about three hours until the train stopped. No buildings could be seen in either direction but I did see the top of a very high wire fence just above the grove of birch trees that filled the view from one window. We had halted at the border, literally. Suddenly, a young, uniformed Russian appeared at our compartment door carrying a sub-machine gun and followed by a large Alsatian dog. The young man, hardly 20 by his face, opened the door, seized the old lady's flowers, opened a window and threw them out onto the rail embankment. He hadn't said a word. With aid of some signs and gun waving, we were all herded out into the corridor from where we could watch him in the compartment through the glass of the closed door. The dog sat watching us.

First, he stood on a seat and used a screwdriver to loosen a large panel in the ceiling. Grasping the edges of the hole, he hauled himself up so he could see into the ceiling cavity. Apparently all was in order because he then replaced the panel before kneeling on the floor and loosening the screws of a like-sized panel. He bent down and looked under the floor. Satisfied (or disappointed?), he replaced the floor panel.

It was a very hot day. The train didn't move. There was no ventilation. All windows were shut. It was becoming very unpleasant. We were asked to go back, one at a time. Kuniko went first. I watched through the door but couldn't hear what was said. We knew "the rules". Each of us had a piece of paper detailing all the money we had plus any "valuables". The youth counted Kuniko's money quite carefully but then he (or more correctly, Kuniko) had a problem. She had recorded 'two rings' but these were in my suitcase, not hers. He wanted to see the rings. A stalemate was quickly reached. Kuniko couldn't comply. I figured out what the problem was and opened the door. The dog growled. I pointed to my case and held out the key. The Russian allowed me to show him Kuniko's rings. He never said anything. Eventually he left, with his dog, and we waited until all inspections were completed. The train began to move, a full hour after it had halted to allow that Russian welcoming committee to get on. The old lady wept.

After a brief stop at the first station in Russia, Vyborg, the train accelerated and ran at high speed through the countryside until it reached Finland Station, in Leningrad. It was just after 7 pm. We stepped onto the open-air platform. No sign of any Intourist person. We walked to the cavernous station building at the end of the platform. I put down our cases in the centre of a large room and Kuniko sat on them while I went searching up and down, inside and outside the station. Eventually I became certain that there was no Intourist office at Finland Station. What in Hell were we to do now?

I approached the ticket windows and waited until it was my turn. There was an elderly lady seated at a window. I explained as best I could (in English) what my concern was. I didn't want a train ticket; I wanted an Intourist office. Eventually, she understood the word "Intourist". She responded but the only word I recognised was "Astoria". We had contact! She was telling me to go to the Astoria Hotel. I knew that there was an Intourist office there, from 11 years previously when I had stayed there. But, where was the Astoria?

The lady told me a bus number and pointed outside. Fine, but I had no Russian money. I held out an empty hand. She put a five kopeck coin in it. I recalled that this was the bus fare eleven years ago – something to be said for the Communists! Yet, I needed another five kopeck coin, for Kuniko who was in the next room. Finally, probably to get rid of me, she gave me a second coin. I don't know what that lady thought, but I knew I would be eternally grateful that she had taken the time and trouble to help me, instead of saying *'Nyet'* like all her countrymen do.

Kuniko and I went to the bus stop. Along came a bus full to the gills with people. We could only just manage to squeeze ourselves and our suitcases on at the back door before the bus left. We stood, hanging to a strap and swaying every which way as the bus went down streets, around corners and over bridges.

Suddenly, I recognised where we were; Nevsky Prospekt. The bus stopped and I told Kuniko get off. I knew that I could find the way to the Astoria but I didn't know where the bus would go next. There was no way, though, that we could make it to the front of the bus and pay our five kopeck coins, so we scrambled off at the back of the bus, watched by dozens of passengers.

One hundred metres down a street and we were at the Astoria. Oh, how valuable my previous visit had been! It was 8:55 pm when we entered the hotel. The Intourist office closed at 9:00 pm, but we got in the door just in time. It took 20 minutes of ringing around by the office staff, but eventually we were told that we should be at the Pribaltiskaya, a new hotel that I had never heard of. An Intourist car was arranged and off we went. It was almost dark, but I sensed that we were heading west, towards the Gulf of Finland. The hotel, a massive building, was on the water's edge a long way from any other building. The sun was setting over the water as we arrived.

Our room was on the fourth floor. I saw that the hotel system hadn't changed; as on every floor in every hotel in Russia, an elderly, fat woman managed the keys. We had to get our room key from her as we left the lift and she wanted it back if we ever headed for the lift. From her seat, she could see any and all movement on her floor of rooms. *"Big Mama is watching you!"*

Food was uppermost in our minds. It was almost 10 pm and we hadn't eaten since breakfast in Helsinki. We found one room that looked like a restaurant, though the people were doing more drinking than eating. Nobody took any interest in us, so we sat down. Eventually, we cornered a waiter who obliged by bringing some food over to our table. At last, the inner man was satisfied. The Russian system, however, was far from satisfied with us. I had no Russian money. Upon arrival at the hotel, I was told the Exchange would open at 9:00 am the next day. Our waiter wanted roubles and I only had dollars. We had eaten, so I stood up and made to walk out. The waiter backed down, took my money – what I judged to be the correct amount – and disappeared. So ended the Arrival Day! Would my patience last the three days?

The next morning, we went down one floor to a breakfast room. It was a cafeteria style and so I stood face-to-face with a cash register and an unsmiling person. The person wouldn't accept dollars. Another guest smiled (he wasn't Russian) and gave me some roubles sufficient to pacify the Russian system. We could eat!

Immediately after breakfast, I changed my dollars into roubles. We then went into the Intourist office at the hotel. It is probably worth noting that we had paid our hotel charge to Intourist in advance, before leaving Sweden. We were travelling *de luxe* and the cost was at least double what a room at the most expensive hotel in London would have cost. Included were transfers from and to the train station (big deal!) and two days of guided tours.

We wanted to sort out these tours and we booked a tour, by boat, to the Summer Palace at Petrodvorets. Armed with a fistful of handwritten paper slips, comprising all the tickets we needed, I went across to the cashier to pay. Problem! Intourist only accepted foreign currency; dollars and not roubles. My patience had run out and it was still early in the first full day! I shouted as loud as I could at everybody. ***Idiots! Imbeciles!*** After some delay, I was persuaded to return to the first desk and she, behind it, was persuaded to re-write all the tickets using a different coloured paper! With this new magic prescription, the cashier took my roubles: 'Oh, what a system!'

Our first guide was a dead loss. She was in her 50's and dedicated her time with us to persuasion. We should become communists. She wasn't interested in showing us what we wanted to see. Rather, it was monuments and inscriptions to the glorious Soviet that we were shown. Fortunately, she was lazy and, when she said the tour was finished – two hours early – we did not object.

We were on Nevsky Prospekt and it was midday. We went in search of a restaurant. We found a magnificent establishment with hundreds of tables, all set with shiny cutlery, multiple sizes of glasses and with yellow table napkins. It was empty, save for the serving staff who sat at a couple of tables at the far end listening to a group of musicians on stage. We sat down. After a while, one waiter came to our table and said 'Closed'. He pointed to his mates at the far end and said 'Eating'. This restaurant was closed while the staff ate lunch and enjoyed their private concert.

We walked out and entered the Hotel Europa, the one place in Leningrad where, eleven years ago, I had found that you could be served. The hotel's restaurant was closed, but a cafeteria was open and we could select from a good range of cold meats and spicy sausages. And, we could get Russian beer. They took my Russian roubles too. We went back there the next day as well.

The second guide was quite young, with a mass of curly blond hair framing a wide face. She was probably in her early 20's, not at all experienced as a guide, but pleasant as a person. Unfortunately, we soon exhausted her knowledge of Leningrad. She did, however, tip us off to the fact that a group from our hotel would be going to a theatrical performance that evening. If we fronted at the right time, we could become part of the group. This we did. Several busloads of in-the-know guests, plus us two ring-ins left the Pribaltiskaya for a theatre somewhere in Leningrad. It was a variety concert, culminating in a grand display of Russian and Cossack dancing. Among the 50 or so buses parked in front of the theatre, we found one that was going to our hotel and so ended an enjoyable – free – evening.

The time had come to leave Leningrad. I wasn't sorry, despite us not having seen a lot that the city does have to offer. I was at my wit's end!

The train left Finland Station and sped back up the line we had travelled those few days previously. We stopped at Vyborg station. On came the same young thug and dog to check us over. This time, we were ordered to stand on the platform while he checked the ceiling and floor cavities of our compartment. Then, we had to front him individually while he checked our "valuables" again.

It seemed to go quicker this time; the train finally moved off from the station and headed west. We passed the border fence and, some 15 minutes later, we stopped at a station. Finland. Two uniformed border staff opened the door to our compartment, smiled and asked 'Anything to declare?' We laughed, they laughed and the train moved off. 'Welcome to the West!'

Flap Flag, Flap
Jennie Herrera

Are we not confusing the form with the substance when we debate endlessly on what we should put at the top of our flagpoles? I would feel the same about my country if we had a dead chook hanging up there. It might even be more appropriate. Chooks, after all, give us unselfish unhurtful and largely unrewarded service and I would more happily salute the 'noble hen' than a piece of cloth probably Made in Pakistan. This would also have the advantage that should I at any time be shipwrecked on a desert isle I could take down the flag and cook it.

What is the real significance of our flag? Is it not merely a collective symbol in the way that family mottoes and heraldic devices are more private symbols, bent on proving that we cannot be dismissed as stateless riff-raff?

What do we ask of our flag? Mainly that it be fun for primary school children, armed with scissors and crayons, to reproduce, and that it should not clash with the Governor-General's wife regardless of what coloured ensemble she has chosen to wear.

Do our hearts swell, figuratively speaking, when we look up at that piece of red-white-and-blue flapping in the breeze? Probably if we are lost and lonely and suddenly espy it above Australia House in London, but I very much doubt if we give it a thought as we dash into the post office for half-a-dozen stamps.

What about the flag itself? Does it represent us as we would like to express our nationhood? Our British heritage is more than our parliament and our laws; it is why we are here and, largely, how we live our lives; it is at the heart of our psyche—it appears in our attitudes to authority, our feelings about the land, the sports we choose to play, our language and how we play with it, our literature, our fondness for gardening, our predilection for keeping pets, the way we drive, how we express our deepest beliefs, the nature of our commercial, social, and educational lives …

If the Emperor of China had pipped Cook and Banks with a fleet of fast junks Australia would be a vastly different place and it is possible that no debate on flags would currently be permitted in this country.

The Southern Cross is a reminder that Australians stood up, at the risk of their lives, to say that fair play, decency and moving towards equality of opportunity, all mattered. They didn't take it far enough of course. They were busy digging up the land, destroying the wildlife, and fouling the pristine rivers of Aboriginal Australia. But the men of Eureka deserve to be remembered, that little fumbled fudged 'revolution' helped set in place the vital concept of accountability.

The Federation Star is dull certainly. But it is a reminder of the checks and balances written into the formal structure of Australia which makes this country better protected than almost any other country on earth from authoritarian take-over. The people of Chile in the late sixties and early seventies believed that after more than half a century of democracy it was too firmly entrenched to be destroyed. They discovered in a tragic way that the checks and balances in their system were almost non-existent. Despite the duplications and waste and sheer silliness that the Federal system throws up it remains a very practical way of keeping Australia stable, honest and open.

Does this mean, though, that our flag is perfect? Hardly. It can be, and often is, mistaken for New Zealand's flag. But, personally, I'd rather risk being mistaken for a Kiwi than to change it and risk being mistaken for a North Korean or an Uzbekistani. Whatever we choose we will probably run the risk of having something similar to someone else. Who, after all, can distinguish the flags of Poland and Indonesia—unless they've had it drummed into them since childhood. Do they lose sleep over the similarity? I doubt it. The 'Stars and Stripes' is surely memorable—but I have known even it to be confused with the flag of Malaysia.

We could go for absolute safety and choose a green and gold spotted kangaroo but I don't feel wildly excited about saluting a green and gold spotted kangaroo.

If we were to take ten people and sit them in front of ten popular designs, chances are that we would get ten different choices. Of course there are ways around this. We could have a different design year and year about, thus pleasing some of the people some of the time and holding out the happy thought that everyone's moment of joy would come.

The question is not whether we should, now, make public our multiracial and multicultural nature; we did that when Phillip disembarked his human cargo and noticed there were quite a lot of black people around. So we could plump for some nice black and white stripes, which would have the useful side-effect that flags could be taken down and waved at footie matches to spur the 'Pies on to glory.

It has always distressed me that we have publicly recognised two hundred years of European messing around but have ignored sixty thousand years of gentle Aboriginal occupation (and it is becoming doubtful whether Australia will be able to survive sixty thousand years of us); that unselfish respect for Australia deserves to be flown in the face of a greedy ruthless exploitative world and the answer is simple—a two-sided flag with Old Faithful on one side and the Aboriginal flag on the other and never mind that the Governor-General's wife has chosen to wear puce.

But, given that our politicians would then waste time and money arguing over which flag should go on which side, I am quite willing to go back to my long-suffering chook and I would suggest a cross between a White Leghorn and a Black Australorp, so that as the band plays and our eyes grow wet with emotion, a great nationwide murmur can rise up towards the sunlit heavens—'Good on yer, Chook.'

Ern

Ant Dry

Flinders Lane on a Saturday morning. Pedestrians bustling, coffee shops heaving. Ern Flavard sat jammed into a corner outside a tiny café, a cup of coffee at his elbow and a newspaper precariously balanced on the too-small table top. He was very content. Life was good. He loved Melbourne. He loved the privacy of the big city, the fact that despite the three million other residents, many of them at his shoulder, he felt alone and undisturbed.

His had been a good life. He'd taught for decades at St John's Catholic School for Boys. It hadn't been a well-paid job, but with the inheritance he had received from his parents, he had lived a very comfortable life.

'Mr. Flavard?'

Ern looked up in annoyance. It was a young man, about thirty, looking uncertain.

'Bloody hell. Sorry Sir, I mean, it really is you Sir.'

The young man held out his hand. 'It's Evans Sir. Left in ninety seven. Bracken Hostel, Sir. Devonshire was my housemaster. You taught me History, Sir. Four years.'

Ern stared at the young man.

'Evans, eh? Ah, yes?'

Evans picked up a chair from a neighbouring table, and sat at Ern's table.

'Gosh, Sir, it's good to see you. I heard you'd retired. What are you up to these days?'

Ern grunted, and shifted in his seat.

'It's wonderful to see you, Sir. I didn't get to say my goodbyes when I left. I'm sorry, I should have done that, but it sort of slipped my mind, you know. Everything was such a rush. Funny how you forget the important stuff. Anyway.'

Evans signalled the waiter. 'A flat white for me, please. Thanks.'

Ern rustled his newspaper, lowering his gaze to the printed word.

'I just wanted to thank you, Sir.'

Ern sighed and looked up.

'I never said goodbye and I wanted to especially because you did so much for me.'

Ern stared at the intruder, raising an eyebrow.

'That chat, we had, Sir, after you had caught me bunking school and smoking behind the change rooms. I've never forgotten that. You know, it was the first time anyone ever spoke to me like that. You know, actually spent time talking to me. Like you actually cared. You made me realise I had to make more of my life. That I was just wasting my time and your time and my parents' time. That there were better things to do than fritter away my talents by trying to be a rebel.'

'Do you know, Sir that was the last time I ever bunked or smoked? It was after our chat that I started to realise that I needed to study more. That I needed to pull my finger out and really work. Do you remember, you told me, that we are the "masters of our own destiny", and you told me to read Henley's "Invictus"? Do you know I've had the poem inscribed on a panel and it hangs on my office wall? It's the defining focal point of my life. I read it every day. I just thought I'd let you know, Sir, I never did say goodbye.'

Evans' flat white arrived. He added sugar and stirred.
'I'm a surgeon now, Sir, recently qualified. Working at the Royal Melbourne. If it hadn't been for you, Sir, I'd probably be on the dole.'

A loud buzzing made the table shake. Evans grabbed his pager from his belt and read the message.

'Oh bugger, I have to go. It was wonderful to see you Sir. And thanks. Again. For my life. I really truly am forever grateful.'

Evans stood, waved the waiter over, gave her some change, shook Ern's hand and left, striding swiftly toward the hospital.

Ern shook his paper again.

He smiled. The old Invictus trick. Yes, he'd used that a lot. He never thought it would work. He frowned. Evans hey? He didn't remember anyone called Evans.

The Blue Chevrolet
Meg Mclaren

1

Selassie loved cars, any make or model. As long as there were four wheels and gasoline in the tank, he could make it go. It was said in Gasparillo that Selassie had only to stand near a car for it to go better. He was gentle with them; his fingers agile and sure as he fiddled with the carburettor, adjusted and scraped spark plugs, all the while gazing intently at the coil boxes. If he had been a gardener, people would have said he had green fingers. He was inspired. He felt the affinity people have for beautiful things. If one looked deep enough into his brown eyes, through the flecked beam of the iris, deep into the blackness in the centre, you could see the vast plains of Africa, and you understood then, that he was a loner.

Cupid changed all that. Standing in the car yard smiling her big, wide smile, her tight, black curls bristling, her brown arms rubbed liberally with coconut oil, a flowered dress with hibiscus swirling around her knees, and red sham-patta shoes covered in dust; she was the only thing that could take his mind off the metal carcass beneath his hands.

'Come Selassie! Leave dat ol' automobile. We can go down de track an' have a cool drink at "Off The Rails". Is too hot to be pullin' on spark plugs.'

He would drop everything and they would run, following the sugar train as it travelled from south to north, loaded with the hard canes of unprocessed sugar.

The first station they came to had a worn out, abandoned look, except when a train was due to arrive. Half an hour before it came to a standstill beside the platform, people would start to arrive. They would gather in groups along the wooden planks or cluster in the areas of swept earth that bordered the track. The women in bright coloured dresses and wide hats of plaited palm leaves, the men squatting on their heels in the shade, chewing on a Chiclet or taking quick puffs of an Anchor Special. Panniers of yams, limes and oranges were piled under the eaves of the station ready to be transported to the market in Port of Spain. There was much talking and laughing together with a rhythm and subtle movement of hips and feet. It seemed that the pulse of Africa was still there beating away.

At the far end of the platform stood a building of old boards and corrugated iron. A tiny niche. A drab, gloomy room owned and run by a round faced Chinese man, his skin crosshatched with wrinkles and deep furrows. Beneath a painted sign that read OFF THE RAILS one entered through a dark doorway, a piece of sacking looped to one side. A mangy dog lay in the corner near sacks of rice and dried beans and drums of cooking oil. A glass fronted fridge was filled with bottles of Coke and Carib Lager, and jugs of Kool Aid and Sorrel and Soursop Juice. A couple of rickety tables covered in plastic stood near a hole-in-the-wall, just a frame without glass and open to everyone's gaze. Beneath a tamarind tree growing outside the window, Chung Li's children splashed and bathed in an upturned turtle shell filled with cool water.

As crowds gather Chung Li becomes anxious and prone to violence should anyone become overly enthusiastic and rowdy; arguing and quarrelling in local patois over a perceived insult. 'Speak Ingrish!' he shouts, soursop juice dribbling in a sticky stream down his chin.

He tosses the pigtail hanging halfway down his back. Rumour is that he beats his wife with the pigtail on a Friday night after drinking his fill of rum. He turns to her now. 'Cheesus!' She is busy blasting a thick mist with a canister of Flit, spraying flies and anything else that moves. 'People everywhere!'

On the Friday before the auction, Cupid and Selassie get there shortly before the train is due to arrive. Cupid sits down at the table nearest the window and Selassie follows with a jug of Kool Aid and two glasses.

'Niiiiice! We go catch a cool breeze here,' he says as he sits beside her. 'Dis time tomorrow we go have wheels. Port of Spain here we come!'

'I's afraid what Babadine goin'a do Selassie. He wan' dat Chevy soooo bad. He goin' to go to any length to get it.'

'You leave one eyed Babadine to me douxdoux. I's well able for your brudder. He already lose one eye due to his badjohn ways. He go lose anudda if he tangle wid me. Jus' be here at de station tomorrow when I arrive to get you.'

2

The morning of the auction is dull and overcast. In the distance Selassie hears the first growls of thunder. The car park is full, packed with every size, shape and make of vehicle: worn out trucks that have seen better days; Dodges, Austins, Chryslers, their seats hot and sticky; Cadillacs with chrome strips from headlamp to pointed tail fins that look as though they could take off skywards. A dark blue Chevrolet sedan, with indicators that pop out of the sides to flash, is parked next to a rusting Model T Ford held together by a hope and a prayer. The Chevy has balding tyres and a meandering crack across the windshield. 'Easy fix,' thinks Selassie, more interested in the engine, which upon examination, proves to be in good condition. 'Dis de one.' He gazes at the car. The sun seems to glint off the metallic roof top and its light bounces up towards the sky – like a golden dream.

He looks across the yard towards the gate. A tall black man is handing out copies of *Motor Sport*, perspiration forming dark circles beneath his arms. People are streaming through, vying with each other for the best spot. Calling out to each other in Caribbean patois. Laughing fondly at each other in appreciation of their own humour.

A bell rings loudly. Silence descends upon the showground and the auction begins. Bidding is fast and furious.

At long last number sixty is called and Selassie puts his hand up. He sees Babadine nearby and they view each other with suspicion, biding their time like rival teams on the football ground. The bids increase until just the two of them are left. Babadine confidently shouts out his final price and looks shocked and furious when Selassie tops it. Selassie crosses the yard to claim his car, unaware of the malevolent looks coming his way. He runs his hands lovingly over the vehicle thinking of tomorrow, Cupid by his side, driving north along the highway.

Then Babadine approaches, the patch over his left eye looks like a black hole to hell. He's waving a bottle of Vat 19, drinking the rum in long gulps and followed by two skinny, stringy young men, tough as nails, one carrying a wrench. Selasse feels a sinking sensation in his stomach. 'Dis goin'a be bad,' he thinks, then is taken by surprise when Babadine hits him in the mouth with his fist – hard! Suddenly they are rolling on the ground and there is the muffled thud of fists. Whaddap!! Punching and kicking. Now a commotion has broken out around them. The air is thick with human sweat. People calling out encouragement.

'You be famous Selassie. You be in de papah!'

'Dey go beat him like a dog!'

'Dat Babadine! He a reeeal badjohn. No mind he have only one eye. I would'na want to tangle wid him.'

Now the two backups move in for the kill, sucking on their teeth, flexing their arms and shadow boxing. They hold Selassie upright, blood spurts out everywhere. His head flops about from side to side. There is a sound of bones crunching.

'Babadine wait! 'Tink about Cupid! She also own de car. She work hard to pay her share.'

'Leave ma sista outa dis. She too good for you Selassie.'
Just then two policemen riding on horseback and looking solemn in uniform, break through the gathering.

'Wha' goin on here?'

'Babadine go kill dis boy sergeant.' One of the spectators speaks up. 'He start de whooole 'ting. All because of dat blue chevvy over dere.'

Eventually, with help from the outraged throng, the whole story comes together. The officers look down at Selassie's battered face. His eyes are sealed and closed, bloated and red. His nose smashed and swollen.

The younger policeman signals to a taxi parked near the gate. 'Get dis man to San Fernando hospital. You t'ree come wit' us. De Royal Jail waitin' for you!'

3

Chung Li sits in front of his shop, on a wooden chair tilted back, fanning himself with a folded newspaper. Cupid sits by the hole in the wall, a flat wheat bread rolled around a curry of goat meat, on a plate before her. It is the same table she and Selassie had last occupied. She has been there for two days and still no word.

When she first heard the news her body writhed and her moans were heartbreaking. 'I go get you Babadine. I go talk to de obeah man, see if he put a spell on you. He gonna bring you bad luck.' She howled, jerking back her head, stamping her heels, a pitiful sight.

Now, on this second day, when the heat of the mid-afternoon sun is almost too hot to bear, she hears the sound of a transistor radio belting out a calypso beat. She runs out to Chung Li. 'Do you hear it?' He nods and smiles.

Selassie is driving as fast as the car will go along a primitive road, the tyres crunching and bumping over exposed roots and loose stones. The sugar fields stretch on either side in ragged rows of tall canes as far as the eye can see, the sweet smell of cane flowers wafting. He can see the station ahead and Chung Li's rum shop. And there, leaning so far over the platform that she is in danger of falling off, is Cupid, a red hat on her head and her dress with hibiscus swirling around her knees, that he loves.

Brakes screeching, tyrcs slithcring, thc blue Chevrolet comes to a halt. Cupid jumps down from the boards and, like sunshine bursting from behind a cloud, the world turns golden around her.

Christmas Magic
Brenda Slavoff

When I was child summer had a special character. There were the days leading up to school break-up for holidays, then the excitement of the countdown to Christmas. Suddenly it was hot; languid days, punctuated with swims, were succeeded by light evenings spent playing or walking on the beach in the hope of a cool breeze. There was the heavy scent of flowers when parched gardens were watered, and lawns were wet under bare feet.

Christmas took the part of a ritual – Santa Claus was real; he visited us and even ate the cake we left for him. No matter what we received for Christmas, it was always something wonderful. As many children do, we tried to stay awake on Christmas Eve in the hope of surprising Santa Claus, but he is nearly always too elusive.

I say nearly always elusive . . .

That long ago night before Christmas, my sister Stella and I lay awake, too hot and excited to sleep, for surely Santa Claus was out and about, having been preparing all year, and he might come at any moment. We had a chimney in our room, and what if he chose that one instead of the living room one? We were aware that he usually waited until everyone was asleep, but perhaps he didn't know that Stella was notorious for resisting going to bed and then getting up again.

My bed was beside the window, and Stella's was against the wall. It was too hot to be under covers, so we were lying with only a sheet over us. Finally my sister came over to the window, which looked out at the verandah and the street, and sat perched at the end of my bed, talking. She frequently kept me up talking, and as she had a difficult temperament I had to oblige her by staying awake or she would get angry and thump me. How old were we? I had started school, so I may have been six, and Stella was more than three years older. I cannot tell how long we sat up, talking and making up stories and games, lit only by the street light outside, enjoying the excitement of Christmas Eve, until the whole world seemed asleep. It was then we heard a strange sound.

It was the sound of faint bells, far away and not of this world; and as we both started towards the window, looking out in surprise, we saw, passing over the verandah side, the shadow of something, moving swiftly. It seemed a shadow of something that was lit up – by the street light? – casting a silhouette that was plainly visible. It was of a sleigh, full of sacks, led by reindeers, as our one glance of it revealed. It passed over quickly, running along the verandah and along the opposite wall – and gone. There had been nothing in the street.

We turned to each other, round-eyed, 'Did you see that?' and both nodded in reply to each other.

Later we pondered over this strange experience. Had we dreamed it? But no, could we both have had the same dream? We compared our memories of it, and they were exactly the same. I can see it in my mind now. We tried staying up for subsequent Christmas Eves, hoping to see or hear something again; but it never recurred. As adults we still remembered it exactly the same. Our mother had told us, when forced to admit that Santa Claus did not actually exist, that the Spirit of Christmas still did, because it lived in all our hearts. I found that a lovely idea.

So – did we dream it? Did we imagine it? Or did it really happen?

Do I hear a "Bah! Humbug"?

Crystal - an allegory about Autism
Dawn Meredith

All her life Crystal had felt alone and strangely different: she was made of different stuff. One day she decided to take a walk and discover if there were others like herself.

She walked and walked. There ahead, a rocky hill rose out of the earth. Crystal decided to climb it. She pushed her stiff, transparent legs up the path to the top of the hill. Her clear, hard feet made a clattering sound as she tried to find a safe and comfortable spot to stand. The sun sparkled on her crystal body, sending shafts of blazing light all around.

Below lay a wide valley of colours, pink and green and yellow and purply-brown. Turning, Crystal was surprised to see a girl standing there; a girl of purest porcelain white, with a rosebud mouth, blue eyes and pale hair. The girl's blue dress looked very pretty. Crystal wished she had a dress like that.

'Hello,' said the girl, in a high, tinkling voice. She patted her stiff dress with a dainty gloved hand. 'I'm China Blue. What's your name?' Crystal stared at the girl's face but said nothing. China Blue was so different. So delicate. 'Do you have a name?' persisted the porcelain girl.

Crystal blinked. 'Of course I have a name.'

'If you don't want to tell me, that's fine,' said China Blue, sniffing, with her tiny upturned nose in the air. This annoyed Crystal.

'I don't have to tell you anything about me,' she said stiffly. China's Blue's eyes glittered like sapphires.

'No. You don't. But it's polite when someone tells you their name to tell them yours.'

'Oh. Ok.' Crystal felt silly now. 'Anyway, it's Crystal.'

'That's a pretty name,' observed the porcelain girl, trying to sit down on a large flat rock. A sweet smelling wind blew gently around her dress but it never moved. Her hair lay in perfect folds around her shoulders, stiff, unruffled. Crystal wished she had pretty coloured hair.

'Where did you get your dress?' she asked shyly.

'My mother gave it to me,' China Blue replied.

'Oh.' Crystal didn't have a mother. So, no dress. She turned and walked away, without saying goodbye, leaving China Blue sitting on the rock. Alone.

Crystal continued her walk of discovery. In a bright forest where sunlight danced among the ferns she met a girl of oak wood, kicking up leaves with her strong legs. As Crystal approached, the girl ran towards her, smiling. Her eyes were golden brown and her hair the colour of honey.

'I'm Goldie,' she said, taking Crystal's hand. 'What's your name?' Crystal stared at the wooden girl, whose twiggy fingers twined around her clear, sharp hand. She pulled away, frowning.

'Why are you touching me?'

The wooden girl laughed and it sounded like the song of a soft wind among pine trees.

'It's spring and my heart is beating faster, with the joy of it!' she exclaimed. 'Isn't your sap running like golden honey in your veins?'

'I have no sap!' snapped Crystal angrily. 'I'm pure, clear crystal. My veins are fine lines of gold and never change.' She turned away. Her square edged heart felt squeezed, as if a giant hand had hold of it. 'I'm going now.'

'But will you come back and play?' asked Goldie. Crystal turned to stare blankly at the girl. Goldie tilted her head and looked suddenly sad. 'Don't you know what play is?'

'Of course I do!' replied Crystal. 'It's where you're in a group and you all tell each other what to say and do.'

Goldie giggled. 'That's not playing! That's… something else.' She reached out curiously and touched Crystal's hard cheek with her finger. 'It's supposed to be fun. Wouldn't you like that? I could show you.'

Crystal turned away. 'No thank you.' She walked on and came upon a sandy white beach. There Crystal saw a paper girl in red shoes dancing on the glittering sand. Curling and uncurling, she bent this way and that in an intricate pattern of twirls. Her papery dress was cut with beautiful designs that blinked in the light as she twirled. Crystal stood and stared.

'Why are you doing that?' Crystal asked, feeling a strange sensation in her feet, as if they wanted to copy the red shoes. The paper girl laughed and it sounded like the rustling of summer grasses in a meadow.

'Can't you hear the wonderful music?' said the paper girl, twirling her lacy dress. She held out her elegant, papery-soft hands. 'Come on. My name is Scarlett. I'll teach you how to dance.'

'So that's what it's called,' mumbled Crystal. There didn't seem to be any point to it. But her feet felt itchy, like they yearned to move. 'I'm Crystal,' she said, watching the patterns the paper girl made. 'Do you think… you could stop awhile and talk to me?'

Scarlett smiled as she waltzed by, circling ever wider. 'It's easy! Just try it! You'll have such fun!'

Crystal shook her head. 'I don't think so.' She looked down at her itchy feet. 'Maybe another time.' And she left.

In a field of buttercups Crystal saw a girl of delicate feathers flutter down from the sky, her wings spread wide to catch the warm summer air. Her face was so small and fine, her eyes sharply beautiful. She called out to Crystal in a voice high and sweet.

'Hello! My name is Pipit. Isn't this the most glorious day you've ever seen?' And she swooped over Crystal, leaving trails of downy feathers. Crystal watched her, silently in awe. 'What's your name, sparkly girl?' cried Pipit.

'Crystal.'

'That's a stunning name!' sang the feathered girl. Pausing high above, she lifted her face to the sun and trilled, 'Sun, oh sun! How I love your warmth on my back and your strength that draws me ever higher!' Crystal rose up on tiptoe, her fingers tingling, her arms out wide. What would it feel like to glide upon air? She wondered.

'How do you do that?' she called up to the feathered girl.

Pipit swooped down and her small feet landed softly in the grass. Her wings out, she bounded forward and before Crystal could stop her, she had put one wing around the hard, transparent girl. The warmth of her feathered body felt strange. And scary. Crystal pulled away.

'I'm… not used to people touching me,' she said, staring at her bare feet, with their hard stiff toes. She longed to be pliant, flexible, to do backflips and fly with the feathered girl in the blue dome above.

'I'm sorry to hear that,' replied Pipit. And her fine eyes welled up with tears. 'How can you stand being so cold and hard and alone?'

Crystal felt a lump in her chest rise up and get stuck in her throat. She wanted to answer the feathered girl. The warmth under Pipit's wing had melted something in her heart. A longing for company. And perhaps the beginnings of trust. But all she could do was stare at the beautiful feathered girl as a single diamond shard, squeezed out of her eye and hung glistening on her cheek. She turned and fled, leaving Pipit calling out for her to come back.

Stumbling now, Crystal found herself in a cave. The dimness was comforting. No one could see her here. She wanted to dance like Scarlett, the paper girl, to forget sorrows and twirl, but her legs were too stiff and her feet too clumsy. She tried to sing with a clear high voice like Pipit, the feathered girl, but all that came out was a croak. She wished for a pretty blue dress with delicate designs like China Blue but when she looked down all she saw was her colourlessness. She wished for invigorating sap running through her lifeless veins and to feel the joy of new life in spring like Goldie the oak girl. But there was no light or joy in her. She wished, oh how she wished to be like them!

Crystal sat down, drew up her knees and cried. Hot, salty, lonely tears gushed out. Her heart swelled like ripe fruit in the late summer. Her delicate feet were cut by the cold rock. Her hair fell gently over her face. But she noticed none of it. Outside the cave, lightning snatched across the darkened sky, followed by a rumble so deep it shook the earth. Rain gushed down, washing away all trace of the day as night crept in. Crystal fell into exhausted sleep, curled up like a hibernating squirrel, tears perched on her cheek like raindrops.

In the morning the first thing Crystal heard was the bird chorus. She opened her eyes, stretched and took a deep, satisfying breath of rain-freshened air. Getting up slowly she walked out of the cave to admire the day. Her feet decided they wanted to go, so she began walking, over the ploughed fields, through the sunlit forest, up to the hilltop, without a single sign of China Blue, Goldie, Scarlett or Pipit. Would she ever see her new friends again? She already missed them.

Somehow the sun was so wonderfully warm and friendly today. She could feel her soft hair swishing over her shoulders. Her arms swung gently by her sides as she walked. She twirled and she realized she was humming. Looking down at her hands she saw they were milky smooth and supple, with white tipped nails.

Clasping her hands to her heart she felt it warm and beating steadily. With delight, she noticed she was wearing a pretty red dress and gold sandals. Raising her sparkling eyes to the sky she felt laughter bubble up in her throat…

And it sounded like the sweetest birdsong in the world.

Message (West Coast, Tasmania)
Graeme Hetherington

To the exclusion of all else,
My handyman-father set great
Store by traditional male skills

I was born totally without,
Irritably dismissing me
As a 'useless arrangement', or

'No hoper', summations that stung,
Eroded personality,
Till in a carpentry class, I,

Disgraced, humiliated for
Pains taken to succeed, began
To glory in his categories,

Perversity climaxing in
A Christmas present that I made
As badly as I could for home,

A letter box we didn't need
Since mail was held at the PO,
Further sabotaging by scant

Application of glue, so it
Beneath my dad's inspecting touch
Stood every chance of falling to

Bits in accord with his idea
Of me. And when by happy chance,
Right on cue, it obeyed enough

To start going skew-whiff, my look
Of hard-eyed, smirking triumph caused
Him at a loss to leave the room.

In The Month That Heralds Winter
Meg McLaren

Everything normal seems suspended
as I walk along the highway,
waiting for Matt's call.
Sun warms the grey stone.
Gardens burdened with autumn palettes
wash over me like a blanket.
Daisies tumble, unrestrained,
over weathered benches.
The Universe is quiet.
Nothing, it seems, will frighten this spirit
as she journeys from the shadows.

Like those Russian dolls
stacked one inside the other,
only your face was visible
when I first saw you.
Your mother, my daughter,
removed the outer covering,
and it seemed that the very essence of life
was embodied within,
and I wonder how old is your soul?
Hands flutter like paper flowers and you
grip my finger until it turns white.

Ancient eyes, unfocused,
glide beyond the outback.
Hovering above the dusty, red loam.
The Celts of old, your ancestors
strong in battle, stand silent around you,
transfixed by your beauty and the power within.
And you seem to be saying,
'I want to live, to touch and see and feel.
To dream glad dreams of wonder.
To gaze at the moon lighting the night sky
until a new day dawns.'

Full Moon: For John Keats
Graeme Hetherington

I'm fairly sure I can make out,
A little blurred, a rabbit in
The full moon, on the squat, ears pricked,

As a reincarnation since
I shot them as a boy for food,
This part of my mind warring with

The ancient Greek philosopher
Parmenides who thought though it
Seemed as big as a silver coin

In truth it much exceeded that,
Wanting to distinguish between
Illusion and reality.

I'm more at home with John Keats, his
'Negative Capability':
'I see, and sing, by my own eyes

Inspired', from the 'Ode to Psyche',
And in a letter to his kin:
'That is when man is capable

Of being in uncertainties,
Mysteries----without irritable
Reaching after fact and reason',

The bunny when I checked tonight
Alert enough so far to have
Dodged astronauts stomping around.

Ayers Rock Incident
Pete Stratford

It was barely a month before the Australian public were to begin struggling with the pronunciation of the name "Azaria", when I stood gazing up the steep face of Ayers Rock. With my wife and two pre-teen daughters we had driven up from Adelaide in convoy with friends whose three children were of similar ages.

Having set up our tents in the campsite, we joined other tourists slowly climbing the imposing monolith while carefully edging past those making their descent, though our children gambolled on ahead quite deaf to our words of caution. Only we of more mature years could foresee the dire consequences that would befall anyone who stumbled or tripped, for there was scarcely half a pace of safe area beside the track before the gradient dropped away sharply out of sight. I was acutely mindful it offered no second chance of regaining a foothold and several small bronze plaques attached at the base of the rock carried names of those who had perished in this manner. Despite my fears we all reached the summit breathless and sweaty but without mishap, then after busily snapping photos of our family atop the Rock, we dutifully signed the tattered visitor's book housed in a stone cairn there. Perhaps this book was destined to the Ranger's rubbish fire when all the torn and dog eared pages were filled, but meantime it held a fleeting record of those who had defied the dangers of falls, sprains, broken bones, or cardiac arrest, to experience something truly magical - the three hundred and sixty degree view. The horizon only interrupted by The Olgas, a close knit group of mountainous rocks protruding from the desert landscape some ten miles in the distance, defying the elements for aeons.

Faces in a crowd are usually not remembered, apart from an occasional one that imprints on the mind for no particular reason and such it was for a couple of young men passing by as they were ascending during our return to the base. One of the pair was slim and tall, with a sallow complexion beneath an oversized Akubra, which I thought a looked a little ridiculous for the few moments we took to pass by, yet never could I have guessed how we two would meet again in tragic circumstances.

Descending was perhaps more terrifying than the ascent, for as we edged past those still climbing I feared the unavoidable that lay before us, that narrow ridge of rock devoid of anything that would arrest a stumble or misplaced step. Fear that knotted in my stomach was not calmed by the sight of a carelessly dropped can of soft drink that cart wheeled over the edge trailing spume as it spiralled from view, but eventually we were safely at the base where we regrouped and I was relieved to know my family were safely on level ground again.

Above us piercing screams suddenly rent the air. Heads turned as one in that direction and I could see what appeared to be a back pack rolling over the edge, but within seconds I saw, to my horror, arms flailing before the object disappeared from our view. A hundred or so people milled about near the base, seeming immobilised by what they had just witnessed. Also shocked by the vision but compelled to seek the answer to what we were all thinking, reluctantly I began the long walk approaching the point where I guessed this unfortunate must surely have ended their fall. Anticipating some horrific scenario, I paused, as if to spare myself the inevitable then from several metres above me, a youthful looking couple called to me, 'they may need help.' My legs robotically resumed the course I'd chosen with only the softly soughing wind accompanying me until eventually small shredded scraps of fabric wafting off the rock face in the breeze drew my attention to where I should search. It heralded a sight forever imprinted in my memory - a near naked fellow reclining awkwardly between two large boulders, arms flung wide. Missing along with the oversized Akubra was a large portion of his skull, the contents splattered over nearby rocks, like some obscene modern art work. As I stood contemplating this scene and what I should do I was vaguely aware of the droning of flies already attracted by the smell of death, a sound which still triggers memories for me. Apart from proper removal of his body he was beyond help, but authorities needed to be notified. Making my way back along the sandy trail I met a Park Ranger, who had already been called to this incident, and I informed him of the location of the body before continuing on my way.

Rejoining my family I simply informed them the fatality was being dealt with by the appropriate authorities, and then attempted to resume the role of a happy camper. Almost an impossible task with graphic images replaying inside my head so to assist getting some restful sleep I self-medicated with brandy. In hindsight that was not a wise decision as I learned that while alcohol incapacitates the body, it does not erase the memory. Next morning we packed up our camping gear to move on, a task not helped by my thumping hangover. Departing Ayers Rock I took with me many memories of wonderment at the beauty of that iconic feature, but unfortunately marred by the traumatic scene I had witnessed there. Years later I was to witness another traumatic death, but that's another story.

A Bad Crowd
Jennie Herrera

A mother says it: he got in with a bad crowd.
That was it, that was what went wrong.
Yes, a bad crowd.

Lurking, always lurking, those influences.

Their cry, as if they could fence sons in—
Or is it a kind of guilt—kept forever silent?
Why didn't I—

Those faces waiting at the court, pretending calm.

At least they've come; it wasn't the cast-out son.
They sit and wait (and wait) for the called name.
The casual shrug.

The ones who collect in summonsed so-what-mode.

The son who is embarrassed by his mum sitting there,
Yet half-glad. (She came.) And the palms that sweat.
Doesn't matter.

Of course it does but nerves can't be acknowledged.

You should've worn your suit, not jeans, I'm sure …
But she doesn't know what will sway the hearts
Of magistrates.

No tattoos, no eyebrow stud, clean fingernails …

At least he's neat and clean … I wish we'd—if only
His dad—we should've put our foot down that time—
We didn't know.

The little signs overlooked—or were we just too busy?

The school, they should've seen, should've told us,
Why didn't they see where this was heading, didn't they
Have a duty?

But schooling stops and the crowd goes on, all that's left.

Jobs. If he'd got a job this wouldn't have … if he was
Tired when he came home from a good day's work
He wouldn't want …

But every place said no, some didn't even bother to reply.

All these people here, rushing to and fro, official-looking,
And the reasons for their rush sit here and wait. A tense
And terminal place.

There must be better ways to unhook the young from …

He grew away from his mum and dad and all at home;
Kids do. Had nowhere else to go but hung around the mall—
They caught him there.

That crowd. Said hey, how's about, and he went along.

Course he went along. I'm sure we did our best for him,
Not our fault but … he got in with a bad crowd, that's the sum
of it,
That's what went wrong.

Didn't have the words, didn't have that self-esteem they talk
about.

Other mums lament, wait, blame, wish, grieve, a refrain, there
Waiting to be called into court. He wouldn't be here if
It wasn't for—

That crowd, that bad lot, those youths with nothing better …

Search and Rescue
Jake O'Mara

It all started with a group of cashed-up young men keen to attend the Formula One Grand Prix in Adelaide. They all worked at Telfer Mining Centre and chartering an aircraft from Port Hedland is the quickest way to get to the big smoke. Their plan circumvented all the plane changes, queues and departure lounge waiting that domestic air travel normally entails.

The chosen aircraft was a middle-aged Cessna 206. It will seat six including the pilot, and there are five lads desperate for some big-city action. The pilot was aware that the 206's engine was due for a major overhaul, and that its oil consumption is therefore higher than usual. The plane left Hedland in the early am, with an hour and a half's flying time to Telfer. At the mine, the passengers boarded, already excited about hoped-for escapades in Adelaide. Next stop, refuelling at Warburton Community, two and a half hours away.

*　　*　　*　　*　　*　　*

Warburton nursing staff bunkhouse, 8:00 am Friday.

I hear the screen door open, and Max appears, he's usually about early, but it's unusual for him to call on me, he won't know I was called out last night, and am still a bit groggy. Neither of us knows that we are about to participate in a comedy of errors, a farce that even Oscar Wilde or Noel Coward could not have dreamed up.

'Morning Jake, how goes it?'

'OK I guess, but I was called out at two am, by a bloke that wanted worm tablets.'

'Yeah, not much of an emergency; he probably couldn't sleep and decided to make someone else suffer as well. Sorry for disturbing you, but we've had a call from Kalgoorlie, a Cessna 206's engine has failed and is down forty nautical miles to the north west of here.'

'Shite, that could be serious!'

'Apparently not. They reckon the plane is undamaged and everybody on board is OK, but they want us to organise a rescue party. We probably need you on board in case there are problems.

I'll go and tell Harry now, ("Harry" is the roads foreman) he's got a GPS.'

GPS is a brand-new technology, and I'm impressed. I start to collect old-school stuff like spare tyres and de-bogging equipment. The health Landcruiser is fuelled already, so I grab some medical stuff, then some food and water and am ready to go.

Ah yes, we're ready, but leaving is not quite that simple. Some Perth-based trainee incompetent out there in Search and Rescue land decides to go for broke and use an aircraft to find and collect the guys, in their haste forgetting that there is nowhere for a plane to land anywhere near the downed mob. Nowhere closer than Warburton anyway.

No, forget all that, they'll send a helicopter from Kalgoorlie. Brilliant! That sounds OK until somebody reminds them that none of the choppers available have enough fuel range to get to the site and back. They use Jet A-1 and we don't stock that at Warbo, so that possibility crashes before take-off.

Right! We'll get a long-range chopper from Adelaide! This is getting better and better! Well, no... the long-range one will need to be refuelled somewhere on two thousand kilometres of Eyre Highway just to get it to Kalgoorlie. That fuel would have to be delivered by road and might take a couple of days to organise. The guys waiting out there in the scrub will be due for the bloody old-age pension before we get to them at this rate!

These prime examples of haste and ignorance and 180-degree turns mean that five hours elapse before we are cleared for our original low-tech mission. The Police from way down in Laverton are in the community on their regular patrol, so we have three vehicles in convoy; Harry, the cops, and me. We set off in the early afternoon, with the roads man and his technologically astute son Chris leading.

Half an hour of dirt road and bush track driving gets us as close as any form of track can to the stricken plane, then we turn off into flat spinifex country. That quickly changes to small rocky breakaways between occasional long sand ridges. The problems begin almost immediately, with one vehicle or another getting bogged, just to break up the predictable monotony of flat tyres. Harry's vehicle has 12-ply conventional tyres and fares well, but the boys in blue and I are running radial-ply tyres which have their soft sidewalls ripped out with metronomic regularity by mulga stumps.

Both vehicles are carrying three spare tyres, and we run around changing wheels like a sweaty, dusty, profanity-uttering Formula One pit crew. Glamorous, scantily clad grid girls are notable by their absence.

In the meantime, a search aircraft has arrived from Alice Springs and is circling over the downed plane, not able to comprehend why we are so slow. On the ground we bash our way through mulga thickets, across gullies strewn with microwave oven-sized rocks and over steep spinifex-covered sand-ridges that look like the man-made jumps on a motocross track. We sweat and curse, our struggling vehicles crawling like ants in the immensity of an ancient land that has reduced all our 20th century sophistication to nothing. We are so near and yet so far from the Cessna.

The plane above us starts flying up and back in a straight line, trying to guide us onto what from the air looks like a usable track, but it is an old geophysical survey line even more overgrown with scrub than the surrounds. So onward we press, the short-sighted leading the profoundly blind, never knowing which of several possible routes will prove to be a dead end and which a means of real progress. It's all trial and error. I keep looking at the lowering sun and my watch to estimate how much daylight we've got, but the real problems have only just begun.

Communication should be a doddle, as all three vehicles are equipped with multi-channel UHF radios. But we soon discover that we have no channels in common, not one, and are reduced to shouting impotently to each other through a hundred metres of scrub. We can't radio each other, the downed plane or the circling aircraft, and none of them can radio us. The plane above gives up and flies off to Warbo for more fuel.

Someone at search HQ then informs the grounded pilot (via the plane's radio) and passengers that if we have not reached them by 4 pm they are to light a signal fire. Never mind that we have a GPS position to guide us to within ten metres of the plane, the technology is too new for procedural bureaucrats.

At 4 pm the guys dutifully light a fire in the spinifex, and we spot the smoke column immediately. It tells us nothing we didn't already know, and we battle on. An hour later the wind has increased, and the search plane returns to swoops low over us. An object falls from the plane, and we dash over to collect it from the metre-high spinifex. It's a note in a soft-drink bottle, and the message is written on a sick-bag;

"Please hurry, fire has turned toward aircraft!"

The wind has changed, turning the fire back on the plane which is standing up to its knees in material that burns like kerosene-soaked straw. In their urging of haste, it's hard to know what the blokes in the spotter plane thinks we are doing, maybe they have spotted our picnic blanket with chicken and champagne. Seriously, a swimmer pursued by a crocodile surely doesn't need to be told to get a move on. We heed the ominous message and become more worried, but it does absolutely nothing for our rate of progress in such impossible country.

Another half hour of desperate crashing about and the plane swoops low again with another soft drink bottle, another sick-bag message;

"Plane in danger of being engulfed by flames!"

We are still struggling through scrub and sand when the white smoke of burning spinifex suddenly becomes a great roiling cloud of black smoke shot with orange flames. The plane's fuel tanks have exploded.

Finally, with the sun just below the horizon and darkness rapidly closing, we drive over the last sandhill and see the plane, now just a smouldering ruin. The centre of the fuselage has gone, as well as the one wing that had fuel in it, while the engine and propeller with nosewheel attached has fallen like a shot cowboy onto its face in the dust. The plane's miserable crew are huddled on a little hill a safe distance away like Napoleon and his generals at Waterloo, but they are very glad to see us.

It has been eleven hours since their terrifying unplanned descent, and five hours since we got permission to leave Warburton. It has taken us well over four hours to cover the 20 or so kilometres since leaving the last semblance of road. The pilot is a pale young man in his early twenties, and he is a picture of contained anger and frustration. He has successfully landed the plane safely and without serious damage in country full of rocky outcrops, small trees and great sand-filled clumps of spinifex, only to see it burn to a crisp before his eyes. That they weren't all killed was due to his skills, and his alone.

We stand around for a while kicking blackened rocks and staring glumly at the smoking remnants of a $200k aircraft, then load the sorry lot into the back of the two troop-carriers and slowly wind our way back to the road in the dark, following our tracks in as best we can. It is after midnight when the dusty, tired convoy reaches Warburton. Luckily, I am the only occupant of the nurse's accommodation, so spare beds are easily found.

Next morning in the clinic I'm doing a wound dressing on a middle-aged Aboriginal lady. She is accompanied by one of her friends who circumspectly raises the subject of the downed plane. Word has got about quickly.

'That one aeroplane, he burnt?'

'Yes, it burnt' I reply.

'Finish?' She asks with a downward flourish of her hand indicating the end of something.

'Yes, it's finished.' The women look at each other dismayed, as though Uluru had somehow turned itself upside down. There is a long, incredulous pause as they try to take in the impossibility of what I am telling them. Then the patient gets a look of sudden inspiration and says,

'…Whitefellas?'

I confirm that the fire was indeed initiated by Whitefellas, and the pair look very relieved, it all makes sense now. God is still in heaven and Whitefellas still know jack shit about managing fire.

Amen.

And Whisper Is Her Name
Dawn Meredith

On a sunny morning a soul passed.
Whisper gently took that last breath
and cradled it in her loving hands
To bear it away on soft wings,
No matter that the day was bright with promise
And the girl who used to be, was already gone.

With pity, did Whisper
look upon the slack face that laughed and cried no more,
The eyes that saw brightness only briefly, before fading.
And Whisper gathered the ruins tenderly,
Along with the sharp, bright joys and the groaning grief.

Whisper asks nothing;
She comes at the appointed hour,
Undaunted by questions, unfazed by horror
And gathers the soul's memories to her breast
as if they were her own;

Whisper does not grieve,
She rejoices. For every breath of life
That was given is a diamond, sparkling with beauty
And the truth of what it means to be alive.
No matter how fleeting or small,

In the end, even a kernel of love, tightly held, matters.

Within the pages of a book...
Pete Stratford

I'm struggling through dense jungle,
tangled greenery all I see
with pursuers closing in behind
I feel I'll die if I don't flee...
as I'm lost amidst the pages of a book.
Gleaming treasure sparkles 'neath the dust
hidden there since middle ages
and our team have just unearthed it
news will splash across front pages...
as I seek amongst the pages of a book.
Cold eyes glow in the spotlight beam
before the hungry croc submerges
to lurk beneath my flimsy craft
driven by dark primal urges...
as I float along the pages of a book.
Deep down where the ocean darkens
I see illumed within the gloom
a decaying sunken vessel
since a storm had sealed it's doom...
and I dive within the pages of a book.
She's a seductress so beguiling
using all her wiles to allure
my resistance quickly weakening
to her intentions so impure...
when I'm lost between the pages of a book.
There are many great adventures
found within a good book's pages
that stir our imagination
or transport us through the ages...
when we're lost within the pages of a book.

Where Should I Be?

Brenda Slavoff

Cold winds are blowing,
Where should I be?
The current is flowing
To the tides of the sea;
The pale moon is waning,
The wind is complaining,
My sad heart is saying,
Where would I be?

**

Wide is the ocean,
Far the horizon,
And my emotion
Like moonbeams reach on;
The breakers are clamouring
The echoes of winds,
My faint heart is stammering,
Where should I be?

**

Searching the distance
Where once the sun set,
Marking the hours
Since day and night met,
Wide is the ocean,
Cold is the wind;
Where would I be, I ask,
If you were with me?

Profit. Or Loss?
Anne Layton-Bennett

there are no winners in this crazy phase
we're living in
where so-called leaders disregard
our planet,
treat it like
a balance sheet
a set of numbers
a political abacus,
a plaything to be abused
exploited, mined for its wonders

then they wonder why the columns
don't add up
they refuse to see it's
their greed, their stupidity
and their fool's gold
that's creating a barren world
where eagles no longer soar
where plains no longer hear a lion's roar
where disease is rife,
and it's hard to breathe
clean air
drink clean water,
or harvest food
free of chemical contamination

Seen from a train
Jennie Herrera

Straight through! A whistle. A place that offers no reason to
stop.
Just a dusty straggle, houses, sheds, tin, brick, board …
the sun on rusting roofs …
Children running on the road. Ragged children.
The parallel road, a track, twin ruts.
Waving children. Ragged children.
Then our speed increases—

The homes, the low hill, the dull dry brown earth.
The terrible nothingness of it all.
A place seen … and forgotten again.
    A nothing place.
'I'm so glad I don't live …' My eyes turned to smeared
windows. So glad. Thank God.

And the children's little legs, bare, brown,
running, reaching, being left behind, with our speed,
slicing through their lives … until the next train …
And then I doze.

The grass, the earth, the spinning world,
that contains all ephemera, all experience, going nowhere
but daily sees … a train …

The miracle of the train which says: other people, other lives.

I dream I live—there. I dream my life is circumscribed.
I feel this terrible aching in my breast that might be dust
and closed windows rattling and might be the fear of being
nothing
in other lives …

David Scholes - 17th June 1990
Graeme Bourke

Today, I met for the first time David Scholes, fly fisherman, writer, painter and World War Two pilot. Everyone has an idol or someone they look up to. I could not help but be drawn to his writing, and to meet the man himself was an experience of a life time. My reason for visiting was to ask some advice about publishing a book (*Come Fly Fish With Me*) that I had written.

The humble white weatherboard cottage both inside and outside expressed a neatness that I felt portrayed some aspects of David Scholes' character, in other words, his striving for perfection in everything he did. The simple style of the building with its uncovered and bare timber flooring, varnished and shining, made me feel very much at home.

I looked down at the fishing magazines that lay on the table in front of me as I waited for David to finish on the phone. I picked up one of the magazines and flicked through the pages. I felt a little nervous in the presence of a man who had fished in many countries, experienced a multitude of adventures and hooked hundreds of trout. I put the magazine down; I couldn't concentrate on it.

Sitting in the cushioned chair with the heat from the open fire pleasantly warming my body, I could not help but be transformed back into the past to when I was a small boy, when open fires were the only source of heating and conversation the only entertainment. How simple were the evenings by the fire in those times when fishing tales went on into the night. I recall struggling to keep my eyes open, but not daring to shut them in fear of missing one word of the exciting adventures that had befallen my elders.

I waited patiently and noticed his slow movements as he put down the phone. The hands that had held many rods moved with obvious difficulty. It is sad to see, but then time stands still for no-one and we all have to face the inevitable, when the hands do not have the power they used to and the body will not stand the rigors of an earlier life.

He was a slightly built man with receding hair that was combed neatly at the sides and he spoke with a firm clear voice when he enquired on what it was, he could do for me. I replied that all I needed was some advice on writing and publishing. With that, he promptly asked me some questions about the proposed book. Then he explained to me all the problems associated with getting a book accepted. He stressed the point that I was only writing for a small section of the fishing fraternity, which could create difficulties in finding a publisher. I felt a little dejected by his negative comments, but deep down I knew that he was right as he continued on explaining the process that works within the publishing industry. I began to understand his wisdom.

As the conversation progressed, I found our opinions on fishing and writing were the same. Scholes mentioned a book written by a local author that was not recognised for its literary excellence, but the book portrayed the true character of the individual and was written from the heart. I have always believed, as David did also, that any writings that will in the future become part of our history and heritage should be treasured as such.

There has been so much of our past lost because nothing was ever recorded. How many tales from around the campfire have been lost forever? What of the stories that helped create our history? What of the days of the Shannon Rise and the early years of the Great Lake? This was one of the reasons why I wrote, so that a small section of our freshwater fishing could be recorded.

Words of a book must flow, explained Scholes. If they do not, then no one will ever remember you as a person of any literary prose. Somehow, I felt that he was talking about himself a little, but I knew that once again he spoke from a vast knowledge and wisdom. Yes, the words must flow, just like the rivers we fish in, twisting, turning, blending and mixing together. Each small stream linked with one another, until finally, they all join to form a mighty river which tumbles on to the ocean.

This was how my book had come together, from bits and pieces that eventually combined to be as one. He spoke of his latest book that was yet to be published. The book, he explained, would be a pictorial depicting his fishing life. It would begin with a photo from when he was only ten years old. Somewhat perturbed, I listened as he spoke of the day when he would no longer be with us. He realised only too well that, once he passed away, all his photos of times gone by wouldn't mean much to anybody else. To him, it was vitally important that words be put to the pictures and thus recorded. For if they were not, then another small but important link with our past would be lost.

Having taken up enough of his time, I bade farewell and expressed my thanks for the small but entertaining moment of conversation. He in turn asked that I let him know how I managed with the publishers. On leaving the house I felt in one way that I had achieved little, but in another way, I knew that it was all up to me. That was the general feeling I had received from David Scholes. Much in the same way as the teacher and the pupil, the teacher can only take the pupil so far.

Later that week I happened to be visiting the local fishing store and while I was there the phone rang and it was David Scholes; he was enquiring about a new rod and reel for the coming season. It really pleased me to know that the old gentleman of fishing was anticipating yet another season. When the book was published, I sent David a copy. Sadly, on the 25th May, 2005 David passed away. His spirit will live on in his writing. That much I can guarantee.

Renison Bell Loners
Graeme Hetherington

Mine manager's son, I would meet
Them on tracks leading through the bush
To the osmiridium fields

To prospect for a small return
While secretly wishing for gold,
Old single blokes he'd sacked because

Of going off the rails as laid
Down narrowly by him, though on
Their so-called 'last chance' when blown in

By God-alone-knew what fate-cursed
Situation elsewhere. Their world
Pile high and clanking on stooped backs,

It seemed like mine, reduced by his
Judgement of me as not his type,
Until this seed of difference sown

Watered by these drifters as role
Models blossomed to dislike of
Family life, becoming a quest

For my elusive home and all
The dreamt of riches it might yield,
As flashes in pans were for them.

Letters Home
Jennie Herrera

'I know you're waiting, dearest father, eager to know
That we are safely moved, that our new home already
Promises familiar trees in saplings' shape that will grow
And beckon, some day recreate the vistas left behind,

Though when I walk my dear husband still adjures me "Take
care"—

And other people, more knowing, longer resident, are keen to
Tell us tales of this world they too fumble to embrace, half-
fearful,
Half in delight, as they grope for words; their experience not
yet
Ours and so I hesitate to repeat hearsay, of whatever kind—

I twirl my pen once more, dip it, dither, ponder, now painfully
aware …

There truly are no words, dearest father, to tell you
How the sun lies on the bay, nor the way sombre
Forests crowd us round, so dark and grim to our
Unaccustomed eyes, and strange and mild when entered in …

And if I tell you that swans are black—will you call me
(fondly) liar?

Where are the words, dearest father, to describe
The bark upon these untidy nameless trees, this bark
That hangs in swaying strips, so we can glimpse delicate
Cream and ivory, secret madder, tan, rich chestnut tints …

Next letter I'll tell you stranger things; your loving daughter
Anna Maria.'

From Horses to Horsepower
Pete Stratford

Old Grandpa grew up working horses, knowing each one's
odd foibles and quirks
all about how to harness and feed them, and how each of their
implements works.
But horses age just as we do, and his faithful old friends
reached the stage
that replacing them wasn't an option, as farms entered the
mechanised age
so Grandpa joined those progressing, investing in a tractor at
last
but was so used to handling horses, had some habits he
couldn't get past.
He struggled with changing the gears, and even more so with
the clutch
though the brakes he managed to master, but he didn't use
them that much.
With the motor roaring full throttle, he'd heave the gear stick
with a yank
which often resulted in stalling, so he'd have to climb off and
re-crank.
Noise from the motor was deafening, unlike horses that he'd
worked before
it didn't matter if someone was listening, for nobody heard
when he swore.
Those crank handles, an evil invention, had a mind of their
own when they turned
to frequently kick badly backwards, very hard on your wrists
one soon learned.
Well, Granpa would then swing that handle, at the tractor and
give it a "whack!"
'if you're gonna kick me, you bugger, then I'm gonna belt
you right back!'
Now that may have worked on the horses, but tractors don't
fear such attacks
but soon became chipped, grazed and dented, with radiator
leaks from the cracks.

It was old Grandpa's mishap that killed it, though very few others would know
he was driving it down near the river, to a spot that he often would go
to hook a snig chain on a log there, then drag it up to his wood shed
a task his horses knew backwards, but a tractor needed steering instead.
So that's how it came to start wandering, heading straight for a deep swimming hole
when Grandpa was slightly distracted, when he took out his pouch for a roll.
Now smoking is said to be dangerous and this time that proved to be true
while his horses would stop at a fence, his tractor just charged on right through
The old chap was yelling his lungs out, but of course it couldn't respond
and continued right into the river to submerge in a deep muddy pond
with him still sitting there swearing and water way up past his bum
a vision that we'd find amusing, but Granpa sure didn't think fun!
That tractor was later recovered, with repairs costing two hundred pound
never driven again by our Grandpa, who claimed he went deaf from its sound.
He retired from farming soon after, moving to a retirement place
repeatedly telling all tenants, tales of Bluey, and Dolly, and Grace.
His memory of horses was perfect, he remembered old Darkie and Hank
but if mention was made of a tractor, very quickly his memory went blank!

That Sinking Feeling
Jake O'Mara

It's quiet in here, silent except for the creaks and pops of expanding metal cladding. Outside the sun beats down with hammer blows from directly above, as if to minimise any shadow that could provide relief. The ubiquitous red sand glares back defiantly, and anything metal will be far too hot to touch. Nothing much moves unnecessarily at this time of day so I'm surprised to hear someone calling me from the driveway. I go to the door, open the security cage on the veranda and greet two women. The older one is Lena, a health-worker in her mid-thirties I've known for a couple of years. She's not had much training but is very smart. The younger one, apparently in her early twenties, is holding a small baby. I have never seen mother or baby before. Apparently, they are related to Lena.

Lena explains that the infant has been curling her foot repeatedly but is not doing it now. They have taken the trouble to call me out and it needs investigating. I go back inside to collect my keys. We walk slowly down to the clinic without speaking. The ground is burning hot, but their bare feet are incredibly tough. I want to ask questions, but they seem not to want the discussion to start yet. The young mother is very shy, with a minimal grasp of English. The clinic is only slightly larger than a double garage, and I lead them into the air-conditioned examination room.

I start with questions about the baby, then about the mother.

'How old is the baby?'

'It's a new baby, Sister,' Lena says. I'm called sister, like every other nurse, despite being male.

'He might be four weeks old.' The child is female, but gender, always difficult in translation, is irrelevant now. They are unable to give a date of birth, it isn't important to them.

'Where are they from?' Lena says the mother is from another community three hours down the sandy track that serves as a road, but it is in the Northern Territory, and we are in Western Australia.

I want information from the Nurse at that community, but it's Sunday, and the clinic radio will not be manned. I start a new file and open a progress note. Everything seems normal, and the baby is asleep. They say it has been feeding properly but I am concerned, and so is Lena. Reluctantly I send them home, with instructions to get me if the foot-curling starts again.

Back in my silent house I start preparing the evening meal. After eating I settle down to watch TV, but the baby is still there in the back of my mind. A little voice in my brain keeps saying 'What could cause that…?' What if…? At about 9 pm the inner voice gets the better of me; I know I will think about this all night. I collect a torch plus my callout bag and head down to where Lena lives. It's about two hundred metres, maybe three.

There are five tiny red metal houses on my way, and each stands dark and silent. They are too hot to sleep in, and one or two have the dull glow of small cooking fires out the front. My feet sound loud on the gravel until a half dozen yapping, snarling dogs confront me, each one daring the other to attack. This happens every time I do a late visit to the camp, so I reach down for a few small rocks and they retreat, but only far enough to give themselves time to dodge a missile.

At Lena's house the only person awake is an old lady, sitting in the dirt beside a few smouldering coals. She seems to know why I'm here and points with her bottom lip to indicate which one of the five or six shapeless bundles on the ground is the new mother. I kneel carefully down beside the blankets and feel under them for the baby, hoping against hope it will be all right. I touch a tiny foot first, and it is curling then uncurling. My heart sinks. I feel further along for the hand. Same rhythmic clutching, same side. Oh shit! There's enough evidence to almost guarantee encephalitis of some sort, and I'm only a poor bloody nurse when the situation needs a neurologist, but the nearest one is two thousand kilometres away in Perth. I'll have to try the Flying Doctor Service in Alice Springs for an emergency evacuation.

I wake Lena and sprint back to the clinic, and she appears soon after with the baby. The mother eventually ambles over, a bit resentful at being woken up. I put my stethoscope to that tiny chest, but the heartbeat is too fast to count, at least 180 a minute, and the breaths are also very rapid. As I listen the heart rate begins to fall toward normal then below, like an electric toy running out of battery. The heart continues to slow, "lub-dup…lub-dup"… to an awful, sickening stop. I listen for what seems like an eternity, willing the sound to restart and just when I've given up hope it starts again and immediately begins its impossible rise to the same blistering level as before. As soon the rate peaks it begins that deathly descent all over again. The child is literally at death's door. I spring to the UHF radio,

'Romeo Lima Hotel, VJD, Romeo Lima Hotel, VJD?' No answer but lots of loud crackling sounds – they can't hear me due to too much static, probably a thunderstorm over toward Alice Springs. I hit the emergency button which knocks out a piercing scream. An indistinct female voice says,

'This is VJD Alice Springs. All non-emergency traffic cease immediately. Can the station using the emergency button please identify over?'

'Romeo Lima Hotel, VJD, over.'

'Station using emergency button please identify over!'

By now I can hear annoyance in the operator's voice, they'll think this is an accidental or prank emergency call. I try again, this time shouting into the mike,

'Romeo Lima Hotel, VJD, I have an emergency, over.'

'Station using emergency button, please identify over!!'

Oh Christ, what the hell can I do? Then out of the darkness comes a male voice,

'Romeo Lima Hotel, this is Mike Sierra Tango, I am about 300 kilometres south of Mount Isa in Queensland and can hear you clearly. Would you like me to relay, over?'

'Go ahead Mike Sierra Tango, are you a medical person over?'

'Negative Romeo Lima Hotel, but if you keep your transmissions short, I can relay verbatim, over.'

Hell's bells, my saviour must be over a thousand kilometres off and it's a bloody miracle, but there's no time to think about divine intervention. My call is patched through to the on-call doctor and she fires off her first question for the stats,

'Where are you situated Romeo Lima Hotel over?'

'I'm at Yiwala Community in the Gibson Desert, fifty kilometres over the West Australian border, over.'

'Romeo Lima Hotel, as you are in Western Australia you should contact the Kalgoorlie RFDS base.' I suppress several expletives and remind her that I am already being relayed to her and haven't a hope in hell of reaching Kalgoorlie Base; it's twice as far as Alice Springs. There is a delay while she considers the new information, then she allows that in the circumstances it might be OK to use RFDS Alice Springs. I provide the baby's approximate age and my findings so far. My panicked state is hopefully lost in the relaying process, and after a few more cryptic exchanges a message is relayed.

'Romeo Lima Hotel, we will medivac the patient. Will advise an ETA when possible.' Then, another fateful question.

'Can you put in an IV line please, normal saline TKVO?' (to keep vein open)

Me?? In a four-week old baby! Are you joking? I didn't say that but replied that I'd give it a go. The on-call doctor is new, and probably has no idea what things are like out here in the sticks. I check the skin for the normal venepuncture spots and of course find no veins worth trying. Ah, despair.

Then I remember that we'd been issued with intra-osseous trocars for this kind of thing. No training of course, just the equipment, which consisted of an IV needle with a big black knob on its head end. The knob was to allow you to push the needle through into the middle of a bone. I never imagined having to use the thing only a few weeks after it was sent out, so where the hell did I put it?

I dive into the examination room, jerking drawers open and slamming cupboards, seeing nothing in my panicked haste. Finally, there it is. I hurriedly read the postcard-sized instruction sheet. 'In infants place the needle into the anterior aspect of the proximal end of the tibia. Bash the thing in with any hammer-like object available.' No, no, that can't be right. Oh hell…'Push until less resistance is felt, indicating the point is in the space in the centre of the bone. Secure in position and connect intravenous line.'

Right, prepare the area, peel the trocar from its packaging. Lena holds the baby in position. I'm metaphorically shitting myself, but there's no alternative. I shakily push the needle in and feel the point enter the centre of the bone. Ominously the child only whimpers slightly. Tape the thing in place, connect the bag of saline, and away we go. The child is still alive, somehow. The radio crackles to life.

'Romeo Lima Hotel, do you have airstrip flares, over?' My saviour is still out there, with the patience of a saint. I answer in the affirmative. Ten minutes later a voice says,

'The flight has departed and ETA is 0030 hours Romeo Lima Hotel, over.' I'm prepared for this at least and send Lena off to find someone to put out the 30-odd Toledo kerosene flares so that the pilot can find us in a hundred thousand square kilometres of unremitting blackness. She comes back looking desperate. No one will budge, they don't want to be involved, even this indirectly, in a death. Perhaps they just want to sleep.

I tear off to get "Warby" the Project Officer and miraculously he's still up. He immediately understands the situation but has no access to a vehicle and has never put out flares before. We dash to my place and load the sinister-looking black spheres into the health Toyota. They're covered in a mixture of soot and kerosene, but this is no time to think about hygiene.

We roar over to the clinic and I check the IV line. It isn't running, at all. Part of the problem is that I've taped the trocar into position a bit too well and the baby's leg is turning purple. I undo the tapes and put a wound pad behind the knee with a tongue depressor stick to keep the leg straight. That's how small this new human is, an ordinary tongue-depressor extends from upper thigh to mid-calf. The IV line starts to flow again, and I tell Lena to shut it off if it starts to flow too quickly, lest it overload that already struggling heart.

Back out to the Landcruiser, leap in with Warby and tear off for the strip, the headlights forming a narrow orange pencil through the mulga scrub, our tail-lights illuminating a red contrail of dust behind. We stop near the windsock, jump out and put a flare at the base of each white fibreglass cone. We are less than a third of the way down the two-kilometre strip when Warby looks up and says,

'What's that light up there?' Bloody hell, it's the RFDS and we haven't got enough flares out! It never enters my head that they have found us and must be able to see the few flares we've put out. We leap back into the car and drive forward, then jump out like robbers leaving a bank holdup. We place more flares, but with panic blurring our minds and a stiff breeze blowing it takes several fumbled matches to light each one.

Suddenly we are brilliantly illuminated by the Cessna Conquest's landing lights. The plane is lining up on final approach, coming at us at 200 kilometres an hour, and the Landcruiser is still in the middle of the strip! I sprint to it and shoot to the side with what seems like only seconds to spare. The plane does a balletic slow bounce ahead of a cloud of dust from the prop wash and they flash past us and disappear into the night. They turn in the blackness way down the strip and taxi slowly back.

We drive up just as the flight nurse and pilot open the plane's door and emerge from the yellow-lit interior into the blackest of nights and a landscape not changed since the dawn of time. I introduce myself, jump back into the driver's seat and speed off down the road. At the dark, still settlement, the glow of the clinic's veranda light evokes childhood memories of a nativity scene, this time in corrugated iron.

Lena has collected a few belongings for the mother and child, and I hang the IV bag from the inside roof of the car. We head out to the airstrip, more carefully this time. When I've completed the few bits of necessary paperwork the flight nurse motions me to come inside the cabin and covertly says,

'The pilot wants to know what the mother might do if the child dies in transit.' I've never been asked this on other retrievals and reply,

'Why, what's the problem?'

'We don't want her throwing things about. She could cause us to crash.' The mother is a stranger to me, so I go back down the steps to ask Lena what might happen if the baby dies.

'She might be angry, sister!' Lena says. Taken aback, I ask who she might be angry with. Lena says, 'With you, sister!' Shocked at this, I ask why. The moment is burnt indelibly into my brain. She looks intently at me and says,

'Did you break that baby's leg sister?' Bloody hell, she's thinking about the tongue-depressor splint! If I had somehow broken the leg it would be the least of our concerns now, but in the young mother's view there is nothing much wrong with her child other than the now bound-up leg. I explain as best I can and Lena relays it all to the mother in Wankatja. She seems to accept the information.

The door slams shut, and the engines begin their rising whine. The plane gathers speed and three points of light rise like bright stars into the endless, primeval night. We drive silently back to the settlement. I drop Lena off at her place, then go back to the strip to extinguish the flares. The two rows of tiny yellow flames extend into the distance, guiding lights to nowhere. They have a surreal, lonely beauty about them. I drive along putting the extinguishing caps on each one. They can stay where they are until tomorrow, I still need to tidy up and lock the clinic. When I finish it is 2:00 am; five hours have passed in a few minutes and I suddenly feel very tired. I trudge home pondering the meaning of life itself. No dogs stir.

Two weeks later the visiting Pediatrician arrives on one of his four-time-a-year visits to this vast area. I describe the situation to him. He looks grave and replies,

'I don't like her chances Jake. By the time there are visible symptoms it's usually too late. She's likely to have profound brain damage; some die.'

My hopes sink, but weeks later when mother and child arrive back in the community, Mischa seems normal enough to my untrained eyes. I return to that community several times in the next eight years, and each time someone presents the child to me, smiles proudly and says,

'Sister Jake, this is Mischa!'

Against all probability she had grown into a normal, healthy kid. I never got to thank the unknown saint out there who stayed by his radio and made it all possible.

Bye Bye M and F – an OPINION
Allan Jamieson

In 2021, the American news organisation CNN published a list of sixty-six "milestones" dealing with one theme and spanning the past 100 years. The intensity of this theme is seemingly increasing.

Decade	20's	30's	40's	50's	60's	70's	80's	90's	00's	10's
No.	1	-	-	4	4	13	3	9	8	24

Here are some of the milestones:

1920's * The Society for Human Rights is founded in Chicago – the first known gay rights organisation.

1950's * The American Psychiatric Association lists homosexuality as a sociopathic personality disturbance. * President Eisenhower bans homosexuals from working for the Federal government.

1960's * Illinois is the first US state to decriminalize homosexuality. * Police raid the Stonewall Inn in New York City; incentivising thereby the gay civil rights movement in America.

1970's * Lambda Legal becomes the first entity legally registered to fight for the equal rights of gays and lesbians. * Maryland is the first state to statutorily ban same-sex marriage. * A 60% majority of the American Psychiatric Association agrees to remove homosexuality from its list of mental disorders. * Kathy Kozachenko becomes the first openly LGBTQ American elected to any public office and Elaine Noble is the first openly gay candidate elected to a state public office. * A Vietnam veteran, Sergeant Matlovich reveals his sexual orientation and is forcibly discharged; a court later awards him back pay and a retroactive promotion. * After undergoing gender reassignment surgery, professional tennis player Renee Richards is banned from competing in the women's US Open; Richards challenged the decision and the New York Supreme Court ruled in her favour. * Harvey Milk is the first openly gay man to be elected to political office in California; 11 months later, Milk is murdered. * The first Lesbian and Gay Rights March takes place in America; at least 75,000 individuals marched.

1980's * Wisconsin becomes the first state to outlaw discrimination based on sexual orientation.

1990's * President Clinton directs that openly gay and lesbian Americans cannot serve in the military. He also bans recognition of same-sex marriage; * A judge in Hawaii rules that the state does not have a legal right to deprive same-sex couples of the right to marry.

2000's * The first legal same-sex marriage in America takes place.
2010's * Obama becomes the first sitting US president to publicly support the freedom for LGBTQ couples to marry. * The US Supreme Court rules that states cannot ban same-sex marriage. * The US Senate confirms Eric Fanning to be Secretary of the Army, making him the first openly gay secretary of a US military branch. * There are at least 41 openly lesbian, gay and bisexual Olympians competing in Rio de Janeiro 2016 (*c.f.* 23 in London 2012). * District of Columbia residents are the first people in the US able to choose X as their gender marker instead of male or female on driver's licences and identification cards; similar policies exist in Canada, India, Bangladesh, Australia, New Zealand and Nepal. * The Pentagon confirms that the first transgender person has signed a contract to join the US military. * The Trump administration bans most transgender people from serving in the military.
2020's *The US Supreme Court rules that federal law protects LGBTQ workers from discrimination – extending protection to millions of workers nationwide; a defeat for the Trump administration. * President Biden signs an executive order repealing the 2019 Trump-era ban on most transgender Americans joining the military.

It is obvious the campaign in the USA by people, who would now be gathered into the cluster known by the label LGBTQ, has been long beset by powerful outbursts against them. LGBTQ, though, is a clumsy alphabet soup term if ever there was; in what follows, I will use "IT" instead (pronounced *it*).

I ask: Does the increasing noise and penetration everywhere by "IT" foretell the obliteration from human society of individuals who consider they are either M or F?

A columnist recently wrote of this possibility. In what follows, my words are included between [   ]:

• The dictionary definition of "woman" – an adult female – is considered hate speech [by some members of "IT". Instead there is] a push to use more "inclusive" terms … such as womxn, menstruators, vulva owners … and individuals with a cervix.
• [In February 2021], midwives at several hospitals in the UK were told to say "chestfeeding" instead of breastfeeding. [Woe betide the husband who enters a UK hospital to see mother and baby – and more pity the poor baby coming face-to-face with a flat, hairy chest.]

• Government bodies [are] making ludicrous decisions in the name of "inclusion". The NHS's pregnancy website advises: "8 in 10 people under 40 years old will get pregnant within one year of trying" … despite only half of them having a uterus?
• Linking motherhood with womanhood is … exclusionary to trans activists who have disproportionate influence on both the public and private sector. … The desire to appease [these] loud activists is seeing girls and women sidelined and bizarrely … [is] championed by the bulk of the modern feminist movement. … Women who do speak up are labelled bigots, transphobes [and worse].

The columnist wrote: 'Anyone who refers to me as a "menstruator" instead of a "woman" would not walk away unscathed'. [Methinks yonder columnist is being very brave.]

For well over 40,000 years, the world has been populated by M's and F's; indeed a great many people consider the world is seriously overpopulated, so the emerging domination of world culture by "IT" adherents has the potential to eliminate this very real problem; one positive outcome from the display of muscles by the "IT" crowd, this might explain why the Green movement supports "IT". We must note, however that "IT" is a peculiar beast; the members cannot reproduce themselves. Instead, the propagation of "IT" depends on a continual influx of new blood, thus it is a non-monetary example of a Ponzi scheme or a Pyramid scheme, schemes that depend on a steady influx of money from new investors.

By amassing more and more legal and political rulings in its favour that are of exclusive benefit to its members, "IT" is developing the capacity to attract an increasing number of members, potentially prolonging and reinforcing its existence for many, many generations.

Will the vitriol continue to escalate? I wonder how long we must wait before "IT" successfully persuades politicians, school teachers and lawyers that the word "generation" is not a gender-neutral term signifying a period of about twenty years, but is a deliberately slanderous slur by M's and F's on some members of "IT". Consequently, any utterance of the word will be outlawed and its users found guilty of a criminal action.

In some notes I presented to guests at my 80th birthday party in 2020, can be found this sentence: 'I've never figured out how to win an argument with a woman!' This referred to an experience of mine at age eleven. Therefore, I will let the aforesaid columnist have the final say:

> 'It's important for the apathetic masses to wake up and stop ceding linguistic territory to radical activists. What starts with words soon manifests in policy.'

Worth Of A Heart
Brenda Slavoff

What's it worth
The heart's trophy?
Offer it on bended knee -
No, too servile.
Throw it at you -
Take it, take it,
No, too forceful.
Beg, plead -
But it's a buyers' market,
Not good business.
Careless -
Don't know where it is,
But maybe . . .
Oh yes, here -
Exchange it,
How's yours? What state?
I saved it for you,
Yes, it's used,
Broken, even,
But strong.
Is there a risk?
Isn't there always?
You could talk me into it,
Or out of it,
But it's still a good heart,
Have it anyway.
What's it worth?

A Bird –Spotter's Day
Lesley Podmore

We're counting birds for Hazel,
  We do it twice a year,
We trudge along vast beaches,
  With all our bird-spotting gear.

We do it all quite willingly ---
  Perhaps you'd call us nerds!
But 'tis for the sake of many
  Endangered little birds.

We're watching what high tides have done
  To nesting sites and grub,
And find if any little ones
  Are hiding in the shrub.

We're looking for those who stay all year,
  And never fly away.
Some beaches have an awful lot,
  But others ---- 'None today!!'

There are teeny little redcaps,
  A-scurrying round like mice,
        (Try not to sneeze or blink,
  Or you might count them twice).

Some love the little hoodies
  All plump and cute and round.
Tread lightly on our sandy beach,
  Or they might go to ground.

There are sooties here in Stanley,
  With pieds amongst their midst,
One time we added ninety eight
  To Hazel's lengthy list.

A flash of terns we hope to glimpse,
  Like aircraft as they fly,
Low across the lapping waves
  Then vanish in the sky.

There are other birds so wonder-ous,
  Who nerdier nerds than we,
Can count in massive numbers
  (With their varsity degree).

They come in flocks from foreign climes
  And nest along the shore,
Near places like our Montagu,
  'Mid roaring fortie's roar.

The years have flown since we began,
  Sand banks shifted here and there,
But still we're glad to come across
  Another nesting pair.

The Dance
Meg McLaren

Abigail dances on pointed toes
before a wall of glass,
light as a dandelion head
when it becomes a fluffy, floating ball.
In a downy trance, she pirouettes on delicate feet
covered by shoes with square, hard heads.
Rich music fills her ears with harmony,
and flies with her to the high fields.
Lifting, twisting, spinning,
an Art Deco sculpture caught in bronze,
exotic and richly detailed,
poised on tiptoe, holding aloft a tambourine.

From a quiet place I look at this
swirling melting pot of inspiration.
The years slip away on a fluent arabesque.
I am eight years old,
yellow hair tightly braided and ribboned.
Wooden floor strumming beneath my feet.
My old skin blooms again, and
like Isadora, I yearn for a silken scarf,
and freedom from the constraints of age.
I long to soar with this child of my daughter,
on an uncradled breeze, into the laughing sky,
head thrown back, arms outstretched.
Aquarius and Gemini united in movement.

'Hey, everyone!
Come and see how good I look!'
Allan Jamieson

It had turned out to be a very pleasant day. A week ago, Mike, Charlie and I had agreed to meet today and play a game of bowls. It was a frequent thing we did, though the weather could disrupt our plans and when it rained, we would meet in the bar. Today, though, we were engaged in our game and it was not certain – with three ends to go – which one of us would turn out the winner and have to shout the bar.

Bowls had long been a popular sport in our country town and the club and its greens were in the main street. Passers-by often stopped and watched over the cyclone wire fence along the footpath.

Mike had just rolled the jack to start the next end when a voice called out from behind us; 'Hey, everyone! Come and see how good I look!' We turned, almost in unison, to see who had called out. There was only one person in sight – a woman, maybe middle aged, around 160 cm tall with dark hair and a bit on the thin side. My mates were probably thinking the same as I was; what was the good thing we were supposed to look at?

Beckoning with one hand, the woman said, 'Come on; don't stand there.' We moved closer. I had no idea who the woman was.

'You don't know my name, do you?' Without waiting for a response, she continued, 'You never knew my name – you only ever called me Stinky, except that you usually repeated the word sing-song fashion, "St-INK-ee, St-INK-ee", you'd call out as you walked to school on one side of the street while I walked on the other side – alone, always alone. You never saw me as a fellow human being, with feelings and wants and desires. To you, I was just like something the cat brought in.'

It came back to me; fifty years ago, there had been someone we called Stinky, but I could not picture what she looked like at that time. I glanced at my mates. Their faces were a blank. It didn't matter, though, because the woman filled in our vacant memories.

'I lived with my Mum on the other side of the tracks – you boys never ventured across the railway line, did you, so you never knew we lived in a run-down, three-room house, only in one room of which were the windows unbroken and that was where we spent our time. When the sun went down the room was pitch dark – we couldn't afford to pay for electricity – so Mum and I would go to bed and I'd cry myself to sleep in her arms.

'I only ever had one dress, the one I wore to school every day. Mum patched it and extended it as I grew taller – I was always thin. It was probably that dress that led you to call me Stinky. It's not nice to bathe in cold water, but you do get used to it and at weekends, when you were outside enjoying yourselves, I stayed indoors while Mum washed the dress and I waited inside for it to dry.'

I noted that Mike, standing next to me, was shifting his weight from one foot to the other. I reckon each one of us was feeling embarrassed, yet trying not to show it. We had not uttered a word.

'You didn't recognise me because I no longer have that dress; these clothes are new. That's why I look good now, "gooder" than I looked fifty years ago. I'm not wrong, am I?'

Before any of us could find the words to respond, the woman revealed more.

'Always alone, I had plenty of time to ponder the meaning of life. My Mum was firm in wanting me to get a good education and I was determined to succeed so I could get a job and help to lift her out of her poverty. I wondered why you boys bothered to go to school; it didn't look like a life and death thing to you and you weren't shy from disrupting the classroom when it suited you.

'Do you know what puzzled me most? The Salvos brought us the food we ate – essentially all of it – and we could never have survived without them. "Thank God for the Salvos" is often said half in jest, but to us they were literally God Sent! My puzzlement was this: How is it that some children grow up and join the Salvation Army or, at least, give them strong support, when all the pupils at school with me were totally unsympathetic to anyone who might be struggling?'

For the first time, the woman gave a slight smile before continuing.

'The Salvos moved Mum and me into a hostel of theirs in a different town. I did complete my schooling and my Mum now lives in a nice unit – with electricity and all "mod cons." But, that's no thanks to you and the others I went to school with.'

With a broad smile, she said, 'Here endeth today's lesson on what life is about.'

We felt about the height of a blade of bowling green grass.

Connections
Pete Stratford

Ever since her strange experience she had been completely distracted from her normal daily responsibilities while struggling to deal with thoughts churning in her mind. Sitting quietly mulling over it yet again, she was initially startled by an urgent rapping on her door, but it hadn't really been unexpected and she instinctively knew what it would be about.

Somewhat isolated from noise the crowds created as they jostled along the streets far below her fifth floor window, she lived very comfortably in a city high rise apartment block and was rarely disturbed by callers. However, she realised it was now time to face confirmation of what she already knew in her heart was true, even as a sense of dread came upon her.

Only two nights before, while cocooned in the warmth of her king size bed and enjoying that half-sleep euphoria, her brother, her twin brother, had come and stood beside her bed. Wordlessly he had reached out and gently stroked his fingers across her forehead as he looked down at her, before leaving the room as silently as he'd entered. Theirs was a kinship which had begun at conception and as they grew into adulthood they'd become so much of one mind, some mutual friends often joked that their communication with each other was by telepathy.

Responding to the repeated knocking, reluctantly she rose and opened the door, then with a barely perceptible wave of the hand had gestured the policeman to enter, before nodding him in the direction of a chair as she sank down onto the couch again. He chose to remain standing with his cap clasped in both hands in front of him, as if self-consciously somehow shielding himself from what may come next. Younger than herself, she guessed, and obviously very uncomfortable with this duty, she felt a slight pang of sympathy for him stir within her.

'There's no easy way to tell you this,' he began in a tightly controlled voice, 'but I have to inform you that two days ago, while they were endeavouring to contain the wild fires up north, your brother and his crew became trapped in their vehicle...'

Although he continued speaking, his voice was fading into a distant blur as she felt herself unable to breathe, yet she had known for two nights now, that her brother had died and she had already been grieving in a way that only twins can really understand.

My Mother's Operation
Brenda Slavoff

In darkness
I am bound to the world
by your tubes and wires
silent as the night
of my sorrowing breaths.

In a world where decay
is hungry for the body
and steals itself a thieves' den
of my life's savings.

Darkness has hidden me
in a sea of deep meaning
whose bonds cannot be severed
in this losing battle of blood,
life's sacrifice.

There is only corruption
of heartbeat and pulse
no permanence of cleanliness;
sterility is death.

Darkness presses closer
personal in watching
as you lie held to life
by medical tubes and wires
within a narrow cylinder of light.

Potholing
Pete Stratford

Darkness, total and utterly blinding darkness, like nothing that happens above ground envelops us as I find myself with a group of "Potholers" who had invited me to join their underground adventure. More correctly named speleologists, but their chosen nickname suited this mixed gender group of young adults all intent on exploring naturally forming cavities underground. Numerous limestone regions of the world are riddled with karsts created by water permeating down through the layers to slowly dissolve and erode the stone thus forming a labyrinth of tunnels and fissures ranging from claustrophobic burrows to yawning cathedral-like caverns that may still have water flowing through or have become dry, the water having created another course to travel.

One with prior knowledge of this particular cave system volunteered as my guide and while the others of the group gained access through another entrance, we two separated from them to enter by following up the stream that flowed gently from within the mountain to form a small crystal clear pool at the base of a rock bluff. Since the water level was only about twenty centimetres below the roof of the cavity through which it flowed our clothes were carried in a tightly rolled wad above the water level as we waded through chin deep until emerging into much shallower water and more space inside the cave, although in complete darkness until lighting our carbide headlamps. Although carrying candles and matches for emergencies, we were reliant on the lamps attached to the hard hats; when burning these gave each of us our own sphere of soft white light, beyond which remained the utter blackness of being underground where no outside light penetrates, neither does any warmth and it was with haste that we re-clad ourselves before following the stream further until we met up with the rest of the group, they having descended by a very long cable ladder thereby staying dry.

After the leader had given a brief explanation on safety, each of us with their own sphere of illumination proceeded to follow the stream along its winding course constantly cautious about the black areas at our feet which may be just shadow, or a gaping chasm of unknown depth. Likewise being aware of the protrusions from beside or above, that would cause injury if carelessly walked into. Edging along narrow fissures water had worn into the rock we scrambled spider like with hands and feet spanning black spaces of undetermined depth to then squeeze through amongst fragmented boulders, some the size of a bus, which had collapsed from the ceiling above when erosion had left insufficient support. Although much of the labyrinth was either water worn or fragmented from falls, there were numerous alcoves and areas festooned with hanging stalactites, and other forms growing imperceptibly to meet a stalagmite coming to join it from below its drip point as dissolved calcite was re-deposited from the water. A rigid rule meant that these pristine formations would remain unmarred by hand marks or foot prints for others who followed our journey into this wonderland. Some of these growths had joined to form columns up to sixty centimetres through, and to see several had been snapped like carrots by earth tremors before being slowly healed together again was not a comfort if one thought about the millions of tonnes of earth overhead and the narrow exit ways. However, being one of the five first humans to view one small "room" previously undiscovered, which was completely lined with glistening calcite formations, some even appearing to flow across the floor like spilled icing, is a scene embedded in my memory. So too, is the silence within these spaces where one's own heartbeat is audible when other disturbing activities are ceased, while drips of water may be heard from a hundred metres away and a match strike sounds like a firecracker.

Eventually we retraced our steps until reaching the wire ladder which others in the group had descended when they entered. Comprised of two thin steel wire cables, about twenty five centimetres apart with two centimetre thick aluminium rungs, set at about thirty centimetres spacing, this ladder could be easily rolled up and carried within confined areas to where it may be required, but being very flexible meant that climbing it was something of an acquired skill. Hugging it to your chest and not tilting your head back to see where the next step was avoided leaving one hanging almost horizontal, much like a sloth, and unable to progress either up or down. But that also meant the naked flame from your headlamp was immediately level with where your hand needed to grab the next rung, and yes, I scorched a finger or two. Due to the concave surface of the wall the ladder hung about a metre out from it meaning that only a very small portion of the wall illuminated by my lamp was visible, so being told the top was twenty eight metres above me didn't really have the impact that was to come until I neared that point. I am not overly keen on heights but climbing in my meagre sphere of light I nervously made my way upwards until when almost reaching the safety of solid ground again, I was dismayed to find the ladder had been twisted so that I was actually on the wrong side of it and trapped beneath the overhanging rock ledge. Despite the presence of a safety rope, which I hoped was being managed by someone trustworthy, there was very definite tightening of the sphincter and much nervous perspiration as I contorted my way to the other side of the wildly writhing ladder without making French fries of my fingers and then finally relieved to crawl onto solid ground again.

Within their fraternity much personal pride is taken for the height of underground ladder climbs undertaken and this particular one was a personal best for most of those involved that day, so on my arrival to relative safety after over nine hours underground, I was enthusiastically asked how I felt about it. With complete honesty and no hesitation, I replied 'bloody terrified!'

A new world order
Anne Layton-Bennett

last year we learned just how fluid life can be
how fragile
it is
here today, gone tomorrow
literally now (thanks to Covid)
for so many

we kid ourselves we're in control
masters of our destiny
Covid mocks that idea, daily
so we pivot,
turning
twisting
tumbling
into new ways of living
and dying

there's no textbook yet
no guidebook, no map or chart
no well-trodden path
to confidently follow
we're all still stumbling
finding our way by chance
by happenstance
learning as we breathe
day-by-day
self-educated

One Less Cat
Brenda Slavoff

'Johnny,' I said wearily, 'I don't want another cat. I'm not allowed to have another cat.'

'It's not a cat, it's only a little kitten –' Johnny protested.

'It'll grow, won't it?'

'But it's so cute –'

'I don't care how cute it is!'

'Oh, come on –'

'No, Johnny, I don't want it. It's hard enough to feed this one, much less myself.'

'They feed 'emselves! It'll be another good mouser.'

'Johnny, this is the fifth kitten –'

'But one died.'

'I know. It was very unpleasant.'

'An' one disappeared.'

'Yes, that was very suspicious.'

'An' one of 'em ran away. So you have to replace 'em.'

'I don't have to replace them, I still have the first cat.'

'What about the rats?'

'I haven't seen a rat since.'

'But you need another cat to keep the first one company.'

'The first cat drove the other one away. Actually, I think she did away with the others too.'

Johnny's little urchin face pleaded with me. He squirmed in distress, wringing his hands inside his ragged jersey. I turned away. I'm an orphan, and I've got my own problems.

'But me mum'll kill me –'

'She won't.'

'She will! She doesn't know about this lot.'

I turned back to him. 'Do you mean you haven't told her about this litter of kittens?'

He shook his head helplessly

'How do you keep this from your mother?'

He sat down on the box I keep for visitors in my little attic room. This was obviously going to take a long time, so I sat down on my bed.

'You see, it's like this. The first two strays come, an' one's a boy. No problem. But the other was a girl cat. Lots o' problems. Me mum says, "Get rid of that one." She didn't have time to deal with it 'erself, what with the shop an' all. But you know, that one was my favourite. I said, "What d' you want me to do?" to Mum, an' she says, cool as anything, "Drown it! There's a bucket of water in the yard."' He looked up at me with his round blue eyes and I sensed where this was going. 'I hid the cat in the neighbour's barn. I went back to me mum an' said, "All sorted," or somethin' like that. An' she was real pleased with me.'

'I'll bet she was,' I said.

'Then the cat 'ad kittens. I could keep the cat out of our house, 'cause she's not stupid, but I couldn't keep the kittens out. They kept wanderin' aroun' an' settling in our kitchen, until me mum says to me, "Get rid of that lot. There's a bucket of water over there." That's when I come to you an' give you your first kitten. She was a real lively one, wasn't she?'

'That's true,' I nodded. I'd been pleased then, not knowing what my gesture was starting. 'And a good ratter, which I needed. Pity she's such a bully.'

'I managed to give all the kittens away, an' when I come home I looked so cheerful that Mum thinks I like killin' things.'

I made a face. 'How could she think such a thing?'

'She's strange, is me mum. Well, the mother cat had another litter. Your second kitten was the best o' that lot. Then one of those kittens had another lot an' that was your third.'

My head was reeling. 'So what's this lot?'

'Nothin' to do with me at all! I told you, me mum got this idea that I enjoy killin' things. Said she'd 'prentice me to a butcher! M' future's all settled. So now she starts bringing other people's kittens for me to drown! An' I can't - I can't - kill anything!!'

Johnny started to blubber, and it's not a pretty sight. I understood the mess he was in, and although he's five years younger than me, he's the only friend I've made since I came to this God-forsaken city to make my fortune. I suppose I'm like a big brother to him. He's a nice kid, and I'd certainly have been eaten up by the rats if not for him and his first cat.

I took a deep breath. 'All right, get me the beast, and then don't come back with any more,' I muttered. 'God knows how it'll survive that bully over there, but that's my problem.'

Johnny's face was transformed in a moment. His eyes shone, the tears dried on his cheeks and, thank God, his nose stopped running. He pulled up his jersey and fetched out a kitten from an inner pocket. Now I knew why he kept squirming. He placed the kitten on my lap, as if he were giving me the greatest gift in the world. He knew I'd take it all along.

I hadn't really liked the previous four kittens, despite the first settling the rats once and for all, but this little blighter was actually cute. She was mostly black, except for some white on her stomach and a little white spot on her forehead. She looked up at me, gave a plaintive mew and began to rub her face against my hand. When I patted her she began a treble purr.

'I don't know how she's going to survive the other cat,' I said gloomily.

Johnny offered no suggestions, but just jumped up, saying, 'Well, I must be getting' home.'

'Why, do you have to drown some more kittens?' I demanded sarcastically.

He grinned and dashed out. At that moment the other cat, Owl, caught sight of the kitten. She stopped dead in her tracks and her hackles went up. This was not going to be good. I hustled her out of the door, and her body was stiff with fury.

The new kitten, whom I called Star because of the little spot on her forehead, settled in very well, probably because she had to sleep in my bed from the first night, to keep her safe from Owl. To keep them apart during the day I even had to take Star out with me. It made life harder, and life wasn't easy to begin with. Then one night Owl started howling, and I put her out in the back alley, hoping she would not return. No use. She was bigger than Star and knew she would win in the end.

I tried to avoid Johnny, not wanting cat number six. The next time I saw him coming to the back entrance, I ran up the back stairs and bolted my door. When he knocked I didn't answer. I should have known that wouldn't work. He just kept on knocking. Nothing stops that kid. So I yelled out that I had come out in spots and couldn't see anyone. That made him run away fast, and I breathed again.

Star became a consolation to me, however. When I was unhappy, which was just about every day since I'd come to this God-forsaken London Town, I would talk to her. Most cats are only interested in themselves, but she was different. She listened to me sympathetically. She washed my face. She kept my feet warm in bed. Only once did I forget about her, when Cook and I had another fight and I stormed off, vowing never to return. I swore I'd leave the city. I'd go back to the country, even though I had no family there anymore; any place was better than here. Then suddenly I heard the church bells tolling the hour and they seemed to be calling me back. Abruptly I remembered that Star was still back in my attic room, and anything could be happening to her. Owl or the cook could at this moment be killing her! I couldn't let her die, and I couldn't drag her across the country like a piece of clothing. So back I went to purgatory. Star was worth it.

Strangely, that night there was much excitement in the house. When I went downstairs to do my chores in the scullery, Cook called me into the kitchen. What now? 'Master wants to see you,' she said gloatingly. 'In the sollar.' I didn't give her the satisfaction of asking her what it was about. Probably I was going to be cast out of the house for keeping two cats. I only had permission for one, and that was because the master's daughter had sorted it out for me. I took a deep breath and went upstairs.

The sollar door was open, and I stood on the threshold.

My master, Mr Fitzwarren, caught sight of me. 'Ah, there you are, my boy,' he said genially, drawing me in. 'Settled in well, eh?'

Yeah, right. 'Yes, sir,' I said brightly. Got to keep up appearances. At least I wasn't in trouble, it seemed.

My master indicated another man, who had a sunburned face and colourful clothes. 'This is my old friend, Captain Parker. We've known each other since we were boys, but he went to sea and I followed my merchant father's footsteps. Now my friend's about to leave for a long voyage, and he's taking many goods of mine to sell, and will bring me back lots of treasure, I hope.'

Everyone laughed.

I touched my forehead to the captain, who seemed the bluff, hearty type. Maybe he wanted to take me aboard? No, that wouldn't suit me. I got sick in the cart coming here; how would I be at sea?

Mr Fitzwarren continued, 'My daughter has suggested that everyone should have an opportunity to invest in something for this voyage; haven't you, my dear?'

Startled, I glanced at the other side of the dim room and saw his daughter sitting by the window, looking almost grown up. Mistress Alice. My face went red. She is so wonderful. She is also kind. She knows I am a charity case.

Alice smiled sweetly. My face went redder. I stammered: 'I don't have anything to invest, Mr Fitzwarren, sir.' London streets, contrary to popular belief, are not paved in gold.

'No savings?'

I hung my head. 'No, sir.'

'What about the cat, Richard?' said Alice lightly.

'The cat?' I said blankly, and she smiled at me again. Then I realised: she knew. She knew about Johnny and his never-ending line-up of cats.

Yes, I thought. Why not? If Johnny can do it, why not I? 'I can give you a cat if you want one,' I said to the captain, entering into the jest.

'Not give,' said Alice, 'invest!'

Suddenly it seemed that the idea was not a joke. They want me to invest a cat, I thought incredulously. Here goes!

'Why yes, you need a cat at sea, sir,' I said seriously. 'The last thing you want is rats in the flour barrels! And my cat has killed every rat from three streets around. And such a lovely nature – ' God forgive me the embellishments! '-- clean and quiet, no trouble at all. I'll go get her for you right now.'

'Are you sure you want to part with her?' queried Mr Fitzwarren.

'I think the captain needs her more than I do,' I said nobly.

'Why not?' laughed Captain Parker. 'If that's all you've got, let's have her.'

I ran up the three flights of stairs as if my feet had wings. I had also just remembered that I'd left the door to my room open and Owl might have entered! I raced in and, sure enough, found Owl had cornered Star, no doubt in preparation for killing her. I grabbed the bully by the scruff of her neck. 'Come on, Owl,' I said grimly, 'you are going on a little journey. You are going to make my fortune!'

She was not in a good mood; I'm sure the prospect did not enchant her. She just wanted to get back and finish Star off. I didn't want to present her in this state, so I detoured to the kitchen, which was empty. I know where the cream is kept.

'There you are, Captain,' I said, returning with a glutted cat. 'Isn't she beautiful?'

He did not seem impressed, but he said nothing.

'Don't you need more than one cat, Captain Parker?' asked Alice.

'I know where you can get more,' I added.

'No, this one will do me,' he said with finality. I could see he was losing interest in the game. Oh well. Anyway, I was pretty sure Owl was pregnant, so there was more where that one came from. And I was distracted by suddenly locking eyes with Mistress Alice.

'I shall let you know how your investment prospers, on my return,' said the captain, still smiling.

Yeah, like it's going to be something big. I came to life again, realising they were dismissing me, and began to move to the door.

'What is your name, boy?' called out the captain suddenly. 'Just in case I need to find you if you leave your service here before I come back.'

I halted in the doorway. Once it was a proud name, but now it means nothing.

'Whittington, sir,' I said. 'Dick Whittington.'

I am woman
Anne Layton-Bennett

some days I just want to block out the world
protect my psyche from all the horrors
and brutality
the insults
the cruelty
and insanity
that's destroying our planet

some days I want to plant a massive
and impenetrable hedge
create an impregnable border
and
have it patrolled by
lions
so
I can live in a bubble
that cannot be pricked
or poisoned
by hate

but one day soon
when I've recovered, and
regained my strength
then listen well
and hear my roar

© 2021 Anne Layton-Bennett

The Secret Box
Dawn Meredith

Twelve year old Lizzy crept down the hallway to Mum and Dad's room, listening carefully to the distant clang of pots in the kitchen as Mum prepared dinner. Dad wasn't home yet and her pesky five year old sister Georgie was in her room playing "horsey". Lizzy sneaked inside and closed the door silently. Her bare toes curled in delight at the feel of soft carpet. Sunlight streamed in through the willowy curtains, tracing patterns on Mum's beautiful white quilt. Lizzy stood, breathing in the joy of delicious, forbidden treasures.

The dressing table was adorned with elegant glass bottles of perfume. A small, blue china dish gently cupped gold and silver rings. Mum's fancy silver jewellery box sat proudly in the centre. Lizzy touched each precious item with her fingertips, wishing she was a grown-up lady. The lid of a lipstick marked "Luscious Pink" came off with a POP! Lizzy smeared it over her lips and lifting a string of sparkly beads over her head admired herself in the long mirror.

Turning, Lizzy spotted a plain, wooden box half hidden on a shelf, high up in the cupboard. Standing on a chair, Lizzy stepped up carefully and lifted the box. It wasn't as heavy as she expected. She shook it. Something hard was sliding back and forth inside. Tingling with excitement, Lizzy stepped down and seated herself on the white bed, the box on her lap. Its corners were chipped, the wood around the clasp was worn smooth. Lizzy pried it open with her clever little fingers and was rewarded with the secretive smell of raw pine and dusty years.

It was disappointing really. Not what she had expected at all. Just four flat pieces of wood, painted with faded scenes. Lizzy leafed through the miniature paintings. They were all fairy tales. The first depicted Goldilocks and The Three Bears. The golden haired girl was, of course, fast asleep in Baby Bear's bed. The bears were lumbering up the stairs to the sunny attic bedroom where the three beds lined up beneath a pretty window overlooking the forest. Father Bear was impressively huge and shaggy, his black fur rippling as he moved, sharp claws hanging beneath giant paws. Mother Bear, slightly smaller, was equipped with disconcertingly long, sharp teeth and vicious little black eyes. And Baby Bear, well, he was hardly cute. The evil grin on his furry face was quite scary. These were not the friendly bears Lizzy remembered from fairy tales. Meanwhile, Goldilocks slept on, sucking her thumb, her golden hair fanned out over the pillow.

'Lithy, what are you doing in Mum and Dad'th room?' said a voice from the doorway. Lizzy spun. Georgie stood there, hands on her hips. 'You're not allowed in here! I'm telling Mum.'

'Go away Georgie!' Lizzy hissed, crouching over the box. 'If you tell on me, I'll tell Mum you broke that vase!'

Georgie chewed her lip, thinking. 'Fine, then.' She spun upon her heel and walked away. I wish I never had a sister, thought Lizzy angrily. So annoying! Lizzy closed the door quietly and sat back on the bed with the forbidden box. She didn't feel bad about Georgie at all. She'd tried to play hide and seek with her this very morning, but Georgie never wanted to be "It", even when she was caught. Complaining to Mum hadn't helped either. I have more fun on my own, she thought.

Lizzy lifted out number two painting, which showed the inside of a witch's cottage. Over the fire hung a big bubbling pot. Two cages swung nearby, containing small children - a boy and a girl. The witch, dressed in black, with green, slimy hair and a pointed hat was laughing. Her bony hand had opened the door to the little girl's cage. The little girl was crying and clutching the bars. She didn't want to be cooked in the big pot.

Lizzy gulped. Fairy tales weren't supposed to be this scary! She shuffled the flat wooden pieces. The third was Jack and the Beanstalk, about the clever boy who climbed the magic beanstalk and sneaked into the ogre's castle. In this painting he was about to snatch the hen that laid golden eggs from her cage. Meanwhile, behind him the one-eyed, toothless ogre had woken up and had grabbed an axe! Lizzy blinked. Suddenly her hands felt very cold and stiff. The little masterpieces slipped and fell to the floor. Lizzy gasped, sitting very still, listening for signs of her mother coming down the hall. But no one came.

There was one painting left. Which fairy story would it be? She gathered the wooden pieces together. But to her dismay, the fourth one was broken! A big jagged crack down the centre had split it in half. In her right hand Lizzy held part of the story of Little Red Riding Hood, of the cunning wolf who had already eaten Granny and was tucked up in her bed. The bonnet hung askew, tied under his hairy chin. In her other hand, Lizzy held the piece depicting innocent Red Riding Hood, knocking at the door, a basket of delicious goodies on her arm. But Red Riding Hood couldn't see the cruel bear trap the wolf had laid for her, right behind the front door.

'Lizzy! Lizzy!' Mum was calling from the kitchen. But Lizzy, entranced by the painting in her hands, ignored it. The bedroom door opened. Lizzy spun, horrified.

'Mum sayth you have to come,' lisped Georgie, pouting.

'Go away, Georgie!' snarled Lizzy. 'You're such a pain!' Georgie was about to say something, then changed her mind. A single tear lay on her cheek. Her bottom lip trembled. The door closed softly. Lizzy laid the paintings side by side on the bed to study them more closely.

It was then she noticed two things.

In the corner of each painting was a sly looking gnome, with gleaming eyes and fat fingers. Strangely, he was not looking at the scene in which he belonged. Oh no, he was looking straight at the person staring at the painting. Straight at Lizzy! It was as if he could see her. A shudder ran up Lizzy's spine. And that was when she noticed something very odd. In the first painting, of Goldilocks and the Three Bears, the little girl asleep in Baby Bear's bed looked just like... just exactly like... her little sister, Georgie.

Lizzy blinked, her mouth falling open in surprise. How could this be? She dropped the painting and ran to Georgie's room. The toy horse was lying on its side on the bed. Two dolls sat nearby, watching, their expressions blank. There was no little sister on the crumpled bed. No little sister cross-legged on the floor. No little sister at all. With a terrible sinking feeling in her stomach, Lizzy ran to the kitchen.

'Mum, have you seen Georgie?' Mum was bent over, putting a dish in the oven. Lizzy tapped her gently. 'Mum?' But her mother didn't move. Her eyes stared at the oven, her arms stiffly extended, her brightly coloured oven mitts holding the dish in mid-air. Mum was frozen. 'Mum!' shouted Lizzy tearfully, shaking her. Mum didn't blink, didn't say a word, just continued staring at the oven, holding the dish. Lizzy looked wildly around the room. What should she do? Her eyes fell on the clock. It was twenty minutes past five. Dad should be home! She raced to the front door, calling his name. Dad stood, frozen, in the act of hanging up his coat, his arm extended in mid-air. 'No, Daddy! Wake up!' shrieked Lizzy. But Dad couldn't move either.

Lizzy was really frightened now. She had to find Georgie. Maybe she was hiding somewhere? She flung open cupboards, checked behind the bathroom door, under all the beds. No Georgie. Lizzy was all alone. She ran back to the kitchen. Mum stood as before and the clock still said twenty minutes past five.

Lizzy trudged back to Mum and Dad's room, tears streaming down her face. What was she going to do? She picked up the painting of Goldilocks and stared at the familiar face of the little girl. Had her own sister really disappeared into this painting? How could it happen? Lizzy's eyes roamed over the painting, taking in every detail, her heart pounding. Georgie, if it really was her, was now trapped inside this fairy tale. And worse, was about to be discovered by three very hungry bears, who looked neither cute nor cuddly and were already at the top of the stairs. Father Bear had his great, black paw on the door handle, about to turn it. Meanwhile, Goldilocks Georgie slept peacefully in baby Bear's bed, completely unaware of the danger.

'Wake up!' shouted Lizzy, even though she knew Georgie couldn't possibly hear her. And then she saw him, the strange little gnome, perched on the end of Mother Bear's bed, legs crossed, waving at Lizzy, a finger to his lips, as if to say, 'Sshh!'

'Help me!' she pleaded. But the gnome just smiled. If he knew how to rescue her little sister, he wasn't telling. Lizzy checked the bears' progress. The handle had been turned. Father Bear was about to push open the door to the attic bedroom. 'No!' Lizzy cried, searching for clues in the painting. But it was the exact story she had heard a million times. It always ended the same way. Except... what if the bears decided to eat Georgie? Lizzy decided to risk taking her eyes off the painting for a second, to check the back, in case there was a clue there. To her relief, she found a verse, written in neat, flowing handwriting:

> Soft as snowflake, hard as bone,
> warm as sunshine, cold as stone,
> freely given, freely heard,
> the power of the spoken word.

Lizzy stared at the poem, confused by its meaning. She read it out loud, her voice sounding strange in the quiet house. It must be a clue. But how could she use it? Turning back to look at the picture she saw, to her horror, that Father Bear had now pushed open the door to the bedroom and his foot was raised, ready to enter. Mother Bear was close behind, followed by pushy, impatient little Baby Bear. Georgie lay peacefully asleep, her golden hair fanned out over the pillow.

'Georgie!' Lizzy gasped . 'Wake UP!' Her tears splashed onto the painting, leaving a dark stain on the wood. It was her fault little Georgie was trapped there, in that strange room, with three hungry bears. 'I didn't mean it, when I said I wished I never had a sister. Please, come back!' But the words were out. Couldn't be gathered again. Lizzy looked for the gnome. He was standing beside Baby Bear's bed smiling down at the sleeping Georgie. 'I'm sorry!' Lizzy whispered . 'Please, help me save my sister. I didn't mean it.' But Father Bear's big, hairy foot was already pressing on the pale blue carpet of the attic bedroom. His eyes were bright with interest. His nose seemed to quiver with the smell of a delicious little girl and Lizzy knew, he was sure to find her.

Father Bear leaned forward with a frown, his furry arm pointing to his rumpled bed. Mother Bear's eyes gleamed and her tongue licked her long snout as if she could already taste the sumptuous human girl. Baby Bear eagerly checked his father's bed for signs of Goldilocks.

While Georgie slept on, two beds away.

And the gnome stood, pointing gleefully at the sleeping girl.

'Please!' Lizzy begged the gnome, her voice cracking. 'What can I do?' The gnome had somehow moved without Lizzy noticing. His hand was cupped to his ear, as if he was listening for something. Lizzy flipped over the painting and repeated the verse written there, feeling sure it was some sort of clue or key.

'Soft as snowflake, hard as bone, warm as sunshine, cold as stone, freely given, freely heard, the power of the spoken word.' And then she added, 'Forgive me, Georgie!'

With a rush of air, the room went dark. Lizzy felt faint, as if she were falling to the floor. Suddenly she heard birds singing. She opened her eyes. The room was flooded with light. Lizzy sat up and blinked. She was inside the three bears' bedroom! Swiftly, Lizzy hid behind Baby Bear's bed. Her heart beat hard inside her chest. She could smell the bears' hairy bodies, smell the earth on their paws. She even fancied she smelled the hunger in their mouths. Seeing Georgie's arm, she tugged it, while keeping out of sight. But Georgie didn't stir. Father Bear stood tall and sniffed the air, his huge, black body swaying. 'Who's been sleeping in my bed?' He grumbled in a deep, growly voice. 'The pillow is on the floor! I bet there are fleas on it already.'

'Well, I mean to say, who's been sleeping in my bed,' complained Mother Bear. 'They've messed up my nice lace coverlet!'

'Mummy, I wonder if they slept in my bed?' Squeaked Baby Bear, as he ambled across the room towards his bed.

'Georgie!' Lizzy hissed, pinching her hard on the arm. 'Wake UP!' Georgie woke with a start and, bleary eyed, glanced around the room. When she saw three black bears she screamed. Lizzy clamped a hand over her mouth.

'Someone's been sleeping in my bed and she's still here!' shouted Baby Bear, jumping joyfully on the bed and pinning both girls with his oversized paws. 'Mummy, come over here!' He cried. 'She looks delicious!'

'Yes, my dear, absolutely delicious.' Mother Bear rolled her eyes at Father Bear. 'He keeps forgetting I'm vegetarian,' she whispered. Father Bear grimaced, his shaggy brows drawn down over his black, deep-set eyes.

'Erm, I don't think they taste very good at all, son. Quite stringy.'

'Help me Daddy!' Cried baby Bear.

'Oh, very well.'

Lizzy felt sick. Baby Bear was pushing down on her stomach. Mother Bear swayed closer, claws bared, reaching out to grab the two girls. The gnome had disappeared. Lizzie managed to get a hand free and pushed at Baby Bear as hard as she could. Georgie whimpered.

'Lithy…' she whispered hoarsely. Lizzie looked around the room for another verse. If one could get her in, surely another could get them both out? On the back of the bedroom door hung a verse, neatly stitched and framed. Lizzy cleared her throat and read it out loud as fast as she could:

> Sun in showers, rain in sun,
> A journey's end has just begun.
> Light as nightfall, dark as the moon,
> Your wish is heard, repeat your boon.

Lizzy grabbed Georgie's hand as hard as she could, closed her eyes and shouted, 'Take us home! I wish to go home!'

A warm wind swirled around her, the same sound as before. The room went quiet. It smelled sort of clean. Lizzy opened her eyes, holding her breath. She was lying on Mum and Dad's bed, the sun streaming cheerfully through the window. But Georgie was not beside her. Lizzy raced to her sister's room, but again, no Georgie. In the kitchen Mum was still bent, putting the dish in the oven. Dad was still in the hall, forever hanging up his coat. With heavy dread in her heart Lizzy returned to her parents' room and picked up the painting. Goldilocks lay sleeping in Baby bear's bed, her golden hair fanned out upon the pillow…but it was not Georgie.

'Oh!' cried Lizzy in relief. She wiped her nose with the back of her hand. Georgie was safe from the bears. But, where was she now? Lizzy shuffled through the paintings and found her sister in the witch's cottage. Squashed inside in a metal cage swinging beside the fire, Georgie's face was tear stained with terror. In another cage nearby swung a little boy named Hansel.

The witch was stirring a large black pot, her back hunched and lumpy. In the next moment the painting changed and the witch turned to smile with glee at Georgie. Georgie was weeping now, as the witch approached the cage. It was time for her to go in the pot of boiling broth. Horrified, Lizzy searched the painting for the gnome, hoping he would help again. There he was, sitting cross-legged in the corner, staring straight at her. His cheeks rosy and cheerful, his eyes gleaming with vicious delight. Quickly, Lizzy turned the painting over and found another verse:

Chocolate fudge, vanilla ice,
Children taste so very nice,
Cooked in broth until they're done,
A hero's task a dangerous one.

A hero? Where was Lizzy going to find one of those? Her Dad was frozen in the hall. He couldn't even hang up his coat, let alone save his daughter from an evil witch! Lizzy fought back tears of helplessness. She had to be brave. She was the only one who could save Georgie. Just like last time, there must be a way to use the verse to get inside the painting. And then, she hoped, the gnome would take pity on her and provide another clue to help them return home. This time she wanted to be prepared. She would take something useful. She ran around the house looking for useful items and returned to her parents' bedroom with a broom, a packet of crisps, a pair of pliers and a sparkler with matches. She checked the painting. Oh no! While she had been busy collecting things, the witch had already taken Georgie out of the cage! Her little sister cowered in the corner below Hansel's cage. The witch was tugging on her sleeve. Lizzy grabbed all the stuff, stood tall and shouted the verse. This time she added 'I'm no hero, but I'll do it!'

Again, she felt faint and the room went dark with a rush of air. But this time she was ready. The light came back and Lizzy found herself in the witch's dim cottage. The smell of the broth was disgusting. Smoke swirled in eddies around the corners of the room. Of course, the gnome was nowhere to be seen. The witch spun round, her ugly face contorted with surprise and anger.

'Yah!' cried the witch and picked up her wand, pointing it straight at Lizzy. Before she could say any magic words, Lizzy knocked the wand out of the witch's bony hands with the broom.

'Georgie, come on!' cried Lizzy. She lit the sparkler and threw it at the witch who shrieked in surprise and fell backwards. Lizzy sprang forward with the pliers and wrenched open the clasp on Hansel's cage. The boy jumped out quickly and made for the door. But the witch was faster. She grabbed him by the shirt. 'Here!' Lizzy threw the packet of crisps at the witch, who had to let go of Hansel to catch it. Tripping on her pointy shoes, the witch fell to the floor, holding up the packet in triumph, like she had just come out of a rugby scrum. Opening it, she shoved handfuls of crisps into her mouth, a look of bliss upon her face.

Hansel took the opportunity to dash out the door. There was no neatly stitched verse hanging behind it this time. Lizzy searched frantically for another verse, or a clue, or the gnome. To her surprise, his head appeared above the witch's kitchen dresser. He still did not speak, but pointed silently to the ceiling. Written in smoky letters was the verse Lizzy hoped to find. She had to read it quickly before the witch finished the bag of crisps:

> starlight white, sunrise gold,
>
> secrets lost, secrets told.
>
> name your enemy, name your foe
>
> homeward bound you shall go.

How could Lizzy find out the witch's name in the next... three seconds? The witch was licking the inside of the crisp packet, her eyes watching Lizzy greedily for more.

'Lithy, take me home!' whined Georgie, hugging close to her big sister.

'I will, as soon as I figure out the witch's name, Georgie.' Lizzy looked again for the gnome's help, but he had disappeared. Where does he keep going? She wondered. And why doesn't he help me now? A hero's task a dangerous one, the verse on the back of the painting had said. 'What's your name?' Lizzy asked the witch. The wrinkled old hag tipped back her head and her laugh sounded like the crackly fire.

'Why should I tell you? Now I have two tender little girls for my pot!'

Lizzy picked up the broom handle and gripped it tight. 'I'll fight you! You can't have my sister!'

The witch's head tilted to one side. 'You think a broom will stop magic?' She laughed again. 'Now, where's that big knife?' She began to rummage in a drawer. 'I'm sure it's in here somewhere. Why does it never stay where I put it?' She scratched her head with a bony finger and looked in another drawer. 'Perhaps a finding spell would work.'

'Gnome, where are you?' cried Lizzy desperately, looking round the room.

'Aha!' yelled the witch in triumph, holding up a large spoon. 'This will do!'

'There!' shouted Georgie, pointing to the wood basket. The gnome was sitting on top of it, his legs crossed, grinning wildly. He was enjoying this very much.

'You!' shouted Lizzy in anger. 'Tell me her name!' But of course, the gnome never spoke. Instead he pointed to the wall. There was nothing there but a crack. Lizzy stared at the gnome. He was cruel indeed! But, Lizzy told herself, a clue was a clue. In the crack in the wall grew a weed and Lizzy knew exactly what it was.

'Daisy!' she cried, holding onto Georgie with fierce determination. The witch spun, her pink eyes ablaze.

'No!' she cried in her crackly voice, her hands reaching out to grab the girls. But a great wind rose inside the cottage and with it a dark fog. Lizzy heard the witch scream in frustration. But as the wind died down and the fog disappeared, Lizzy saw that she was again safe in her parents' room. Alone.

Lizzy raced to Georgie's room. Again, her little sister had not returned. This time Lizzy didn't even bother to check on her parents or check the cupboards. She already knew exactly where to find Georgie. Lizzy stared at the painting of Jack and the Beanstalk. Georgie, dressed in Jack's clothes, had climbed up the beanstalk and entered the ogre's castle. While she watched the painting, it shifted slightly. Now Georgie had clambered upon the ogre's table while he slept. The little hen who laid golden eggs perched in a gilded cage at the other end of the table. Georgie was carefully reaching for the little hen, totally unaware of what was going on behind her. The ogre had woken up! He saw a thief about to steal his prized hen. His big hand reached out to grab his axe, glinting sharp in the candlelight. Lizzy's heart fluttered in her throat.

'Georgie, look out!' she shouted. But with a smile upon her lips, her eyes alight with joy, Georgie crept closer to the little hen. The ogre rose huge and gnarly behind her. 'Georgie!' shouted Lizzy. She didn't want to take her eyes off the painting, but she knew the only clue would be the verse, written on the back of the wooden panel. With trembling hands, Lizzy flipped the painting over to read the verse she hoped was there. It read:

> Golden promises, silver dreams,
> Children's laughter, children's screams.
> poison pen and poison dart,
> an act of theft breaks an ogre's heart.

An act of theft? An ogre's heart? It didn't make sense. She looked around her parents' room anxiously. What weapons did they have here? The simple answer was - none. Lizzy would have to sneak in to the ogre's castle somehow. Her only advantage was her small size. She searched for the gnome. And to her relief she found him. There, standing near the ogre's door. His face was ruddy and shiny, his eyes dark with mischief. He'd helped her before, would he do it again?

'Please!' Lizzy begged him. 'Tell me what to do!' And then she saw that his hand pointed to the ogre's wife, who had somehow appeared in the background. Despite her scary husband, Mrs Ogre had a kindly face. And now that kindly face was awash with tears of sadness as she gazed upon the little hen. 'She loves the hen...' whispered Lizzy out loud. The heart that would be broken by the thief belonged to the ogre's wife, not the ogre. 'I'll make sure she keeps the hen! Please!' Lizzy pleaded with the gnome. But it wasn't enough just to say that. Something more was needed. The room remained flooded with daylight. Lizzy had not been transported anywhere. Now she saw that Georgie had turned her head and realised the ogre was bearing down upon her with his axe lifted high. His great mouth opened in a silent roar. Georgie's face was white with fear. Lizzy screamed. This time she was powerless to save her little sister.

'I promise we won't take the hen!' Lizzy begged the gnome. 'We won't break her heart, no matter what happens to us!' There was a rush of air. The room darkened. Lizzy smiled. It worked! She blinked several times. The castle was quite dim. She couldn't even tell where she had landed. She looked up and saw wood panelling above her head. 'Georgie!' she shouted. 'I'm here!' Two massive feet stomped right next to where she sat huddled. Slowly the ogre's body bent until his giant face appeared. Scrabbling fast, Lizzy escaped the swipe of his great hand. 'Georgie!' she screeched.

'I'm up here!' Came her sister's frightened little voice.

'Get down!' Commanded Lizzy.

'No! I can't leave the hen!'

'You have to! It's the only way we're getting out of here. Leave it! Get down somehow!' Lizzy climbed up a woollen jumper sleeve and hauled herself onto the table. Unbelievably, Georgie was still trying to get her hands on the hen.

'What are you doing?' Lizzy, rushed towards her sister and grabbed her shirt. 'You have to leave the hen behind. The ogre's wife loves it! Now do as I say!'

'No...' whined Georgie. 'I want it. She'th tho cute.'

'Rar!' roared the ogre, his hairy face rising beside them, then his broad shoulders, then his glinting axe. 'I'll have you little fingerlings for my supper! Wife, is there room in the pot?' The ogre's wife was drying her tears with her apron.

'Yes, my dear, plenty of room. Oh, why do they want my little hen? She's mine, my lovely one!'

'We won't take it!' shouted Lizzy, unsure if they could hear a voice as small as hers. 'We just want to go home.'

The ogre cocked his head. 'Wife, I do believe one of them is speaking.'

Lizzy let go of Georgie and cupped her hands around her mouth. She shouted louder. 'We won't take the hen!' The ogre's face darkened. Lizzy quailed at his anger.

'LIAR!' he roared and the castle shook with his rage. He pointed a huge stubby finger. Lizzy spun. Georgie had tucked the little hen under her arm. Lizzy put up a hand as if to stop the ogre.

'Wait!' She turned to Georgie. 'Put it down, NOW!'

'No!' said Georgie firmly. 'Thee's pretty and thee needth a good home.'

'It's stealing!' thundered Lizzy with all her strength. 'It doesn't belong to us. Look around you, Georgie. The hen has everything she needs. Fresh straw, good seed, fresh water.'

'But I want it,' Georgie stubbornly insisted.

'If you take it, they will kill us. Now put it DOWN!' Lizzy stomped her foot on the table. Georgie knew she'd crossed some kind of line with her older sister. Lizzy grabbed the hen. It squawked and flapped. She shoved it back in its gilded cage and locked the door. Then she wrapped her arms around Georgie so she couldn't get away. She searched the room with her eyes. Where was the gnome? How could she get back home? Was there another verse somewhere? The ogre was breathing heavily, his bushy eyebrows low over his deep-set eyes. The axe shone dully in the light and Lizzy could have sworn she saw blood on its worn blade.

The girls crouched, holding onto each other. Lizzy's heart hammered wildly inside her chest. She felt dizzy. The ogre's deep-set eyes were like two dark monsters, hiding in caves. His stubbly face split into a grin and Lizzy saw his blackened and yellowed teeth. Ugh!

Time was running out. She had to find that verse. The ogre's wife reached for the gilded cage. She cooed to the hen, who clucked back contentedly. She seemed to have forgotten about the two intruders already. And then, Lizzy's sharp little eyes saw the verse. It was embroidered on the ogre's apron, in blue thread. It took only a few seconds to read it:

> Fawns are brave, fools are wise,
> not all is visible to the eyes.
> pay the price, pay the fee
> And winging home you shall be.

For once, Lizzy wondered, couldn't the verse make sense immediately? The cunning gnome had disappeared, but Lizzy was used to his treachery now. Hints. That's all he was prepared to give. The rest she had to figure out by herself.

'We have to pay a fee,' she said to Georgie.

'Huh?' Georgie looked up at her with big eyes. Lizzy let go of her sister and scratched her own head.

'It's ok Georgie. I'll figure it out.'

'I want to go home. Where'th Mummy?'

'Mummy's...' Lizzy wanted to say, 'Mummy's frozen in the kitchen. So is Dad. So is time itself, there.' But she thought she better not frighten Georgie. 'We'll get back. Soon. Don't worry.' Lizzy bit her lip. Her teeth sank into the soft flesh until it felt numb. What fee did you pay an ogre to escape his castle?

'So, you came here to steal my hen. But I think you'll do nicely for our supper.' The ogre reached down and picked up both girls with his huge, stubby fingers. They screamed and wriggled and clung to each other and sobbed. 'What say you, wife? Some rosemary and garlic?' He said calmly, as if he couldn't hear their screams at all. Mrs Ogre looked up from stroking her little hen.

'Methinks they are too sour for rosemary, husband. What about sweet basil?' She got up and went to the cupboard, emerging with a jar of snails and a packet of dried leaves. 'These would do nicely as a garnish. What say you?'

The ogre nodded, as the girls gasped and tried to get their breath. The ogre had them suspended in the air, like two insects. Lizzy's mind spun. The fee! The fee! What price do we pay? How Lizzy wished the gnome was here! How could he stand to watch two little girls suffer and die at the hands of hungry ogres? He could point to something, anything! Surely? But there was no sign of the nasty gnome. Lizzy would have to figure it out by herself. She cupped her hands around her mouth and shouted as loud as she could:

'How much to let us go?'

The ogre bent his head to listen. His breath rushed over the girls like a fetid wave. 'They're speaking again, wife,' he said, putting them down not-so-gently on the table. Lizzy took a deep breath to calm herself. She cupped her hands around her mouth once more.

'What fee? We will pay anything if you'll let us go!'

The ogre scratched his head. 'Trinkets. That's what we like.' Lizzy remembered something. She reached in her pocket and pulled out her mother's beaded necklace. It sparkled with black onyx, blue crystals and a silver clasp. She held it out to the ogre. His eyes lit up and he reached out with his massive hand to gently take the tiny offering. He made a cooing sound. 'Look, wife... see what they gave us...' He held it up to the light. 'You have more?' He asked, a dreamy expression on his face. Lizzy shook her head, held up her empty hands and stuck out her bottom lip to indicate she was sorry. The ogre's face scrunched up with thought.

Lizzy felt for Georgie's hand and squeezed it. Then she whispered the verse on Mrs Ogre's apron.

> Fawns are brave, fools are wise,
> not all is visible to the eyes.
> pay the price, pay the fee
> And winging home you soon shall be.

There was a rush of warm wind, the room darkened and Lizzy squealed with joy. 'We're going home, Georgie!' She shouted. But as the light returned her voice echoed inside their parents' bedroom and she found herself once more alone. With a sob of exhaustion, Lizzy flung herself upon the bed. How could she find the strength to rescue her little sister AGAIN? It just wasn't fair! Why did this keep happening? She was sorry, sorry, sorry for what she said. Why must she continue to be punished for those few, hasty words uttered in anger?

But even as she had these thoughts, Lizzy was sitting up, sniffing and reaching for the last painting, the broken one. She felt sick in the stomach. Would the magic still work if the painting was broken? Would Georgie be stuck inside the story of Little Red Riding Hood forever? Would her parents be frozen forever here at home? Her hands trembled as she picked up the two halves and put them together. The bright sunlight outside did nothing to cheer her. Not even the sound of someone whistling as they walked down the street, or the birds squawking over bread crumbs in the bird feeder outside the window. Everything went on as usual in the outside world. But nothing was as usual here in Lizzy's house.

There stood Georgie, dressed in a red cape, a basket of cakes on her arm, knocking on Granny's cottage door. Behind that door glinted a steel trap big enough to stop a bear from getting away. And in the bed, tucked up and wearing Granny's bonnet, was a wolf, licking his lips.

The gnome. Where was he? Lizzy scanned the painting carefully. There, sitting in the corner of Granny's cottage, his eyes gleaming with mischief, looking straight at Lizzy. Red Riding Hood had already begun to open the door. Behind it the shiny, steel trap gaped, ready to grasp Georgie's little foot in its jagged jaw. The wolf would catch her easily! The gnome grinned, his cheeks shiny and red as apples. His finger now pointed to the door. Lizzy frowned, concentrating. Another poem was written, inside the painting, on the back of the door. Lizzy had to get Dad's magnifying glasses to read it:

> Sour as lemon, bitter as kale,
> sweeten your words to end this tale.
> Brave and quick, strong and true,
> much now will be asked of you.

The door opened wider. Georgie's foot was already inside. She'd be caught in that horrible trap! The wolf had sat up in bed. Saliva dripped from the corners of his long mouth full of long, white teeth. Granny's bonnet hung askew, tied under his hairy chin with pink ribbons. The gnome sat as before, watching. Lizzy quickly said the verse out loud, clenching her fists until her fingernails dug into her palms.

But nothing happened.

Georgie's face appeared round the door, her expression happy to see her grandmother. Her other foot was stepping inside.

'Don't step on the trap!' Lizzy shrieked, but herself was trapped, outside the painting, looking in. All she had was a silly poem that made no sense. Her little sister was about to die, for real this time. The gnome kept smiling. 'What do you want me to do?' She yelled at him. But he remained mute. 'I'll do it! Whatever it takes! I'll do anything!' Still nothing happened. Lizzy sobbed, staring in horror at her sister's little head appearing round the door. Sweeten your words.... 'Please! It's so unfair!' Lizzy pleaded. 'Georgie doesn't deserve this, she's only little. Take me instead!'

A welcome rush of dark wind signaled Lizzy's passage to the other side. She was inside Granny's cottage! And she had to think fast. Seeing her, the wolf yelped with delight and flung back the bedcovers. Georgie screamed, dropping the basket and stumbled forward, straight towards the deadly jaws of steel. Lizzy lunged towards Georgie. But she was so intent on saving her sister she forgot about the trap.

CLANK!

Lizzy screamed and fell to the floor. The pain around her ankle was like hot embers. She couldn't speak. The wolf rose up to his full height and howled, Granny's bonnet dangling, the ribbons undone. He dropped to all fours and padded towards the fallen Lizzy.

'Two little girls! This will be a lovely picnic,' he rasped.

'Leave her alone!' cried Georgie, dropping to her knees beside Lizzy. She put her arms around her big sister.
The wolf growled. 'Two for one trap. Now, which little snack shall I have first?'

Lizzy couldn't think, couldn't move. She was defeated. The wolf's face was inches from hers, his hot breath smelling of dead things. The fur on his face was worn and patchy where he had fought with other wolves.

'I will not let you eat my thithter!' Shouted Georgie fiercely.

'Georgie, run!' gasped Lizzy. 'Save yourself!'

But Georgie shook her head. 'I'm not leaving you, Lithy.' Tears streamed down her little face. Lizzy could see she was scared out of her wits, but she clung to Lizzy and would not let go. How does this story end in the fairy tales? Thought Lizzy numbly. Something... someone...

The door was suddenly bashed open and a big man strode into the room carrying an axe in his broad hand. The woodcutter! With a roar, he swung at the wolf. Lizzy closed her eyes, whimpering and held on tight to her little sister. She did not want to see what happened next. There was an awful screech. Then the room went silent.

Lizzy opened her eyes. She was back in Mum and Dad's bedroom. She looked down at her leg. The trap was gone and so had the terrible pain. But best of all, Georgie was sitting next to her! Lizzy hugged her little sister.

'You were so brave, Georgie!' Lizzy cried, tears of relief sliding down her cheeks.

'You're my thithter, Lithy.' Georgie said simply, her blue eyes big and round. Lizzy wondered, was it over now? She reached for the final painting and put the two halves together. Red Riding Hood had a stranger's face once more. Lizzy gave her sister another squeeze.

'Let's go and see if Mum and Dad are ok.'

'What happened to Mum and Dad?'

'They were frozen. Until I got you back, time stopped in our house.'

Mum called from the kitchen. 'Georgie! Lizzy! Dinner's almost ready.' Lizzy sighed, her heart full of gratitude. They ran to the kitchen, laughing and jostling each other. Lizzy wrapped her arms around her mother and buried her face.

'I love you, Mum! SO much!'

'What's all this?' Dad walked in. 'Where's my two favourite girls?' He asked, sitting down at the table. They jumped on his lap and told him what had happened.

'And Georgie saved me in the last one,' Lizzy was saying. Dad listened politely, but he didn't seem to believe that four small paintings had magical powers. Lizzy caught Mum's eye. Her mother had a wistful smile upon her lips and a faraway look in her eyes.

'You never know what could happen,' said Mum. 'But you have to be brave and quick, strong and true when much is asked of you.'

Lizzy smiled at Mum. Then she looked at her brave little sister and knew that it was indeed true.

The Great Pyramid
Pete Stratford

Struggling to ignore the stench wafting from the nearby camels and their un-bathed handlers, I stand in awe at the enormity of the tower of squared rocks positioned so uniformly in front of me. The stinging of sand being whipped against my legs by the erratic wind adds to my discomfort as I swelter under the noon day sun. Suffering the incessant badgering of cameleers and numerous hawkers of paltry souvenirs, I am but one of the many hapless tourists who have come from afar to gaze upon this edifice of man's creativity, a pilgrimage enacted by countless generations of travellers before me.

My day had begun before 3:30 a.m, having risen to leave the comfort of my cabin aboard a cruise ship, then take a seat on a crowded bus which travelled along beside the Suez Canal northwards from Port Tewfik to Cairo. As my sleep befogged brain slowly cleared, I took in the scenes as we passed beside drab settlements, most of their buildings once painted in bold colours but badly faded, flaking and dilapidated, yet evidently still in use. Many of them deeply pock-marked, a silent witness to the conflict commonly referred to as the "Six Day War". While a few inhabitants appeared to be intent on some purpose, others loitered idly smoking, or simply sat in small groups on the dusty ground ignoring the passing traffic. Eventually, as our bus entered Cairo city, there was a marked change in the density of buildings and numbers of people. So also were many vehicles of all descriptions, each jostling haphazardly as they sought a space on the road. Mingling amongst the motorized vehicles were emaciated horses, donkeys, or bullocks stoically pulling overloaded carts while their driver perched atop seemingly oblivious to the tooting of horns, as they slowly plodded an erratic course through a haze of exhaust smoke and diesel fumes.

Finally I stand beside the pyramid, while all around me the cacophony of voices in so many languages loudly pleading, haranguing, or abusing some other, a din made bearable only by the wind dispersing these sounds away across the desert. Huge hand-hewn blocks of stone, each fitted intimately against its neighbour, have been ravaged by the elements over eons, erosion partially reshaping many. Meanwhile, sand has filtered into any crevices or landed on ledges, only to be moved elsewhere in a constant state of flux by the desert winds. Standing here, one cannot help but ruminate on the enormity of the workforce that once toiled on this very spot to build, block by block, this monumental structure, widely regarded to be the grave of Cheops, perhaps the most highly venerated of a string of pharaohs from a long-gone empire. Known locally as "Khufu", this pyramid was erected some three thousand years ago, long before the calendar by which we measure time, came into being. Now, as I move closer to the huge blocks that form the base at ground level, my eyes focus on a segmented spiral shell deeply embedded within the stone. This fossilized ammonite is said to have lived during the Jurassic period, over two hundred million years ago. Yet, at some time in pre-history it became embedded in the sea floor sediment, which in turn solidified over time to form the rock that now entraps this shell. Although still in awe at the size of this structure, strangely Khufu doesn't strike me as being quite so ancient after all.

The Day The Water Ran Out
Ant Dry

Nothing lowers my IQ more than having to do without water.

Nobody in Australia really understands what I am on about because they have never really had water cuts.

We had a water cut this morning. We woke up, opened the tap and there was no water.

It was inexplicable. It was like waking up and the sun hadn't risen or opening the door and finding out that someone had stolen the front lawn. It was one of those, 'I just…. I don't know what to say' moments. We were stunned. Both of us.

Then the awfulness of it all set in. We had no water.

I say again - nothing lowers my IQ more than having no water.

An over-reaction perhaps? An overstatement of the problem? Perhaps, but then also, perhaps not.

Maybe a shrink would tell me it was a version of Post-Traumatic Stress Disorder.

There would be merit in this line of thinking, because, it had been the lack of water that had tipped me over the edge some ten years ago.

Everyone knows the story of the frog in the pot. He happily sits in the pot on the stove and doesn't notice as the heat goes from cold to warm and then to hot. He only notices when the water boils. He notices spectacularly by exploding, in a great firework type of a display, with green and red blotches flying all over the place. At least I assume that's what it would be like – never having actually seen a frog explode. The point is that, as his troubles build up, he hardly notices. It's only when he reaches saturation point that he feels affected.

It was the water cuts that did it for me in Zimbabwe.

I put up with the petrol rationing. That had never been a big deal, it had always been a part of my life.

I put up with the petrol cuts.

I put up with there being no petrol.

I put up with the deteriorating roads

I put up with the gradually disappearing traffic lights.

I put up with a Police force turning from a proud force-to-be-reckoned-with into a bribe-taking ineffectual rabble.

I put up with a government turning from a magnanimous power sharing group of fine men into a corrupt sycophantic and unruly mob.

I put up with there being no milk in the shops

I put up with there being no meat on the shelves

I put up with having to hunt for bread

I put up with gradual power outages. I had even bought a generator that turned on automatically, such that when I came home at night I knew if the power was on. If the lights were bright, the generator was on. If the light was such that I felt I had to feel my way into the house, groping and parting the darkness before me, the mains were on.

I put up with all of those things, and more.

But when the day came that I turned on my tap and nothing came out, I lost my marbles. My frog exploded.

Perhaps I am too fastidious. Perhaps I was an odd child that always liked to be clean and developed into an odd man with the same inclination. I don't think it odd, but I'm sure some people do. Perhaps I am odd because I like to be able to flush the toilet, I don't know. Perhaps I'm odd because I don't feel clean or able to operate without brushing my teeth. I don't know. There are degrees of oddness, degrees of madness. Perhaps I am just showing the degree to which I am insane. Again, I don't know.

All I know is that when there was no water, my IQ dropped.

You know the expression "to see red"? For the first time ever, I understood it that day, the day the water ran out. A film of redness actually set on the rim of my vision. I never thought it was a real thing. It is. I found that out the day the water ran out.

But here's the thing. As I sat there, enraged, my eyes engorged with blood, too furious to properly articulate how I felt, and too apoplectic to communicate the same to my wife, the true real horror of it settled on me like a wet, cold fog.

There was absolutely nothing I could do about it. I was completely powerless.

I couldn't complain to the City Council. They would shrug their shoulders, indifferent to the fact that their incompetence had allowed the pipes to age so much that they simply disintegrated.

They would be uninterested in the fact that the pump station at the city dam had been giving trouble for years and needed to be replaced, and that it had not been replaced because it was more important for the city funds to be used to buy the Mayor a new Mercedes Benz.

Rage needs an outlet.

There was a tree in the back yard that my wife had been wanting removed for a while. I had been resisting its removal, for a reason I fail to remember. In my mist of fury, I found the axe. It was blunt, but I didn't care. That tree never knew what happened to it – I didn't know what happened to it either.

What I do know is that some hours after the water dried up the tree was down, and stumped and my mind was made up.

I'd had enough. I couldn't put up with it any more. We were going to leave Africa.

Paradise Gondwana

Lesley Podmore

From vastly beauteous branches green,
Amid the gale-blown leafy scene,
Peep pairs of eyes.
Hushed thought a-plenty,
Watching, pleading, intuitively knowing
Their future role on Earth depends on man,
On man in "suits with petrol legs".

Their fortress from the age of ice
Now washed with rain, or brushed with mist;
Oft touched by roaring forty's galeful blessing,
Feel drips of gentle peace, caressing
Fern and litter, skink and pebble.

Tea-like streams pour into rivers.
Rivers roar and surge forever,
Gouging rockface,
Swirling eddy.

Here canoists try their skill,
And pit themselves against whose will?
Come they with reverential awe,
Appalled to hear a log truck's roar?
Do they stay, --- drink in the peace?
Contact realms in meditation
Known to few now, in this nation?
Would we all could know this pleasure,
Find our inner kingdom's treasure.

The wake-up call has been about
A few years now ---
Do I need to shout?

Hands
Brenda Slavoff

He passed her ground floor flat every day, always in a hurry to get to the stairs and up to his own flat. Sometimes her door was simply ajar, but mostly she was standing in the open doorway, caressing a drink with her frail hands. At first she just looked at him, the slight young man with the long curly dark hair – it was the late 70s – but soon she would nod, lift up the drink and smile. Then came the 'Guten Tag!' and Heinz would smile back, wave his hand, as he disappeared round the stairwell. Then it became 'How are you? What's it like out there today?' As it came close to Christmas, his replies were, 'Snow today! Just a light fall.' She noticed his softer Austrian accent.

But suddenly, caught up in the rush of young busy life, he pauses. She had asked him about himself. He stopped before the next flight of stairs, and took a few steps back.

'I've come to Germany to work; I'm an engineer.' He blushes. He was living with his high-school sweetheart, who was a teacher. Actually, he is glad to impart the startling news that she has just discovered she is pregnant . . . and he is fixing a nursery in the flat. He likes to turn his hands to practical things. 'I hope my hammering doesn't disturb you on weekends,' he apologises. 'We're just above you.'

'I don't hear anything.' She clutches her glass. 'Would you like to come in for a drink?'

It is nearly Christmas – why not? Andrea is out shopping, he could look out for her and carry the things up.

The flat is surprisingly tasteful, with beautiful antique furniture.

'What will you have? I only have alcohol.'

He accepts a cognac. She doesn't add anything to it. He lifts the glass to her; she lifts hers.

'Merry Christmas,' he says.

She shrugs. 'It's just another day.'

There's a fine portrait on the wall. The woman beside the man in it is obviously her, but young, her features pure like silver.

'My husband. He died last year. He was in the army.'

Heinz makes a sympathetic sound.

'I was beautiful,' she says dully. 'And so was he.'

The woman in the portrait is indeed beautiful, but time has devoured that reality.

'I hardly drank before. Now I never stop.'

He thinks of Andrea, in her fresh prettiness.

'He had the most beautiful hands I've ever seen in a man. I would watch them doing things, how he moved them when he spoke. I miss them touching me. Hands talk.' She gulps down her cognac. 'They did bad things during the war, signed papers that sent people to their deaths – but what choice did he have?'

Heinz does not answer. He glances at her own hands that now only live to hold a glass. Suddenly he sees his mother's hands, limp over the coverlet of the hospital bed. He had not been able to bring himself to touch them, though he knew he'd never see her again. His father had bent down and kissed them.

She looks at him appraisingly, and he drops his gaze. She is looking at him with dull desire. The outer door bangs and Andrea enters in a flurry of cold air. His hostess slowly takes his empty glass and motions him out. Her eyes linger a moment on his handsome, boyish face and then drop down to his hands.

"My Diary"
Allan Jamieson

I met a man once who explained how he'd published books and relied solely on selling the copies overseas. I reckoned his expertise was in knowing how to market something on the internet. Perhaps it was also in keeping a straight face; brazen was certainly a descriptor that could apply, though by confining his business to other countries he never needed to show his face to prospective or actual customers. I'll call him Fred and what follows is more or less what he told me.

He arranged to have copies of a book printed "on demand". They were paperback in format, with a plain white cover on which was placed large, black letters declaring "My Diary." He priced the books in his internet ads such that the price covered not only the printing cost, but also the postage cost to those countries he had targeted. Oh, by the way, the number of pages in a book was such that it just managed to weigh less than 250 g, thus eligible for the "letter rate" and the quoted sales price to secure a copy was attractive despite it including an "insurance cover", for a reason that will become clear.

This seemed to be a simple business model – as long as his marketing strategy proved well founded. It was!

For instance, he had anticipated that some copies of his book might go missing in the mail; a customer who queried the non-arrival was quickly assured that a *free* replacement would be soon in the mail. This was a part-reason for the "insurance" cover hidden in the original sales price.

So far, so good!

There was, though, a second category of customers who complained; these were people who had received their copy. Indeed, they were the main group of complainants. Anticipating these complaints, Fred had a ready response. You see, these people complained, because while the title was clearly visible on the front cover, every page between the front and back covers was blank and unnumbered. Fred's response went like this:

Wait a moment! You are now the proud owner of a book boldly declaring "My Diary." on the cover. This is your book and there is plenty of space on the cover for you to add your name. I've left my name off – it's not my diary!

You can imagine that quite a few email exchanges stopped at this point; these customers recognising belatedly that business over the internet did not always end happily for the purchaser. Fred silently blessed them for conforming to a key part of his marketing theory; international transactions via the internet were inherently risky and provided a good modern-day example of that adage from two millennia ago – *caveat emptor*. Fred often tried to envisage the circumstances back then which gave rise to that phrase, yet he was confident that, had he lived in the days of the Roman Empire, he would have found a way to make a good profit.

This left the persistent complainants, who would invariably feel grieved; who had wanted to read of Fred's life story, as clearly outlined in the synopsis Fred had placed in his advertisement. For these people Fred had yet another stock answer:

> So, you're interested in the life of a person unknown to you; a life of travel to exotic locations; of wild sex parties featuring seemingly impossible gymnastics; of the insides of courts and prisons; and of miraculous escapes.
>
> I've always believed 'it takes one to know one' so I reckon your own diary would be a "best seller". Start writing! I'd be happy to type up your draft and have my printer produce proper copies for you. I don't charge much and my name will not appear anywhere. What say?

Anyone not insulted by Fred's answer could either give up – *caveat emptor* still applying – or take up Fred's offer. He was ahead financially anyway, but now could emerge the prospect of a bonus – all along a part of his strategy – to top off the profit.

It did not much matter; either the overseas customer did have the urge to write a book and the ability to write it (lacking only the knowhow around how to get books printed and marketed), or the urge was there to have one's own book, but knowing how to put this urge into practice was not there.

Whichever it was did not trouble Fred. He invited his 'newly hooked' customer to send an email with a brief outline of the person's life and Fred would provide a quote to produce the books – including a 'modest' profit for his input, naturally – and ending his quote with these words: "Of course, my name will not appear anywhere on your book." He kept to himself the fact that his printer had agreed to supply Fred with a finder's fee, a few cents per copy, each time he secured an overseas author.

Fred could not lose! His income might vary from month to month (and with the relative success of each "My Diary" advertisement), but he assured me he never lost money.

It is a few years since he confided this story to me. I don't know where he lives nowadays, though a gaol cell isn't altogether out of all likelihood. I did hear on the grapevine that the Tax Office was hounding him over undeclared income and they don't waste their time – and our moncy – on pipsqucaks.

The Daughter
Brenda Slavoff

Cathy dressed very carefully, in a new dress that showed off her figure. Was there too much cleavage? Why not, she thought naughtily, adding a necklace to emphasise it. The material of the dress was clinging and sparkling with sequins. It suited her bright personality. Her make-up was perfect, eyes and high cheekbones defined. Her hair, no longer strawberry blonde, had blonde tips to cover the grey. It actually suited her better than the original colour.

So good of him to accompany her to the Christmas dinner dance! He didn't usually go to such things. Good of him to go dancing with her at all, because she knew he was really only interested in his medical career. Yet they'd even taken dancing lessons together. Was it to be a typical case of the nurse ending up with the doctor? Cathy giggled. Very different from her previous marriage to an electrician. Everybody had been surprised at her marrying him. Not because of his profession, but because they'd really had nothing in common, apart from sex. In the end all they had in common was the house, which was sold. So much for young love. She'd had so many boys interested in her, too! Now, twenty-five years down the track, she was much wiser. This relationship was perfect, and it would last.

She was meeting him at the venue. He couldn't get away as early as she could, but he promised not to be late. She took a taxi, because she didn't want to limit her drinks tonight; she was determined to have a good time. Her colleagues were already there, husbands or wives in tow, and cocktails were being ordered. One of the doctors bought one for her. She saw the ambulance driver, looking jealously out for her, as she talked to others. He'd been after her for years, and though he accepted being just her friend, he could never resist putting an arm round her shoulders or a hand to her bright hair.

She was in the middle of a noisy chattering group when the doctor arrived. Cathy saw him immediately – not surprising, as he was a head taller than all the other men – and he was looking out for her too, pleasant, easy-going despite his strong presence at work, his mouth turned up in a slight smile, his eyes observant behind steel-rimmed glasses. That smile broadened when he caught sight of her. She waved to him eagerly, and then her hand froze.

Who was this behind him? A tall young girl came through the doorway behind him, her face averted in shyness. Sleek black hair fell to her waist. The dress was beautiful, a simple V between small breasts, a slit in the skirt revealing long brown legs. Cathy watched her enter, and suddenly she recalled him telling her about his fifteen-year-old daughter coming back from a trip to India with her mother, his ex-wife, who had returned to her home. His ex-wife was a doctor too.

He came across the room eagerly to her, his daughter following awkwardly. There were amazed stares from other people, who looked quizzically at her now, shrugging questions. He was at her side, and he kissed her quickly on the lips. In the six weeks she had known him, he had never showed much affection in public, though he was different in private. Whenever he answered her phone calls, in reply to her, 'How are you?' he always answered softly, 'Better for talking to you.'

His joy was stronger tonight. He introduced his daughter proudly, explaining that she had returned two days ago, earlier than was expected, because she had hated being with her mother's family, and didn't get on with her mother at all. 'She's going to stay with me,' he said happily, and went on to say his son had decided to stay in India. She knew it was very important to him that she and his daughter meet at last. She turned to smile warmly at the girl, trying to put her at ease in this roomful of older strangers, remembering how boring such gatherings had been in her own youth. The girl seemed more shy than bored. No wonder she was shy; everyone was staring at her beauty! The girl responded to Cathy's friendliness, saying hello and nice to meet you, but she only looked up briefly. Such great dark eyes, almost black in colour, and long lashes, flipping up once and then down again. The girl was already as tall as Cathy, a good height. Cathy offered her hand to the girl, her fair, freckled hand, to the girl's smooth golden one. 'No one believes this is my daughter,' the doctor laughed; 'they all say, how did an ugly guy like you have such a beautiful daughter?'

The girl obviously took after her mother. What did she look like? But Cathy protested laughingly, 'No, you are good looking!' and he pretended not to be gratified.

They moved towards their seats. On the way, one of her friends held her back and whispered to her, 'Is that his daughter? My God, she's simply stunning! Just like a model. She must have the world at her feet.' Cathy found herself retorting, 'If only life was so simple!' and moved on. The doctor sat between them, talking more to his daughter than to her. When he went to get a drink, Cathy tried to be friendly to the daughter, asking her about herself. What did she like to do? The girl didn't like sport, wasn't interested in swimming or running. She played the violin.

'I learned the piano for a while when I was a child, but I don't think I could play now,' said Cathy. Her mother couldn't afford the lessons after her father had left them.

The daughter liked maths and science, and was hoping to be a doctor herself.

'Girls hardly thought about being doctors in my day,' commented Cathy. She had turned to nursing as a good way to get a profession whilst earning some money, and she enjoyed it.

The daughter chose the pasta dish. She was a vegetarian, against her father's opinion. Yet he was apologetic at ordering steak. The girl glowered at him and said, 'Some poor animal suffered for that.'

'It won't come back to life, love.'

'Daddy, I can't believe you're going to eat that in front of me!'

How strange that she called him "Daddy" still. It seemed very immature. Cathy leaned towards him defensively, 'He had better eat it,' she said lightly, 'otherwise its sacrifice will have been in vain.'

The girl didn't answer.

'I love animals, too,' Cathy tried to make amends. 'I have a border collie that I got from the dogs' home.'

The music started, and Cathy waited impatiently for him to take her to the dance floor. This was what she had looked forward to the most, showing him off, showing herself off. She felt him rise to his feet and turned to him, smiling expectantly. But the girl was also on her feet, her father's hand under her elbow. They left the table without a glance in her direction.

She watched them dance. The girl did not know how to dance, she shuffled ungracefully on her feet, merely holding onto her father as he moved. He looked radiantly happy.

The ambulance driver was at her side. 'What planet did she come from?' He motioned towards the daughter.

'How do you mean?'

'She's more than mortal! But you can't get a word out of her.'

'Why do you want to?'

'I'd love to ask her out. She's the best-looking person in the room!'

'She's only fifteen,' said Cathy repressively.

His face fell. 'That'd be right,' he said, disgruntled.

'Go and have another drink,' she advised lightly.

Father and daughter came back to the table. Another dance started up, and he took Cathy's hand this time, but she pulled back. 'No, not this one,' she said, 'I can't do this one.'

He nodded and sat down, relieved. She talked around him to the girl, asking her about India. What was it like? 'It's dirty and crowded,' the girl said, making a face.

'So you're glad to be home?'

The girl nodded and smiled. Her teeth were perfect and white. How ridiculous it is that a girl's looks matter so much, thought Cathy. It isn't like that for boys. They don't get treated to celebrity status merely because their looks correspond to the current fashion. And a good thing for them, too. They get on with their lives.

How would they all spend this weekend? Cathy had spent the last two weekends with the doctor, their first nights together. After the second morning he had said, 'I want to do everything in life with you, not just make love.' But did she want the same thing? It had all been too hasty, she now thought.

Dessert was coming round. The daughter was so slender there was no worry for her about her weight. Cathy had to be more careful. Her friends were always envious of her figure, but she had to work at it. Lots of exercise, a careful diet and, of course, she had never had children.

They still hadn't danced, but it was getting late, and she was a morning person; she could feel herself drooping. She shouldn't have had that last drink. Time to get a taxi.

'I'll take you home,' the doctor said.

Cathy shook her head. 'You don't want to leave this early.'

'We're ready to go,' he insisted, with a look at his daughter.

'No, I'll take a taxi.'

He was on his feet, helping her into her jacket, as he always did, saying, 'I'll be over in the morning.'

'No, don't; I plan a morning run.'

'Lunch, then? I'll come at eleven.'

'What about -?' and she indicated his daughter.

'She wants to visit her friends.'

He was so eager, she had to answer, 'Oh, I'll let you know.' She decided she would get out of it somehow tomorrow morning. She needed to draw back, things were going too fast.

He insisted on seeing her to the taxi, and before they parted, kissed her lightly again, like a shy schoolboy with his first girlfriend. Yes, that's how he was. It took her back to her early dates as a young girl, when boys had fought over her at dances and pubs. The relationship was uncomfortable, not what she wanted. She knew it was over. She felt very experienced, mature and wise.

Fears for our near future
Anne Layton-Bennett

a friend creates poems
from our marketing man's
political parlance

she scribbles his earworms
of propaganda -
his fast and phony phrases
that are
meaningless and deliberate
distractions -
an ad man's ploy designed
to tread grooves in our psyche
persuade us his misleading mantras
about climate, coal
and gas
(and sun, wind and water)
are compatible with health, wealth
and a future that burns bright

Answered
Lotta King

'Do you miss him?' I enquired.
The young widow's eyes held mine,
as she replied, 'Well,
there are all sorts of missing.
There is running for the train
as it moves faster and draws away
and becomes small and distant
beyond everything.

'There is jumping from the high diving board
and somehow your body becomes
disconnected from your intentions
as you fumble, splashing
evanescent, into the pool.

'Then as a child running in the playground
to catch someone and just
not touching, both continuing
with empty arms.

'And there is aiming for something,
drawing back your arrow,
releasing and misplacing it,
your target not within
your physical capabilities.

'And then, there is missing like
living in the city
and scarcely remembering
a baby echidna, or the scent of wild roses
or the cries of black cockatoos.

'Then there is the feeling a man has
during a life sentence, when he misses hope,
promise, his life and the whole world.'
'And do you miss him?' I asked again.
'Yes, those ways I miss him. In those ways, I do.'

Manoeuvres
Jennie Herrera

It's the first lesson the novice learns: pawns can afford
to be lost.
Pawns are moderately expendable.
Don't give them away unnecessarily but don't mourn their
loss.

And then it's up the chain: what each one does, what each one
can't …
'Like an army,' one father tells his son.
'Like big business,' another gathers in his heirs.
'Never forget where true power lies.'

'Know your staff. Put them in positions where they can
enhance your profit.
Use your personnel to grow your company.'
'There's no glass ceiling when you play,' a female CEO tells
her daughter, 'but you've got to know your people inside out.'

'Decide what of your equipment is most valuable; never use
your best to man the frontline … decide who's expendable
before you announce your intentions.
Never go to war if you're under-strength.
A defensive game can win, come from behind, know how
attrition works.'

A military map doesn't look much like diagrams in books
entitled:
How to Play Chess
but they are curiously compatible when the killing's done and
the
rag-tag survivors finally carried off …

The Crystal Cleaner
Edith Speers

He was pale and skinny, medium height, with black hair and dark eyes. They say no one has black eyes, not really, so I told the cops they were really dark brown, so dark they looked black. Not true. His eyes were black, truly black, because no light was reflected from them, ever. Flat dead black. Black like the black holes in outer space that suck in everything that comes anywhere near them. A dead end for everything, including light. This is not the kind of description that cops want to hear. Tell them something like that and they give you a look. Just a look. No facial movement, no lifting of an eyebrow, no jokey or questioning comment. If they were going to take me seriously and not write me off as a drug-addled candidate for the psych ward I had to be careful what I said. But without looking like I was being careful. I had to pretend to be normal.

How ironic is that. For over a month now, everything I did was to get out of being normal. Normal is boring. Normal means not cool, not a stoner, not a trouble-maker, not suicidal, not a cutter or a tragic and troubled product of a dysfunctional family. Not anything. And I was sick of it. I mean, I've seen older people go through their high school or college year books and point to faces and tell stories but some faces they just say 'She was nice' and move on. Or worse, 'I don't remember her.' One day, the summer between Year 11 and Year 12, I got up to another boring day and looked at my boring face and couldn't stand it anymore.

And this was my big chance. Home alone. Parents who trusted me as long as I video-linked them every few days, I was so responsible, mature for my age, never been in trouble. Also they'd paid for me to go to tutoring twice a week all summer. So here I was, with more freedom than I'd ever had in my life and was I really going to waste it just being normal? No way.

I started with my hair. Cut it all off. Cool. That would save me all that time with the ceramic plates getting the curl out of it — the curls were gone. Then I dyed what was left. Only thing in the bathroom were some spray cans of temporary colour. Couldn't decide between black and poppy red so I did both. Time to get an outfit, something to match my new look. I tore the legs off my oldest jeans – had to snip through the seams – and put them on over black tights. Not bad. I pulled out some of the threads so they dangled. My Doc Martins were brown, boring brown, boring and brown as my whole life, so I sprayed them black. A black crop top then a black... No, not black again. This was getting too predictable. A shirt of my dad's from Indonesia that mum never let him wear except at barbeques – tie-died purple and red and green. Covered my freckled cheek bones with mum's foundation and lashings of blusher, slathered on the eye-liner, and used lime green zinc cream as lipstick. Added a fake nose- piercing. Okay, this would do while I cruised the op shops, which is where I got this khaki sort of cotton jacket with a hood and a lot of pockets. No wonder Ivor found me irresistible. So did a lot of other guys but by day two I'd worked out the details.

The first day I hung out at the mall – not an indoor multi-storey place, an outside one with a glass ceiling. No fear that anyone would recognise me – but the voice almost gave me away. One of the guys asking a smoke off me said, 'You have great diction, don't I know you from that drama workshop at the Peacock Theatre? Last March?'

I said, real bored, 'I don't do that shit.'

Oh I knew him alright but no way did I want to pick up anyone who might know people I knew, let alone anyone who used a word like 'diction' and asked for smokes instead of offering them, so when he asked me if I wanted a coffee, I nodded, he got me one – a short black, of course, the new me would never touch milk – then I said, 'Now you can piss off.'

The next guy asked me if I was on Facebook. Dumb question. Of course I was on Facebook but my parents were so worried about my electronic footprint, and how my career prospects might get damaged by anything 'inappropriate' it was even more boring than my normal life. Which is the exact opposite of what everyone else does. So I said, 'I don't do that shit.' After five minutes of his nerdy lameness I said, 'You're boring me.' Finally I had to say, 'Piss off.'

So, on Day One I learned that I could manage just about every situation with just three phrases. This also protected me from anyone recognising my voice – and, just as importantly, it stopped me from saying too much that might give me away. I also learned to mute my phone and keep it zipped up in an inside pocket. Even when it vibrated I ignored it until I was on my own, in a toilet cubicle. This was because people also ask to borrow your phone and I didn't want anyone running off with it or flicking through my photos or checking out my text messages, all of which almost happened.

Late on Day Two was when Ivor finally made his move. He told me later that he'd been watching me the day before. Anyway, the street lights went on, which means it must've been past 8pm and aside from having all these guys coming onto me, and a few women as well, and having them buy me smokes and food and stuff, and getting felt up in a movie, the day looked like being a dead loss. Then someone was looming over me. He said, 'Let's go to the park.' I said, 'Piss off.' He said, 'This place is for normals.' I said, 'You're boring me.' He said, 'I got a few cones.' I said, 'I don't do that shit.' Oh crap. Had I missed my chance?

Silence. I hadn't really looked at him, I'd been doing the bored 'whatever' routine. I looked at him. He was hot. He looked dangerous, like a junkie or a vampire, he was so pale, with those eyes, and his hair was thick and silky, so my fingers itched to slide through it, and he was so lean his hips were sort of hollowed out at the fronts like they were waiting to get mine locked into them like puzzle pieces. I went to the park and we smoked a cone, then another, then he took me to a party full of weird people and I got drunk and then he disappeared. I got a cab home and couldn't wait until the next day.

I slept in, but that didn't matter. I knew he wouldn't show up in the park until the street lights came on. For almost four weeks we did everything I'd never done before but wanted to do. Except sex. I mean, I'd done sex before but that's the one thing he wouldn't do. He didn't like being touched and if I tried anything he'd just disappear. Once he said, 'That's for normals.' Another time he said, 'Sex will end everything.' He reached out and stroked my neck with the tip of his finger, then he licked his finger, very slowly. Then he walked away. I knew better than to ever follow him. Of course he must have followed me, he knew exactly where I lived, found out my real name, what my parents did, who their friends were, everything.

Our whole thing was to never ask questions, right? So when he opened up to me, my heart started jumping. He told me about his gypsy parents, and what they taught him, and how he made money by doing Tarot readings and crystal healing. He took me to this old house with all the windows boarded up and he showed me the cards and told me to pick one and it was a big red heart with three swords going through it. How cool was that. His card was Death, which was even cooler. Then he opened a battered old biscuit tin and showed me some of his relatives and ancestors, who all looked like something out of an Addams Family movie. There were no modern pictures, none of him and his parents, and I figured I knew why. Finally he showed me the crystals and let me touch them. 'Now I'll have to clean them,' he said, 'or I can't use them with anyone else.' It had something to do with vibrations, which I totally understood because my aunt's an alterno hippy sort of person.

Each crystal had to be cleaned in a different way so that's what we did after that. Every night we went out and cleaned a crystal. Ivor said each crystal had different needs. Like some need white light, or moonlight, or have to be buried overnight, but always in a special place, like where certain flowers or herbs were growing. Others can only be washed in a certain type of bottled water. Others needed salt water, not just any old sea water, but water with special types of mineral salts dissolved in it. The weirdest thing was that some needed smudging, which sounds like you're making them dirty but is just the opposite. Special sage – white sage – with just the right vibration, is picked fresh then dried and bundled up, sometimes with a certain type of lavender, and the smoke is waved over the crystal. Anyway, all this stuff was complicated and sometimes expensive so he had to raid people's gardens or sometimes even get into shops or houses to get what he needed. It turned out I knew where he could find some of this stuff so then I just had to find out when the people would be away from home and it was all a lot easier. I stayed out front somewhere, on a verandah or behind some shrubbery or something, to keep watch.

I'm not a total moron. I knew he had to break and enter some places. I didn't know he was doing a B&E on all of them. I mean, I never saw him with suspicious bulges under his jacket or in his pockets or anything like that. Turned out he specialised in cash and jewellery.

Anyway, the last time we went out together was when he needed a crystal bowl – a crystal singing bowl he called it, because when you run your finger round it, on the inside, it sort of hums – and it so happened I knew these people down the street had a huge one, right in their front window. He'd been gone for ages and I was getting bored so I went on Facebook on my phone and there were so many postings to catch up on I sort of forgot to watch the street. I got caught. He didn't.

As soon as I saw the cops in front of me, I screamed. One stayed with me and the other went round the back of the house. I burst into sobs, and howled, and snivelled, and scrubbed tears from my face with my shirt tails. Blusher and green zinc cream and eyeliner wouldn't show up on that thing. I had my hoodie up, too, all the way to the cop shop where I begged to use the loo. My luck was in. No women cops available so this cute young guy stood guard at the door. I ducked my head under the taps and scrubbed like hell till my hair was boring brown, with pale pink highlights, then I dried it under the hand-dryer. It was quick and easy – I did the same thing every few days, just before I conferenced with my parents or went to tutoring.

In the mirror a scared young girl with freckles stared back at me, pale and pathetic, heart-broken because her boyfriend had lied to her and tricked her and then left her all alone to take the blame. I was going to take off my fake nose piercing but what I saw in the mirror made me stop. Yeah, that would work better. So when I was slouched miserably in an interview room, my big sad eyes downcast, I slowly took off the piercing and, with a little catch in my breathing, somewhere between a sigh and a sob, I tucked it into my pocket. It totally worked. The cops exchanged glances, asked questions, made notes. A gentle caution and they sent me on my way.

So it was an awesome summer. Only one thing I missed out on – but there's a week left. And I know where that cute cop lives. Found out when his shift ended and followed him home. I learned a lot more from Ivor than how to clean crystals.

Faerie Dawn
Graeme Bourke

If ever there was a place where I would expect to find a hobbit, a pixie or an elf, it would have to be at Lake Burbury on the West Coast of Tasmania. This is a truly magnificent place with an unmistakable aura that weaves nature's magic in an awesome way; it is a fairyland of beauty. Let me tell you of just one of my fishing experiences that had me literally holding my breath in more ways than one.

At five o'clock in the morning I crawled from beneath the warm blankets and quietly dressed myself so as not to disturb my partner, who would probably sleep for another two or three hours. I gathered the fly rod and made my way down to the boat that was tethered at the shore. I looked across at the calm stretches of water around the tiny islands and knew there would be trout feeding in those waters. There was no wind, and everything was shrouded in the greyness of the pre-dawn. The land had not yet woken from its slumber.

I pushed off from the shore and started the motor; then I steered the boat towards the two tiny islands in the middle of the lake. Reaching the calm water, I cut the motor and just drifted. Eyes scanned the milky calm for any sign of feeding trout. At first, I saw nothing, which had me somewhat perplexed. I was so sure that there would be trout here.

Eventually, I noticed the telltale sign of a fin protruding from the top of the water like a tiny sailboat. The only problem was that the fish was actually moving away from me, and this would make it very difficult for me to present the fly. Still, I had to try. The grey seven-weight intermediate line snaked out across the water, the two flies I had on landed to one side of the fish. But alas, the trout continued on his way, quite oblivious to the flies.

Standing there in the boat and searching the water in the eerie stillness of the early morning, I cast out the line in the forlorn hope that a cruising fish might see the flies. Then, I saw a fish take some tasty morsels off the top of the water just in front of the boat. The line sped through my fingers as I pulled the flies directly into the trout's path. A subtle pause allowed the flies to sink a little, then, a slow retrieve. The fish must see the flies!

Suddenly, the line tightened and the rod bent over sharply. There was a feel of strength, power and energy at the end of the line as the rainbow trout leapt out of the water, shaking its head and twisting its silver and red flanks in defiance as it crashed back into the water. Line screamed off the reel, but the hook was set, this fish was going nowhere. After a great fight the trout was brought to the net and boated, a fine rainbow of around a kilo.

It was then I noticed the glow on the top of the hills to the west. Soon the sun would be spreading its golden rays across the land and onto the water. I had to work fast if I wanted another fish. I knew that once the sun hit the water the fish would be gone. Keen eyes once again scoured the water. I saw several more fish, but they were out of range, so I started the motor and moved along the wind lane (a calm river-like area in a lake) to another spot.

It wasn't long before I saw my next target. The fish was swimming across the front of the boat with its fins clearly visible on top of the water. I cast out some two metres in front of the fish and allowed the flies to sink, then, the slow retrieve. Once again, the line tightened and the fish was on, another rainbow. This trout wasn't as big as the first, but still, it was a nice fish, and it fought me every inch of the way. As I put the net under the fish, I noticed that my leader was tangled. On closer inspection after I had put the fish in the bag, I saw that the leader was indeed a right mess. And the two flies, a Black Woolly Worm on the point and a Brown Woolly Worm as the dropper, which was the fly that both fish had taken, were stripped of their hackles and were now useless. I cut them off and discarded them. I then managed to untie the mess even though I still had a couple of extra knots that shouldn't have been there, but time was of the essence. Tying on two more flies I began searching the water again.

The sun was now reaching out and caressing the mountain peaks. My attention was drawn to the brilliance of golden sunlight as it slowly crept down the mountainside bringing life to the purple cliffs. Suddenly, the fishing became a secondary option as I continued to admire one of nature's magnificent scenes. Every contour and crag on the side of the cliffs now visible as the creeping sun sought out every niche, as if to say good morning to the animals and insects that would probably come out and bask in the warmth of the morning sun. A fish came in range to my left. I put out a tentative cast, which landed far too close. The fish continued on its merry way, totally ignoring the flies.

My eyes returned to the picture unfolding before me as the grey dawn yielded to the brightness of the morning sun. The sun was on the water now and the two tiny islands lit up in all brilliant detail. The rock formations reflected their greys, browns and silver colours, the trees became alive and the bright green rushes waved gently as a wisp of wind passed by.

I sat down in the boat and laid the rod down. I would fish no more this morning. I half expected the rosy red face of a hobbit to poke his head out from within the thick foliage and say a cheery good morning to me. Or maybe a Leprechaun would appear in his bright green clothing and dance a silent jig on the placid shores of the island as a gesture of peace and tranquility. I sat there in the eerie silence and drank in the aura of this magical morning. Not a sound could be heard. I thought of the people back in the camping ground snug in their beds, what a sight they were missing. For a brief moment, on one of her most auspicious occasions, I was sincerely touched by Mother Nature.

Through The Back Fence
A story for children
Lesley Podmore

<u>Over the back fence</u>

Over Joby's back fence was a paddock. On this particular Saturday he was peeping through the gap beside a loose paling to see what was happening. There was always something going on. The farmer had horses there sometimes; and often sheep with all sorts of brownish wool.

Today there was a noise Joby didn't know. He could hear it; it was rather raucous, and coming from the dam. Joby wished he could squeeze through that gap to find out.

'Joby! Joby!!' Mum was calling. (They were going shopping) 'Do I haff ta come Mum?' he yelled. 'It's awfully hot, and boring. Can't I go to James's?' 'Well,' said Mum, 'I'll find out.' So she did, and it was alright. James was lots of fun, and his mum made awesome pizzas. Joby couldn't wait.

<u>The Paddock.</u>

Now, James's house wasn't far away. In fact it was seventy six Joby steps down the street, and it also had a fence backing on to that paddock. And, instead of a loose paling or two, James's fence had a gate. A gate into that awesome place.

Usually it was out of bounds for James because his father thought he'd be trodden on by horses or sat on by sheep; and his nanna thought the sheep would get into the garden and eat all the bushes. But James's mother thought it was perfectly alright to go exploring as long as she came too. Besides, the farmer was her cousin, and he didn't mind.

Soooo, after pizzas (with lots of pineapple, yum-oh), Joby and James and his mum put on gumboots and sunhats and set off to see what the racket in the dam was all about.

Joby and James had a long way to go down to the dam. On the way they ran round a clump of trees and scared the local possum. They raced around the water trough, and nearly tumbled into a wombat's hole. And they played 'I'm the king of the castle' on top of a large rock. All this time the great racket was coming from the dam. Thud-up! Thud-up!

over the fence. 'Where's my carrot?' he was saying. 'You can give it this time,' said Joby to James. 'I'll go and get one.'

Now, while Joby had been stuck inside during all that wintry rain, Uncle Fred had been making a new friend who followed him about everywhere. She seemed to love him and became his little shadow. In fact she was the right colour for a shadow. She was greyish black and looked like a box with four legs. A woolly box. It was one of the sheep. She too poked her head through the hole, munching. 'Mair, mair –urr-rair,' she said.

'Well!' said Dad, 'she's too wide to fit through the hole. I wonder if Mum will name her too?

Come on boys, inside! It's starting to rain again.'

What's All This About?

It was a Tuesday afternoon and Joby was in bed. He was sick. He had a nasty sore throat and a pounding head, and his tummy felt funny. His mum was fussing around with glasses of water and very small Vegemite sandwiches. She also put a bucket near his bed. 'For just-in-case,' she said.

The next day Joby was a little better, but Oh Dear!! His mum had caught the nasty bug, and now she was in bed. 'Just play with your Lego or put on the telly if you want,' she said. 'I'll be in my bedroom.'

From the lounge room window Joby could just see into the paddock. The baby geese had all hatched and were quite big now. Uncle Fred was still there. But best of all there were little lambs. Their mums often maired loudly to tell them to stay close.

Joby was busy building a castle with his Lego, when he heard another great racket from the dam. This time it was a sheep mairing very loudly. Joby was about to build the turrets when he realised this sheep sounded very upset. She kept on and on. Joby stood on the sofa and peered down the hill. The sheep making all the noise was Mary. (You guessed it! Joby's mum had been busy with names). Mary was by the dam and seemed very upset. And here came Uncle Fred at full gallop to Joby's fence. 'Neigh! Neigh! Neigh,' he called, and banged the fence with his front hooves, 'Neigh! Neigh!!'

'Oh Joby,' called mum. 'Go and tell that horse to be quiet. My head is pounding.' So Joby went to tell Uncle Fred to shush. However Uncle Fred kept roaring in his horsey way and banging the fence some more. He reared and galloped towards the dam, looking over his shoulder at Joby as if to say 'Come quickly!!'

'Oh boy,' thought Joby, 'he wants me to see what's up. I can just about get through there if I go sideways.' So he put on his gumboots and squeezed through. 'What's wrong, Uncle Fred? What do you want me to do?'

Joby To The Rescue.

Joby ran down the hillside all the way to the dam. Uncle Fred and Mary were both looking into the dam and yelling in their own way. And then Joby saw why. Stuck in the mud was a tiny lamb!! Now Joby was upset too. The poor little thing was covered in mud halfway up its sides and couldn't move. 'Oh Mary, is this yours? Mum, Mum!!' he yelled. But she couldn't hear. She had pillows over her head.

'Neigh! Neigh!' called Uncle Fred.

'Oh, mairy-airy-air!' called Mary.

'Blaa, blaa, blaa,' went the lamb.

'Mum! Mum!' yelled Joby. 'Well,' he thought. 'I'll go through the tunnel.' So he began pulling himself through on his tummy. 'That was easy. Now to reach the lamb,' he thought. The mud was very soft, and Joby's left gumboot became stuck. Now what was he to do? He couldn't quite reach the lamb, and if he trod with his right boot, that would get stuck too!!!

'Oh! Mum Muuum!'

'Mairy, mairy, mairy!'

'Blaa! Blaaa! Blaaa!'

'Neigh! Neigh! Neigh!'

Joby suddenly noticed the pump beside the water. It had a little shed about it. And this shed was made from roofing iron. 'It's a bit like Dad's drum,' thought Joby. 'I'll bang it!' So with one step with his right gum boot, and another step with his bare left foot, Joby reached the pump. He picked up a broken branch and banged and yelled.

Now all this extra racket was heard. James's nanna heard it and came running. The farmer was home for tea. He came running, with his wife behind him.

'What do you think you're doing, boy!!' he yelled. Joby pointed to the little lamb. The farmer leapt the fence and scooped the little thing up. 'Well done, Joby,' he said. 'You saved a life.' He took the lamb, with Mary following behind, to clean him up.

James's nanna lifted Joby back over the fence, gave him a big hug, and took him back home to clean him up. And the farmer's wife fished out the gumboot.

<u>Now All's Good.</u>
Later that day, when Joby and his dad were eating dinner, pizzas of course, and Mum was still in bed with a bucket beside her for 'just-in-case,' there came a knock at the door.

'Any-one home?' called the farmer. 'You have a very brave boy there, Gavin,' said the farmer. 'He's saved a little lamb. Did he tell you?'

Dad was very proud, and Mum felt she had better not get sick ever again. The farmer had come with a big bag of Mary's wool he'd kept from last year's shearing, for Joby's mum to knit a special jumper, and the farmer's wife brought a large bowl of strawberries and icecream for every-one to share.

Well done, Joby.

Cautionary tale

Adam Stokell

Jack jumpers stretch already thin strands of belonging.

Workers emerge from the nest at dawn and scatter in a starburst of directions, each ant hooking or crooking good things to clean-and-jerk back to the We: ichneumon fuselage for the next gen to chew on, hundredweight of sandstone to help summer-white the roof.

The danger is that all that time alone out rambling the known world, the thousand days and different ways of being they encounter and kill, will eventually give rise to several tall Ideas, sirens out into the I.

Luckily for local nests, I remain ego-bound to the same dry plot – part scarecrow, part cautionary tale.

What's in a Word?

Allan Jamieson

It happens to me sometimes that a word comes to mind, or I'm attracted to a word, and later – next day or soon after – a quite independent situation arises and this word occupies "centre stage".

Take a word like scorpion. I haven't seen a scorpion for years, nor read of one in a book or in the news, so it did seem surprising that in bed just two nights ago I 'saw' a scorpion moving beside my head on the pillow. It was a vivid scene, yet it had to be a dream, because the bedroom was quite dark and I could not have seen a real scorpion – nor was I bitten.

Today, a friend called in at my office and we talked of many things. At one point, she told me she had received her first injection against COVID three weeks ago and she suffered a strong feverish reaction that lasted some hours. I said I would have my first injection in four days' time and I could recall receiving an injection some 55 years ago against yellow fever, prior to travelling through the Panama Canal on a passenger ship. I had suffered a strong feverish reaction soon after that injection and considered myself fortunate in being able to walk home from the doctor's surgery and up two flights of stairs to my bedroom without fainting or falling down the stairs. The fever lasted some hours.

My friend said she was familiar with injections for yellow fever, as she had lived for some years in the Caribbean where that disease is rife. She then told me this childhood memory:

We had a gardener. He was a black man, a very nice man, and I enjoyed talking with him. He used to go hunting in the hills and one day I saw a large welt near one of his wrists. He explained that before going hunting it was a custom to brush the tail of a scorpion across the lower arm. This built up immunity against scorpion bites, which could be lethal if one was bitten while in a remote part of the island. This was a traditional immunisation method brought to the Caribbean by African slaves.

What are the odds of this somewhat rare word – scorpion – coming independently to mind twice in a mere two days?

I don't know the answer, yet this coincidence prompted me to recall a situation from the 1950's when I was boarding at a university college in Melbourne. I had a close friend also boarding there and we spent many hours together, playing billiards, or table tennis, or just talking of diverse things.

One Friday evening, around 10 pm, we adjourned to his study after playing billiards. I should explain that Frank, my friend, shared the study with a fellow student, Ted. They each had separate bedrooms across the central corridor of the long building. The building had thick stone and brick walls, dating from 1887 and all the rooms had double doors facing this corridor, to minimise noise. When we entered the study, Ted wasn't there and Frank said Ted usually adjourned early to his bedroom most nights.

This evening Frank and I debated whether mental telepathy was a real phenomenon. I thought it was, so we set out to test this by various means. A simple test was for one of us to think of a number, say from one to ten or some such, and for the other to name the number. This and similar games occupied us for maybe an hour and the evidence was mounting statistically that mental telepathy *is* genuine.

Emboldened, we decided on a "real" test. We began silently 'calling' for Ted to come into the study. We sat with our minds working for about ten minutes, after which we talked of several other things. We fell silent, though, when Ted walked into the study. We were astonished, even more so when Ted said he had come to get a drink of water. There was no water in the study, yet each bedroom had its own hand basin and water tap.

Ted was destined to live a very successful life, so our unconventional way of getting him out of bed that Friday night did no obvious harm.

[Ted gained a science degree with honours in mathematics and physics from Melbourne University, after which he worked as a geophysicist, exploring the Savage River region in Tasmania and working as Chief Geophysicist in Canada. He obtained a doctorate from Oxford University. Later he was to advocate an integrated approach to animal welfare, bringing together scientists, politicians, lawyers, and animal protection organisations to address injustices to animals. He died aged 77.]

To this day, I will argue that mental telepathy is real!

In the early 1960s, I was boarding with an Anglican minister and his family. He was an avid reader and, at the time I knew him, he had a special interest in ghosts. Not the common or garden type that everyone imagines look like an erect white sheet with two black holes for eyes, but the essentially invisible poltergeists [German for "noisy spirit"]. These "troublesome spirits" make themselves known by causing objects, such as plates, chairs, etc. to move or in causing pictures on walls to hang at odd angles, or in creating loud noises at unusual times.

I don't wish to imply that the minister believed in these ghosts, but he did have reason to be interested in them, because there have been many recorded instances in history where poltergeists made their presence known in church rectories, especially if adolescent girls were also living there. The minister's family comprised his wife and teenage daughter.

Given my "confirmed" belief in mental telepathy, I was primed to have an open-minded interest in poltergeists too and I provided a good listening post for the minister. I'm sure each of us would not have been surprised if a poltergeist had made its presence known while we sat in the living room discussing theories. Nothing such happened while I lived there, but in writing this story now, I contacted the minister's daughter. A great grandmother these days, this was her reply:

> I do believe that the vicarage was haunted but not by a noisy ghost. It was on the fourteenth step of the staircase, just before the bathroom landing, that I became aware of a cold and clammy feeling, like being in a fog. It was decidedly eerie and a somewhat frightening feeling, particularly to a young teenage girl of 14 or so. This feeling was so intense, that I would count the steps while ascending and then jump that particular step, in order to avoid it. I did mention this phenomenon to my father, who agreed that it could well be so, but he assured me that whatever it was would cause me no harm. I later found out that a daughter of a previous vicar had died in the house many years previously. Was her soul still searching for eternal peace? It is interesting that Richard, who was my boyfriend in the later 1960's and became my husband, also experienced the same weird feelings around that fourteenth step!

I can't recall a cold step on those stairs, but who am I to question the daughter's experience. Perhaps that spirit held back in my presence; I was not "family".

Last night, I asked my wife if she had ever experienced something unexplainable. She referred to her childhood memories in Odo, a tiny village some 40 km east of Nagoya situated on a hillside overlooking the Yakagi River – an extremely isolated place. We have been there a few times and I remember it being very peaceful.

When my wife was about four or five years old, she and her mum were living with her grandfather and grandmother at Odo. Grandpa was a doctor who had his own general practice and my wife said she used to play in his surgery for hours. This explains, I reckon, why my wife has a very broad grasp of medical issues and we have several medical textbooks in our house in Japanese, German and English.

Anyway, Grandpa had built a small hospital further up the hillside above his surgery and there was a Shinto shrine in that vicinity as well. Of course, as befitted such a location, a graveyard was also sited there. My wife recalled how the four of them happened to be sitting outside the surgery in the cool of the evening when a flickering blue light appeared up the hillside. The incident happened over 70 years ago, but the image is still vivid in her mind.

There is, of course, a scientific explanation for this light and I put it to my wife that it was probably a "will-o'-the-wisp"; methane gas. She acknowledged this point of view, but she argued that cremation of bodies has been practiced in Japan for millennia and the likelihood is that the graveyard comprised solely granite headstones with recesses to hold the ashes. What would produce the methane?

My wife then showed me an article in the most recent edition she had of *Shukan Asahi*, a Japanese weekly magazine. The article was written by a medical doctor associated with a hospital in Kawagoe, a history-rich city north of Tokyo. He wrote of visiting America with a friend and they went to a Hopi Indian reservation in Arizona. The Hopi are widely known for their spirituality and beliefs rooted in Animism (the attribution of a living soul to plants, inanimate objects, and natural phenomena). A guide pointed to a carved image on a rock and told the two Japanese that this was sacred. The doctor tried to take a photo of the rock, but his camera shutter failed to function. He borrowed his friend's camera, but that too did not operate. The two Japanese moved on to other places later and noted that their cameras now worked fine. In the article, the doctor made these three points:

a) There are many things in life that are not explainable;
b) If we assume there are many mysteries of human life, we can accept strange things;
c) If you freely allow these wonders to exist, your world will be open and full.

Recently, I read a truly excellent book by a senior lecturer in Indigenous Knowledges at Deakin University, in which he tells of a conversation he had with a Tasmanian aboriginal:

> We yarn about the sentience of stones and the ancient Greek mistake of identifying dead matter as opposed to living matter, limiting for centuries to come the potential of western thought when attempting to define things ... They viewed space as lifeless and empty between the stars; our own stories represented those dark areas as living country, based on observed effects of attraction from those places on celestial bodies [but] western science came late to discoveries of what they now call "dead matter", finding that those areas of dead and empty space actually contain most of the matter in the universe.

This brings me to the point of my story. There are and always have been a variety of happenings that at the time defied an obvious explanation, thereby giving rise to the concepts of "magic", "spirits", "ghosts" or "mental telepathy". The world is populated with individuals who believe they know everything and who, upon hearing tales like the ones I've described here will readily propose explanations; sometimes these need to be "constructed" and it needs a good dose of faith to accept them, especially when they come from people who were not there at the time!

The world would be a better place if we followed the advice of that Japanese doctor and allowed the "unexplainable" to exist. In Australia, we don't have to go far to find a culturally rich civilisation that has lasted for tens of thousands of years longer than has our cold, hard western civilisation.

One Hundred Percent Dog
(a tribute to a chihuahua)
Brenda Slavoff

The wolf begat you
and as God marks the sparrow's fall
you fell into my lap -
my one hand, in fact,
took all of you in its heart.

They say that humans
and dogs evolved together
in a blood relationship
of love and destruction.
A dialogue of sympathy,
teeth bared, you hunted our presence
in fear and fascination.

What did we do to you,
eternal puppy,
your bark worse than your bite,
wildness in a package,
civilisation without a message?

Flesh of my flesh,
What did you do to me,
binding me with your endless
love and helplessness
to a meekness you don't want?

Lawless relationship,
survival is a leap of joy.
Bred to be a plaything
I live through you
dreaming of your creation
through humans.
So I think.

Because only God
gave you that joyful tail.

Last Man Standing
Pete. Stratford

While chatting with an old chap
down the street quite recently
he said; 'Young folk don't realize
how lonely being old can be.'
My parents died when I was young
all my siblings have gone too
so I'm the only one left standing.
Lord knows how I've made it through.
That blood bath our lot served in
was followed up by other wars
where plenty of my good mates died
for someone else's cause
but my number didn't come up
I was among those surviving few
but still carry nightmare memories
just like most old soldiers do.
Back wearing civvies was a struggle
we didn't fit into that scene
and those who hadn't been there
couldn't grasp where we had been.
But we struggled through with effort
to carve ourselves a better life
some with a wife, then children
though some others got in strife.
They simply couldn't settle down
remained haunted all the time.
Blokes even took their own lives
or turned to a life of crime.
So, here I find myself alone now
without any of my peers.
I should have joined them long ago!
(please forgive me these few tears)

You simply cannot understand
unless you've been there too
the memories that us old chaps have

or the things that we went through.
When I look back on those tough days
I remember good mates like Mac
Willie, Blake, and best mate Blue
great pals, that didn't make it back.
We were more than brothers
as we stood together side by side
all battling bravely for the cause
as good men beside us died.
All I do now is quietly wait
until the Lord receives my thanks
that when His last bugle calls me
I'll march beside them in their ranks.

The Primrose Path
Brenda Slavoff

Once upon a time there was a princess who wasn't beautiful, or clever; who was, in fact, so ordinary that no one would have believed she really was a princess, except that her father was a king.

No good fairies attended her christening with gifts and graces to bestow. Princess Primrose wasn't ugly, but she was quite plain. She grew into a chubby young girl, with a round face and narrow blue eyes that almost disappeared when she laughed. She had tow coloured hair and she was very short. Being plain was not necessarily a curse, however, because it meant her stepmother was not jealous of her. No poisoned apples for Princess Primrose! Of course, not being clever was embarrassing. She wasn't good at reading or writing, couldn't play a musical instrument, didn't dance and had a voice like a frog. She didn't like frogs, either, so she was certainly never going to kiss one and win a handsome prince. She was no good at ball games, so she would never be found playing with a golden ball under a lime tree, nor be tossing several as she set out to rescue a prince. She was no good at spinning; but at least that meant there was no danger of spindles or needles on her sixteenth birthday. What was she good at? Well, nothing at all, really, but she did like playing hopscotch with the steward's son.

The King didn't care much for her. He was as nondescript as Primrose, but it didn't bring them closer together. Her mother had died giving birth to Primrose, so perhaps he didn't like to be reminded of that. The stepmother was very beautiful, and she had borne a son, which assured the succession. This half-brother, a spoiled brat in Primrose's estimation, liked nothing better than playing with wooden swords and wacking servants over the head with his weapon. They had to pretend they thought he was very cute, or they would hear about it from the Queen. 'Dear boy,' they'd say between gritted teeth, nursing the latest lump on their forehead.

Prince Michael tried wacking Primrose over the head once, but playing hopscotch regularly, she was very good at ducking and swerving. Then she wrested the wooden sword out of his hand and chased him with it all over the castle until he ran screaming into his mother's private boudoir. The stepmother would normally have had

Princess Primrose walloped for daring to lay a finger on her darling, but something strange was going on in the boudoir. She had a visitor, Count Horace, a handsome new arrival to the court, and somehow the expected punishment never eventuated. And little Prince Michael never tried anything with his half-sister again.

Despite having an unpleasant stepmother, Primrose was in no danger of becoming a Cinderella, because after all she was a princess. Besides, she was no good at housework, either. At banquets she sat at the royal table with her father, stepmother and half-brother. No one paid any attention to her, but a place was always laid out for her with a golden plate and she could eat as much as she liked and think what she wanted. She noticed how everyone stared at her stepmother. What must it be like to be so beautiful that you didn't have to do anything but sit there, and everyone thought you were wonderful? 'I could tell them,' she thought, 'that she puts henna through her hair, and that she wears rouge. It's not all natural.' She had discovered these facts because she sometimes looked in on her stepmother, out of curiosity. The Queen never noticed her. Once when another of the Queen's handsome male visitors questioned why Primrose was not ordered to leave, the Queen had just laughed, 'Oh, she's too stupid to do anything wrong.' Primrose did acknowledge that even without henna and rouge, her stepmother would still be stunningly beautiful. Nothing could detract from her brilliant eyes, her undulating grace, her captivating laugh. Oh well, the food was always good at banquets. No point envying anyone.

Primrose wondered how it would have been if her own mother had lived. Would her mother have been able to teach her to sew, to dress prettily, to talk charmingly to others? Then a handsome prince might have fallen in love with her and taken her away. Nothing was happening in that department either. Here she was, nearly sixteen, and no princes from other countries had asked for her hand. There was not even a cousin who thought she was a good bet. 'That's because I'm not'' she thought dolefully. The only thing she was good at was hopscotch. She had learned to play chess with the steward's son, but she was no good at that, either. Would she have been pretty and clever if her own mother had lived? Her old nurse had told her that when Primrose was born, her mother had whispered, 'She's perfectly beautiful,' before she died. Every night Primrose said goodnight to her real mother, pretending that she was alive. But in the morning she knew it wasn't true. And unfortunately she didn't have a fairy godmother, and there were no magic trees growing in the garden.

She knew her stepmother was not to be trusted. She knew terrible schemes were being planned in the privacy of the boudoir, because she heard snatches of talk coming from there. More and more men seemed to be meeting there. She tried to tell her father of her suspicions, but he wouldn't listen to her. 'Just because you're jealous, you mustn't make up such awful stories,' he reprimanded her. But one day the poor King found out about the stepmother's plans to take over the kingdom, and it was a day that would live in Primrose's memory forever. She had gone to skip the squares of the marble floor in the main hall, though she was really too old to play such games, when she came across her stepmother in the arms of Duke Carl, in the middle of the hall, of all places. She stopped dead in front of them, thinking, 'What's wrong with the boudoir for doing this? Why are you blocking my path?' when the duke noticed her. He released the Queen at once and, looking down at Primrose, said in a menacing voice: 'That girl, she'll talk!'

The Queen just laughed, 'Don't be silly, she's half-witted; besides, your men are outside.'

But Duke Carl ignored the Queen's remark, whipped out his sword and advanced towards the princess. Poor Primrose was taken completely by surprise, but she knew this was no game, that it was deadly serious. She ducked, swerved, dodged and ran. Hearing her screams, the old steward hurried into the hall, saw the duke with his sword in hand, chasing the princess, who was running for her life. The steward stood frozen at the door and yelped for help. This distraction halted the duke for a moment and gave Primrose the reprieve she needed. Soldiers entered the hall, but they were Duke Carl's men. One of them ran the steward down where he stood, before the palace guards could come to their rescue, but Primrose dodged all of them and ran for her father. Duke Carl died defending the Queen, the Queen died defending herself, the King died defending his kingdom. It was all very horrible, but the insurrection was quelled.

Life goes on. The next day an emergency meeting of nobles, statesmen and councillors was held. 'Who is to rule us?' they demanded in a panic. After much tactful deliberation, they agreed that Prince Michael was most probably not the King's son at all.

No point going into it, but they needed to be on the safe side. That left only Primrose. She was sitting in the garden when she saw the procession of men march towards her. They bowed and laid the sceptre of state at her feet.

She held her first parliament within the week, and her poise and common sense were praised extravagantly. Primrose felt rather sorry for Prince Michael, whether or not he was her half-brother. After all, his mother had died violently and the man he believed to be his father had also been killed; his whole world had collapsed around him. She patted him on the back and sent him, with a good settlement, to his mother's relatives in a distant kingdom. He certainly didn't look at all like the King, but then he did not look like Count Horace or Duke Carl or any of the handsome foreign visitors her stepmother had been conspiring with. In fact, he looked an awful lot like the head gardener, but Primrose was not going to pursue that train of thought. She sent him off with her kindest blessing, poor kid.

However, the government feared trouble from the banished prince. 'What if he should decide to use force of arms to claim what he thinks of as his inheritance?' they demanded. Primrose was about to giggle, 'Why would he want to control the gardens?' but she stopped herself, remembering decorum. 'He has been given a generous settlement,' she reminded them.

'But the relatives of the late Queen are a turbulent lot, and there are already rumours that they are planning vengeance,' they chorused. 'And you, your majesty, are but a young girl, untrained in arms.'

'That's true,' thought Primrose. 'I'm good at avoiding swords, but I don't think I could handle one.'

Finally the head statesman came forward. 'We believe that if your majesty would marry, the kingdom would be far safer.'

Yes, but whom to marry? Primrose thought about it, long and hard. Finally a solution came to her and she said, 'I will marry no foreign prince who may plot against us as my stepmother did. The only man I will accept is the son of the steward, who died like a hero in saving my life.' It was the least she could do to make up to her old playmate for losing his father.

So it was arranged. He was a nice young man, and they had always enjoyed playing hopscotch together when they were children. As they joined hands before the altar he gave her an appreciative smile, grateful for her generosity. They liked each other's company and he often let her win at chess. She knew he was letting her win, but she still enjoyed the triumph. They came to love each other dearly, and they lived happily ever afterwards.

Horror Vacui: Fear Of Empty Space
Graeme Hetherington

Judged dangerous to power lines,
The ancient eucalypt that spread
Protectively above my flat,

About to be enfolded, borne
Away with me on windy days,
Gloriously high, was cut down.

And as I took in emptiness,
Withstanding shock of it not there,
Panic at nothingness, the thought

That death invalidates all swept
Through me as when my wife was felled
By cancer to the stump of self,

Then that by fire to barest of
Irreducible minimums,
And I'm unable still to view

The void with equanimity,
Bow to it as a fact, since there
Is no eye to this frightening storm

Of feeling to stare down and quell,
No something to help make peace with
The enormity of a life

Extinguished just to disappear
Forever without trace, absence
The cruelest presence to endure,

Urn filled with ash, hand fine sawdust
The most mocking of substitutes
For loved one and tree once embraced.

In the blink of an Eye
Jake O'Mara

On a hot January day, a mounted escort and a small coach bumped slowly along the Bathurst road, headed for Sydney town. Everything, man, beast and plant, seemed to stagger under the weight of the burning orb above. No bird sounds were heard, and nothing moved in the baking bush. Even the trees seemed to be pleading for mercy as they waited, still and mute, for the cool of the evening.

Two horsemen were seen in the distance, and Mounted Constable Rem Wayborn, riding just behind the coach, squinted at them through the heat haze and the sweat and a horde of flies. He observed that the approaching men were faring no better than he was; they also looked listless and defeated. They seemed to be headed up into the foothills where it was likely to be even hotter. He glanced toward his companion officer, Mounted Constable Nathanael Pinnock, but the older officer appeared to be suffering even more in the desiccating conditions.

One of the approaching riders looked up briefly when they were about a hundred yards off but resumed his drooping posture seconds later. Their horses slowly closed the distance and drew opposite the coach team's leading pair. Suddenly they drew revolvers and shouted, 'Bail up!' at the coach-driver. The Constables were caught unawares and had no option but to raise their hands. The nearer bushranger dismounted and pulled open the coach door, but in his haste he had not disarmed the officers first. The older, vulpine-faced felon remained mounted. He aimed a pair of revolvers at the officers and snarled,

'Get out, all of you!'

As the passengers stepped down onto the dusty earth, the attention of the younger bandit was momentarily diverted by a pretty young woman. In that instant Constable Pinnock drew his revolver and fired. Someone cried out as the man was hit, but he went down on one knee, firing wildly as he fell onto his side. The other bandit fired at Pinnock and missed; a second later Wayborn fired at the mounted robber but disabled only his right arm. The pistol fell from the man's hand, but he returned fire with his left, then wheeled his mount and galloped toward the cover of nearby trees. Wayborn took aim and fired as he went, but neither horse nor rider faltered.

Constable Wayborn leapt from the horse and rushed to the distraught passengers, only then noticing that the young woman was slumped on the ground, bleeding profusely. Kneeling, he turned her onto her back. She looked straight at him accusingly, then stiffened slightly, and was still. As a ghastly pool of blood spread out from under her onto the road, his whole world seemed to stop, and a strange roaring sound filled his ears. Then, movement from the wounded and prostrate bushranger broke into his consciousness. The felon had reached into his shirt and grasped the butt of another pistol. As if in a dream, the constable turned and placed the muzzle of his revolver against the man's head.

In that awful moment, Rem Wayborn abandoned the God of his youth and fell headlong into an abyss. There was no sound but he felt the weapon buck in his hand. A flurry of dust was kicked up by the muzzle blast, and the man's body convulsed as the ball passed through his skull. Only then did Constable Wayborn hear the cries from the other passengers, but they were faint and distant, in another world. In less than a minute the whole world had changed, and all subsequent events happened in a strange half-darkness, as though all the rules of the physical world had been suspended.

Wayborn thought and felt nothing, save an overwhelming emptiness and disbelief. It was a dream, a void, silent and meaningless, in which time stood still. He had taken a life, and everything would change. He had lost a life, but the change so wrought was incomprehensible. He felt his very soul reaching out, pleading '…Come back, come back!' and wanted to cry out, to somehow change those awful, irreversible seconds. His wife, the very reason for his existence for the past four years, now lay lifeless and helpless, jolted roughly about on the floor of the coach, and it would be up to others to explain what had happened. Constable Wayborn could not speak. He opened his mouth, but no sound emanated from it. The coach, heavy laden with a soured cargo of Bathurst gold and monstrous grief, creaked slowly toward the new railway at Penrith.

Then there was the trial for the unlawful killing of the convict Elias Plant and eventually a verdict of justifiable homicide, plus the suggestion that Rem leave New South Wales. But the emptiness continued, following him like a bloodhound, as he sought somewhere far from the memories, the pain, and the pitying looks of others. He was aware of whispered conversations, of huddles and furtive looks occurring wherever he went. He knew what people were saying; sometimes he could almost hear their conversations, but it was difficult to know if he was dreaming. Reality and dreams began to merge, but the words were always damning. 'You might as well be dead, Remus Wayborn. There is nothing here for you.'

Maurie's Cartoon Challenge
Ant Dry and Allan Jamieson

Before he passed away, Maurie was President of FAWNW. At a meeting in 2014, he showed the members an image (below) and challenged them to suggest what led to the man's predicament.

In 2021, two of those members searched their archives for the stories that follow.

Bert
Ant Dry

Bert stood in the kitchen transfixed with indecision.

Garlic bread or herb bread? Which one? He held the garlic bread in his left hand and the herb in his right. He couldn't remember. He began to sweat.

He turned to his computer. He'd better check.

He called up his "date on line" account and clicked on "Angela". He scrolled through their recent conversation. Garlic or herb? Garlic or herb? Oh where was it?

With a flood of relief he found it. She liked garlic. Hallelujah. The herb bread went back into the freezer.

Just then a "ping" sounded. He rushed to his screen. It was her!

'Can't wait!' she had written.

'Me too!' he typed back. He looked at his watch. 4 o'clock on the dot. She'd be here at 6.30. So much to do. So little time.

Who had said that? Cecil Rhodes? Or was it Einstein? Whatever, who cared. Better get dinner on.

Love had come to Bert late in life. He had not been gifted with good looks, and his body bore more resemblance to a piece of knotted string than it did to anything else. He was bald except for a little tuff that sprouted from the top of his head like the leaves on a beetroot. He had worn glasses almost from birth.

He had always been passionately interested in girls, but had never had the courage to so much as speak to one. The girls at school had made fun of him to the point where he couldn't even look one in the eye. If one happened to speak to him, he would wriggle in a paroxysm of nervous embarrassment and the buzzing in his ears wouldn't allow him to hear anything that she was saying.

It hadn't been much better after school. He'd found a job at the car park, handing out the tickets as people drove in and collecting their cash as they drove out. Everyone, especially the women, would deal with him as if he did not exist. He may as well have been a machine, he thought. All of his workmates were men or boys, and be began to despair of ever finding himself a mate.

It was Charlie, one of his co-workers who had put him on to "Date-on-line". Charlie had boasted how the site had found him chick after chick who just wanted to be banged. Bert had gone purple with embarrassment at Charlie's descriptions of his conquests, but he had listened intently. He had agonised for weeks before venturing on to the site for himself.

He nearly hadn't completed his registration. One of the last requirements was that he had to put a picture of himself on the website. The thought of that turned his insides to water, and he had had to spend some time in the toilet before he could pluck up sufficient courage to continue. He eventually found a photo that his mother had taken of him. The light had been poor and his features blurred, so on the whole, he thought he looked okay.

Angela had been the first and only "hit" he had had, and they had both taken it very slowly. Her picture was a bit blurred too, and seemed to have been taken from a peculiar angle, but at least she had shown some interest.

That had been three months ago. Initially they had messaged each other daily and then twice a day. After a few weeks it was an hourly process. Bert's life began to revolve around his computer. He moved it from the lounge area in his bed-sit to right next to his bed, so that he could message her late into the night and could wake up to a message from her in the morning.

He would delay his departure for work until the very last moment, continually looking across at his computer screen to make sure he didn't miss a single message. He was listless at work, and left his post on the dot of the finishing time, rushing home to re-communicate with Angela.

He had taken to talking to her as he fussed around his bed-sit. He would tell her about his day and what his mom had said about her next door neighbour's dog the last time he had seen her, and various other fascinating topics. The computer just sat and listened, and then later he would type the same and tell her the same things all over again.

Bert had desperately wanted to progress the relationship to the next stage and actually meet her, but he was frightened that it may somehow all go wrong. Did she actually exist, or was she some cruel figment of his imagination?

Eventually, two nights ago, he had popped the question.

'Shall we meet?' he had typed.

The screen stayed silent for longer than it had in ages. He sat frozen in front of it until the pins and needles became too bad and he had to get up to allow the blood to properly circulate.

"Ping" went the machine as he straightened up from a stretch. He whirled around.

'OK' appeared on the screen. He felt weak with relief. He leaned over the computer and lightly kissed the top of the screen.

'Thank you.' He whispered, gently stroking the plastic cover.

They had arranged that she would come over to his place tonight at 6.30.

Bert bent over the stove. Tomato soup for starters, with garlic bread. KFC with coleslaw microwaved for mains, and then ice cream for dessert. A well designed menu with a touch of panache.

An extra touch of class was needed though. This was important. What to do? A table cloth. That would do it. He looked under his bed, found his spare sheet and threw it over the table under the window. The stain in the middle he covered with a pot of plastic flowers. He looked at it. Yes, it was most chic, but it needed just a little something else. Ah, yes, Candles, that would do it. He scratched around in his cupboard and found the packet of candles he had had to buy the last time they had had a power cut. They were yellow with age and a bit crooked, but they would still be romantic.

He found a saucer, and wiped off the remains of an old dinner and lit the candle, waiting for the grease to drip a bit on the little plate so that he could secure it in place. He placed the candle on the edge of the table.

Perfect.

Actually, it would look better if he allowed it to drip a little more, it would look more romantic.

He looked at his watch. Oh my god, it was six o'clock. He'd better have a shower.

He took off all his clothes, threw them under the bed and leapt into the shower.

He'd bought some shampoo. He usually just used soap, but tonight was a special occasion. He'd also bought some deodorant, but as he stood in the shower, he couldn't remember where he'd put it. Never mind, he'd find it. He soaped himself all over and rinsed off the suds. A quick shave? No need. He'd done that last week.

It took five minutes only and he had finished. He pushed his glasses back onto his face and threw back the door of the bathroom.

He stopped dead in his tracks, panic flooding through his veins. There were flames everywhere. What was going on? This was a nightmare.

It must have been about two seconds but it seemed to take an hour for him to realise what had happened. The candle had fallen over and had lit the table cloth. The curtains and the table itself were now ablaze.

True love makes heroes of the most timid of people.

Bert was galvanised into action. He must save Angela. He took one final horrified look at the blaze, turned, grabbed the computer and leaped out of the door, taking Angela to safety. He ran down the stairs and onto the lawn in front of the unit.

The flames grew and leapt into the ceiling, licking the outside walls at the same time. He watched as the unit slowly disappeared into itself. With a great sigh it collapsed, dust shooting into the sky along with the flames. In no time at all, all that remained of his unit was the charred stumps of the foundations.

Slowly realisation washed over him. He was standing naked in the middle of the lawn just off the street, holding his computer to his chest.

Carefully he placed Angela on the lawn, and sat down drawing his knees into his chest and wrapping his arms around his legs.

Now what?

===//===

I should have seen it coming
Allan Jamieson

The policeman looked down at the naked man squatting on the lawn.

'What happened to you?'

'I should have seen it coming, constable.'

'How so?'

'Well, years ago my wife started complaining; this grew and grew; eventually just about everything was wrong here. The trees, for instance: "Those gums – ugh!" she said. "Why can't we have a row of beautiful English elms? Symmetrical, elegant, seasonally alive. Not like your bloody gums that are anything but nice to look at – stubborn evergreens, yet they still drop leaves and bark – messy things. Chop them down!"'

'So, your wife's not from here?'

'That's correct, but in the early days all went well – until.'

'Until what?'

'Until, I guess, I retired.'

'What happened?'

'Well, I think she expected to have me at her beck and call all the time, but I'd always had a list of things I wanted to do – you know, when you work for others they dictate your time 24 hours a day, seven days a week most weeks. Now, I had the chance to do what I wanted to do!'

'And?'

'And she wanted me to do what she wanted instead. Dig the garden, cut down those trees, and so on. But I set up an office away from home and spent my days there. She wanted the house painted, a new kitchen and all sorts of other things.'

'Umm, seems to me your wife had a point.'

'Yeah, I guess so. As I said, I should have seen it coming.'

'And, as I said before, what happened to you?'

'I think it was my pet tarantula that did it. She'd never liked him. A couple of flies a month kept him happy and I quite liked having him around. I called him Geoff, after my brother, so I could converse with Geoff as if my brother was in the room – you know, man to man – but she'd never been comfortable with the spider.'

'It seems to me that your wife had a point there too. And?'

'I came home last night – no Geoff. I asked where he was. Silence. I should have known better but I asked again. "IT'S DEAD! You care more for that spider than you care for me. I never liked your Geoff, so there!" I thought it prudent to keep quiet after that and went to bed in silence. This morning when I was in the shower, the house caught alight and I just managed to escape – no time to find my clothes. I reached the lawn and waiting for me was my computer and a squashed Geoff. What beats me is how she cut down the gum trees. She must have had an accomplice.'

'From what I've been told, your wife used a chainsaw on those trees. Nobody helped her.'

'Well, like I said: I should have seen it coming.'

From Different Planets
Pete. Stratford

His parents went their separate ways while he was still at breast
Mum said they were from different worlds, both thought it for the best.
So he'd been raised a city boy, at private schools, a scholar,
then worked his way up through the ranks 'til earning a top dollar.
But as he read through the letter, as so many times he had
just pencil on rough paper; "why not come and meet your dad?"
Strange feelings rose within him, all mixed with trepidation
'til finally he found himself boarding at a railway station.
Off the train, he was left standing by a rusting wayside shed
his Armani suit dust covered, and filled with a sense of dread.
Then from an awkward stranger; 'G'day, they call me Jack'
who shook his hand near off his arm, as he slapped him on the back.
He thought he'd mumbled some reply, as dust clouded off his coat
but was unsure if words came out, or stuck there in his throat.
He stumbled dumbly behind Jack, his mind gripped in a fog
while Jack just tossed his suitcase on the ute, beside a dog.
Days dragged by so slowly then, for this old man and his minor
as the wall between the two of them stood like the one in China.
At college he'd been "top shot," shooting with the small bore
and held the Marksman Trophy, scoring ninety eight point four.
Jack took him out spotlighting, a part of the country rhythm
to cull some kangaroos, for the land was crawlin' with 'em
but on a range the targets don't move about or change
and though he kept on trying, it all seemed very strange.
Then, one night he drew a bead, was all ready to let fly
when a big 'roo looked back at him, just stared him eye to eye.
He couldn't pull the trigger; found he didn't have the heart
to kill this docile creature, which then fled into the dark.
He stole a glance at Jack, with spotlight held on its dust
and was sure he saw across his face a look much like disgust.
Days later, yarding cattle, all bush bred, mean and wild
as they tried to separate them Jack's language wasn't mild!
When a scrub bull breaking from the mob tried to leave the yard
its hooves flashed out and kicked Jack, and kicked him bloody hard.

Splints were strapped on broken bones while in dung and dust Jack
laid
so unlike the college rooms where he had learned First Aid.
Then beneath some meagre shade until Air Ambulance removal
he noticed Jack's face wearing a faint look of approval.
So while the gulf between them remained quite outback vast
both knew that if they stuck at it, they stood a chance at last.

Two Women
Jennie Herrera

An old woman stood beside the road, a squat figure in shabby black skirt and patched blouse and scuffed leather shoes with no laces. Around her, the straw-coloured grass rolled across the dry foothills and up to the snow-capped sierra. A stream, rushing milky-white in the Spring thaw, was busily carving a new bed in the wide grey gravel of the valley floor. A kite hung over the hills and she spread her fingers across her eyes to catch its flight against the morning sun. It soared, then hung suspended, grace without motion. She understood—the tiny creature waiting, frozen; the betraying shift among the grass stems, the swift rush of wings. Yes, this she understood.

As a little girl she'd watched too, many times. But then it had been the condor soaring on an updraft, his keen eyes in the bald head searching the tumbled country below. Country where a couple of small skin tepees huddled among the huge boulders. Country which was home. There the campfire spread its thin smoke fluttering away to the east. Their flocks of scabby sheep grazed the dry hills, moving through the prickly calafete bushes with their tart blue berries, leaving little shreds of grey-white hanging.

It was a long time since she had seen a condor—and she never would again. Only in memory.

That little girl came back to her clearly—the one who had stooped to follow on silent feet the snuffling track of an armadillo. (And there, near, was Lago Argentino with its blue-white icebergs—but her people had called it differently—and over it, over her, over everything the racing ragged cloud of a Patagonian sky.) Or the one who had come face to face with a newborn guanaco nestled, hidden safely from prying eyes, in a hollow of grass and scree with its ears flicking back and forward in fear and mingled curiosity. And, for a suspended moment, the two little creatures gazed at each other with soft dark eyes—alive to each faint rustle, the sough of the wind, the moving cloud shadows ...

But most of the guanaco were gone now. She didn't ask why—or how—or when.

She had gone away from that childhood home with a young Italian store-keeper, an ambitious young man who planned to do more with his life than sell low-quality bombachas and boots and scarves to hard-drinking hard-riding gauchos. And who had no intention of remaining womanless while his plans and hopes for his future grew and matured. He had brought her north with him when he moved to a better position. And then—her usefulness to him outlived—he had abandoned her with her baby son, without apparent regret, on that estancia north of Esquel and set out unencumbered for the capital.

That was forty years ago. Her son, touched with a little of his father's ambition, had started a small business in Buenos Aires. And now she'd left the estancia cookhouse for the last time to go and live out her old age with him; left the dingy room where she'd helped to prepare numberless mutton asados, tonnes of rice and potatoes, thousands of loaves of coarse bread. Left without regret.

And in those forty years her people had vanished like summer snow off the pampas and into the pages of Argentine history.

The bus was coming now. She could see the dust as it snaked its way across the flanks of the foothills. A small dark speck which would take another twenty minutes to travel the wide clear landscape to where she stood, waiting stolidly and feeling no particular emotion as one part of her life ended and another part prepared to begin. She got down in El Bolson where the bus stopped for lunch and watched the other passengers file into a small restaurant. But she made no move to follow them. For only twice in those forty years had she ventured out—to bury her infant daughter and have her son baptised—and she wasn't certain of the way the world worked (or why water on her son's head would bring him prosperity); nor did she know what the crisp roll of peso notes in her pocket might buy.

So she stood near the bus, seeing the mountain peaks where the dry grass gave way to dusty bamboo and stunted pine and then to snow, and the wind still funnelled cold in the mountain valley.

It was late when the bus reached Bariloche where comfortable hotels looked out over Lago Nahuel Huapi, brooding in the evening light for those who had venerated its restless water, and her son waited patiently for her arrival. His dark eyes scanned each alighting passenger and showed a mixture of relief as she stepped down and a kind of shame that this squat heavy-featured old woman should be the one he waited for.

***

The people in the square jostled and pushed against one another, crowded together as they were under the watchful eyes of the police. Then they grew still as a beautiful woman stepped out on to the lavishly-decorated balcony. She was dressed delicately in gold and white with shining rolls of blonde hair under a tiny white hat with its demure fall of lace.

(The people of Spain had cheered her, wild and tumultuous in their welcome.)

'Who is she?' The old woman watched but betrayed no curiosity in her gaze.

'Evita—of course.'

The man beside her spoke impatiently, his voice low. And even as he spoke the crowd began an ecstatic cry of 'Perón! Evita! Perón! Evita!' as a tall man, floridly good-looking, joined the lady on the balcony.

'Who is Evita? And who is he?'

'Be quiet, Mama!' His voice had acquired an edge.

'Don't you think she's pretty?'

The couple on the balcony were waving now, their smiles fixed, their eyes calculating as they ranged the motley crowd below; calculating the numbers, divining the mood and the response.

A kindly-faced woman dressed in black turned, listening interestedly to the low exchange between mother and son, and said mildly, 'Eva would understand. She is an angel.'

(But the crowds in Naples had cried angrily 'Give us bread!')

'No. She wouldn't.' The man's eyes echoed the snap in his voice, the growing fear in his heart.

Others pressed in against them were listening now, a nervous irritable listening. Why didn't the old Indian woman go away before she got them all into trouble with her stupid ignorant questions? The police shifted and moved, hemming in the ragged edges of the crowd. And the waves of unease grew (for who should dare to ask those questions) and became hostility; grew and threatened to engulf the old woman in the folds of anxious hysteria.

She looked around, puzzled, watching their faces and she spoke softly in Tehuelche like the dry rustle of autumn leaves. But the unknown words might've been the sigh of the wind across uninhabited plains.

President Perón was clearing his throat, beginning his speech, and the people crowding her in turned away with avid ears and tremulous trust in his promise, loud across the Plaza... The promise of a new Argentina. For if the old is trampled down … obsolete …

And perhaps she'd said, 'Why do you bother to hate me? The future is yours.' But if she'd known why (and how and when) the condor is rarely seen and the guanaco herds grow sparse might she have added 'Treat it well'?

(The crowds heard the boom and crackle, they heard …)

Granny Gertie's Grave
Pete Stratford

While researching an old mining town
from back in the eighteen thirties
a name that came up frequently
was that of "Granny Gertie's"
so I delved a little deeper
and learned that in that town
a pioneer lass named "Gertrude"
became a woman of renown.
She had sailed out from England
to escape its winter's cold
and join those hardy miners
seeking fortunes finding gold.
She'd had to grow up quickly
for being young and quite naive
had not gathered many life skills
before of home she'd taken leave.
She had questioned an old miner
who to her looked old and wise
but failed to notice when he spoke
there was a twinkle in his eyes.
He said she'd be the only one
he'd told the secret of his life
and she must never tell another
even when she became a wife.
'Every morning, on your breakfast
take care you never miss a day
sprinkle it with gunpowder
and you'll never grow old and grey.'
She took this sage advice to heart
doing just as she'd been told
then lived a long hard working life
until she grew very old.

When she passed away at last
her children numbered near a score
while grandchildren even doubled that

and great grandkids even more.
She'd had so many birthdays
some say over ninety eight
when she finally received that call
to enter in through Heaven's Gate.
She'd always claimed it was the secret
which she'd kept hidden all her days
had kept her body fit and active
and stopped her hair from going grey.
When I enquired where her grave was
where they'd laid the mortal bones
of that famous pioneering woman
revered as "Granny Gertie" Jones
I was told there was no headstone
but where she'd been taken to cremate her
I'd find her name upon a bronze plaque
beside a forty two foot crater!

Tyenna River transportations
Adam Stokell

Young December:
tea-trees blow the willowed banks.
Countless blooms exhale as one
galactic spell. It's almost evening.
Old young sunlight slips between
the willow-walls. Tannins stroked,
honeyed water keeps a log.

Lost watching constellations fledge
this corridor, sssvit,
I'm swallow-pinged. Blooms detach,
become a swarm of whitewings
whorled above the river's tick.

Cloud of cloudlets, global plume
out of which the single insects –
some strange roster – feather down
and sip, scratch some itch
of river-rash, sip.

Most lift again, regain the swarm,
whorl till night rewinds them:
blooms asleep on peeling branches,
white abiding.
   Unless …

This old new world still reeks
of transportation. Of willow-words.
Of trout shipped round the world
in freeze-framed streams, local manna lapsed
on stained-glass ceilings.

Trout that mime Tyenna stones;
trout that crouch as paddle-tailed
duck-billed planks of wood drift by;
trout that pounce
when whitewings land in reach.

Dreamcatcher
Ellie Goss

Walking the length of tables and displays was the perfect way to spend a Saturday, Macey thought to herself, while taking in the smells and bustle of the scene surrounding her. It was comforting to hear the friendly banter between stall holders. It made her heart feel a little lighter knowing that the market's popularity was growing on the back of ideas for health and well-being that were as much about the past as they were the present.

'Hey Madge!' Macey said, smiling at the fifty-something year old woman, with her well-rounded figure bustling about her stall.

'Ah, sugar pot, it's so good to see you. You have been away a few weeks I think, yes?' Her friendly approach was one of the things Macey found so endearing, the two hugged a tight squeeze of hello.

'Yes, working overtime I'm afraid. Just like everyone else, hospital staff get sick too. I've been covering some colleagues who have come down with the flu. But they all seem to be back on the mend now. Unlike my cupboards which are getting bare. If I wait any longer, I will be eating peanut butter for breakfast as well as for dinner,' she laughed only half joking.

'You're a good girl Mace. Wait a tick, I have something here I set aside for you. I can't tell you how long I've had it or even where it came from but as soon as I spotted it, I knew it was for you.' Madge left her post guarding the table, where people entered her nook of bric-a-brac, treasures just waiting to be discovered. Madge had been a marketer for several years, and now was even more content with her new spot under cover. It had become a nightmare for the woman, trying to unpack and pack each week. So, when a slot in the market building had become available, she had jumped at it, making the stall uniquely her own.

Re-emerging from a chest that was overflowing with brass trinkets, embossed metals from around the globe and sparkling objects like window charms she triumphantly exclaimed, 'here it is.' She held the object out for Macey to investigate.

'Oh my, Marge. It's beautiful, it really is!' Macey was enchanted by the intricately adorned piece. With obviously hand crocheted lace at its centre, ribbons, lace and semi-precious gems adorning it; they hung like heavy dewdrops found on an Autumn's morning. It was the most beautiful dreamcatcher she had ever seen. It had an element of antiquity to it as the hook was a gorgeous fitting of worked silver, while the beading that held the iridescent gems added to its glamour.

'Oh, I knew you'd like it,' Marge exclaimed, pleased with herself.

'Like, I love it. Could you wrap it for me while I have a little look around?'

'Of course, my dear. You help yourself now.'

After about an hour Macey was ready to leave the market and return home. She gave Marge a quick hug and a kiss on her cheek before leaving with the day's treasures, which had included not only the fruit and veg from the other stall holders but, four tea cups with floral designs and a lampshade that was made of glass beads and brass clasps.

Walking through the front door of her one-bedroom cottage, Macey made for the kitchen where she dropped her Saturday market buys on the wide wooden counter. Home sweet home, she thought to herself. From the corner of her eye, she noticed the answering machine flashing, so she resolved to make a cup of chai, and while washing her fruit & veg, listen to her messages.

'Hi darling, mumsy here. Just calling to let you know that we will be away for a little longer than we had first expected, with several other show bookings springing up. I'm sure you understand, but we won't make it back in time for your birthday sweetheart. We promise we'll celebrate when we return, ok hon. Anyway, we love you! Got to go, bye.' Macey's eyes rolled, her parents the stage actors, gypsy feet and carefree ways and absolutely nothing like her. But she loved them all the more for it. As footloose, creative and upbeat as they were, she was a both-feet-on-the-ground-type, stable and secure; that's why she had chosen nursing. Secure and wise choice she had been told on more than one occasion. A job she loved more than anything.

Picking up the last of her hand sewn shopping bags she moved off towards her bedroom. As she reached the room, she looked about for the perfect spot for the contents of the paper wrapping. She considered placing the dreamcatcher above her upholstered bed but thought better of it when considering that it would require a long-term commitment of a picture hook. So instead, she tied a ribbon to the intricate silver hook and looped it over the centre of the curtain rail. The heavy drapes currently hung to the sides of the large sliding doors that separated her room from the cottage garden and patio that led from it, the envy of her best friend Kate. Of a night during her days off, she loved leaving the drapes open to let the moonlight shine in and the twinkle of the stars, sooth her into a restful sleep.

After a quiet night in, that included her fav flash meal, chicken noodles, a dish she had picked up while on holiday in Bali several years ago, a yoga session because she felt guilty for having missed several classes recently and a movie it was time for bed.

She stood dazzled by the light captured and played upon the ceiling and walls by the gems that hung from the dreamcatcher. The moon was full and added to the enchanting scene, with its own white glow showing through the still open drapes. It looked like something out of a fairy tale book she decided. She walked over and closed the slightly ajar door and went for a hot shower before climbing into her pre-warmed bed; the blessing of an electric blanket was never undervalued in her home.

***

Macey felt a little stiff and sore as she lifted her body, feeling heavy and sluggish as she made the attempt. The first thing to strike her as odd was not just the burdensomeness of her own body but the constricting coverings. Normally she slept with a medium weighted doona, with a coverlet at the end of the bed, for use later should the night call for it. But for some reason she felt pinned down. She rolled over to see if she was tangled in her bedding only to discover that she wasn't in her own bed with her own coverings. Instead, a mass of mis-matched blankets covered her, knitted and patchworked. While the mattress she was laying on was hard, at a guess made of wooden slats, adding further to the dilemma was the discovery that she was not actually in a room of any sort that she could recall. As she investigated further, she was shocked to find she was in fact in a wagon of sorts. It was fitted with what appeared to be a kitchen, complete with a stove and cooking utensils hung along a wall, as well there was a fold away table. It was the discovery of a pair of leather boots at the canvas flap, which acted as a door that she felt a sense of panic begin to surface. I'm dreaming, she thought. There was no other explanation, and then she spotted something that drew her curiosity. There dangling at a corner to the opening of the wagon was a dreamcatcher, not any dreamcatcher but hers.

Breaking her from the spellbinding shock was the familiar smell of tea and something cooking that made her stomach growl. With bare feet she paddled across the rug strewn floorboards to pull back the canvas drape, all the while with an eye on the dreamcatcher.

'Morning buttercup,' came the friendly greeting from only metres away where a small campfire was lit and warming pots sitting on the rocks surrounding it. 'You might want to grab a jacket off the hook beside you, it's a might chilly out here and slip those boots on I left for you, don't want to be stepping on anything nasty. After breakfast I'll be taking you to see your patient.'

'How is it that you have my dreamcatcher?' she asked, while thinking that of all the things to ask that was probably the one that should be delegated to the bottom of the list.

'You what?'

Lost for a response, she gently plucked the ornate object from its hook and held it at arms-length towards the man cooking breakfast.

'Oh, that, well it came with the wagon actually,' he replied unfussed, turning away again to stir a pot to ensure the contents didn't burn to the bottom.

After breakfast Macey was sent back to the wagon to dress and then directed to a young boy who had broken his wrist. She worked all morning trying to help the boy, firstly to bandage the bones in a way to help them set where they should and then to keep him from becoming feverish. Exhausted from the work she ate lunch with the boy's mother before being sought out to help others in the camp with their ailments. That night she returned to the wagon and tried to explain to her earlier breakfast companion, that this was all really above and beyond her level of authorisation. But that night she slept soundly only to wake in her own bed the next morning.

***

'Gee, you look a bit wrecked Macey. You, ok?'

Nothing like a friend pointing out how crap you looked thought Macey.

'I'm fine Kate, just having some weird dreams. They're, well ...' she stopped while trying to think of the right words. 'Well, they feel real. More real than any dream I've ever had before and then I wake up feeling like I haven't slept.'

'Yeah, well you're right. That does sound weird. You haven't been hitting the wine bottle or anything?' Kate asked, already knowing the answer. The reply she received was simply a look, one that spoke volumes of what Macey thought of that question. Not in their line of work.

***

It was around the third month that Macey stumbled upon the beginnings of an answer.

Unable to sleep Macey stood leaning against the open sliding door of her bedroom and looked out on the still warm night. The previous two nights had been very busy, she mused. Having travelled continents, to find herself in the home of a young girl of about six, to whom she was apparently brought in to aid in her recovery from pneumonia. What in her own time was considered quite manageable, in the late 19th century was all too often fatal. The girl had been frightfully ill but after two days and nights the worst had passed. As Macey went over it, thinking about the treatment, the things that could be done better in the manner of a self-appraisal, something bright made her eyes flinch, an automatic reaction. Turning, she watched as the moonlight touched the gems hanging from the dreamcatcher. As she watched, it looked as though the gems were capturing the moonlight, before an illuminating and intricate web formed. Then a moment later she was standing in a foreign room with vaulted ceilings held up by plinths, and scatter cushions made of rich materials casually strewn all about.

Across the room, hanging in the open breeze with the moonlight streaming in was a matching dreamcatcher to her own, but before she could contemplate this further, she heard whispers coming from a corner of the room not far from where she stood.

Within moments there were several scantily clad girls surrounding her as she leant down to discover what was causing the mournful sobs that had erupted from one of the girls. Unable to understand them, nor them her, didn't prevent Macey from assessing the situation. The girl had obviously been beaten and was covered with bruising; the swelling had already closed one of her eyes. Taking action, she went to a large open bowl, she could smell the perfume in the water but decided it would be better than nothing. Grabbing a nearby cushion she soaked it and returned to the girl, placing the cushion to help reduce the swelling. On seeing this one of the girls grew aggressive and attempted to remove the cushion and within moments the situation began to deteriorate as sides were taken. One of the girls pushed Macey out of the way, while another produced a poultice for the abrasions. Macey could smell clove and rosemary as they were strong components of whatever was in the mixture. As things began to calm, Macey once again felt drawn to the dreamcatcher and within the blink of an eye was transported back to her standing place by the open door. She had suspicions about why it was that this occurred for five days, she knew or guessed why it was every month, she was sure it was triggered by the full moon waning and the new moon ascending but she didn't know why.

It was not until three months later that she discovered the answer. She had decided that night at the moonlit door that it would be best if she were to arrange her roster around the dreamcatcher moon time travel, although she had decided not to explain why or even to talk of the strange happenings any further to anyone. In fact, she had become so well organised that she had developed a quilted body sling that was comfortable enough to sleep in while it held basic items she might need, but now most times she waited by the door seated in a comfy chair.

She had gently fallen asleep, exhausted, and excited about what the night might bring. Sometimes she woke in unfamiliar places, sometimes she was transported awake and alert, often those she first met, seemed to know her, while yet on other sojourns she remained nameless. Like the time she had found herself in wartime. The full five days had seen her work in conditions that broke her heart, bringing what little comfort she could while working under doctors who were under-staffed with little or no medical supplies. She had traversed the ground of so many emotions and yet she never felt more alive than she had during the past six months.

When she awoke, it was within a grand building with paintings hung on the walls, ornate and filigreed timber castings, with drapes almost two storeys in length. She twirled taking in the grand scene, like a picture in a magazine and then she realised she must be in Italy. Screams broke through her reverie, she knew those screams, she had served her initial internship in the maternity wards and if she wasn't mistaken someone would soon be ready to deliver a new life into the world.

Without any trouble she found her way to the woman in labor. For hours they struggled together, one in the pains of labor the other soothing and preparing the way. Macey had quickly discovered that the baby was in the wrong position and had coaxed it, first by instructing the mother to allow the belly to pendulum and then manually, preventing a potentially fatal delivery. It was in the early hours of the morning, as the sun awoke to stream through the giant windows, that the baby was born. A healthy baby girl, who was quickly fussed over and wrapped in swaddling by the other woman in the room.

As both mother and nurse slept a man stole into the room, but the movement caused Macey to wake. The man brought a finger to his lips to indicate quiet and so Macey watched as he hung an ornate dreamcatcher over the bed, only to have the light captured by it and sent dancing across the bed and spilling a shimmering rainbow coloured kaleidoscope into the room.

The scene in its entirety was beautiful Macey thought, but she soon felt like an intruder to this private moment and so she crept from the room finding herself in a large hallway. She walked just a short distance before being joined by an elderly looking woman who pushed a letter into her hand.

It had taken several weeks for Macey to decipher the contents of the letter and even then, she decided to send it away for translation. She discovered that the dreamcatcher, while a gift, had not been directly from the husband whom she had met during his intimate encounter in the birthing suite, but rather the woman in the hallway. She had made the dreamcatcher by hand for her daughter. As she did, she wove old spells and enchantments into the fabric, ones that she had learnt as a child, carefully selecting gems known for their special qualities; of safe passage, of wellbeing and adding them into the gift. As she had great fears for her only daughter's safety during childbirth, convinced that their luck must soon be at its end, as they mother and daughter had come from such humble beginnings before the marriage and their elevation to such a grand station.

Macey had read the translation several times and was still in awe All she could assume was that the spells and chants written into the dreamcatcher were powerful although they may have needed a bit of tweaking but they had certainly worked their magic, transporting her through time and place, even if for just a fleeting time.

A small noise caused her to turn from the moonlit night where she stood pondering the year past. Nestled in the warmth of the cradle was a four-month-old baby, just readying herself to wake for a night feed. Macey smiled wondering about the magical tale that she would have to spin, of a father, in a place beyond the reach of space and time. Closing the door, she went to the infant collecting her into her arms, but then again that was a problem still moons away.

The End

Madonna Lily
Brenda Slavoff

Your name is a vision of quiet cloisters,
Pale hands stilled, white banded heads bowed
  Candles reaching upwards,
  Verses rising in soprano hymns.
Light is penetrating narrow archways
And incense wavering in benediction
As soft voices recite prayers in unison:
  White paged books are open,
  White fingers lead the way for eyes,
Concentration hovers as a dove in landing,
Still airborne, peacefully held aloft,
  Beyond earth, within reach
  Of hope and faith, encompassing love,
Wings opened in charity to the world.
  Madonna Lily's petals stretch upwards and out
      In ecstatic abandonment.

Plague Proportions
Jennie Herrera

I remember when someone mentioned the accusations against Colleen McCullough in our writers' group someone else said, 'But how could you prove you hadn't pinched someone else's work?' and I replied, 'Surely you are innocent until proven guilty in this as in other things? It shouldn't be up to you to prove your innocence.'

Yet while you are waiting for the verdict, or even if you are never formally accused, that precious thing, your literary reputation, may be tarnished.

Plagiarism in non-fiction is often easier to prove—'Where, sir, did you get your facts?'—than in fiction with its less tangible stock-in-trade of ideas, characters, storylines, style and wit. Charles Darwin and Alfred Wallace came independently to their theories on evolution and with mutual respect and courtesy agreed to publish simultaneously. But they were rare men—and I wonder if that would happen in today's dog-eat-dog world of academic publishing.

Agatha Christie and A. J. Cronin both named a novel *A Pocketful of Rye*, a Hobart historian and an English explorer both chose *A Question of Survival*; Sally Morgan used *My Place* for her autobiography while Nadia Wheatley chose it for a children's story. So it is fortunate that titles cannot be copyrighted or there would be even more literary back-biting. It becomes less clear with the names of characters. H. Rider Haggard created She-Who-Must-Be-Obeyed—L. M. Montgomery dropped her in casually as a nickname for her landlady in *Kilmeny of the Orchard*—John Mortimer took her to comic heights in his Rumpole series. But did She-Who-Must-Be-Obeyed still belong to Haggard or might she be said to have entered the public domain, like Dracula or Scrooge, before her copyright expired?

Montgomery was accused of pinching Mazo de la Roche's domineering grandmother for her book *Magic for Marigold* to which she responded tartly, would no one be permitted to portray a domineering grandmother in the next hundred years of Canadian letters. But she was on shakier ground when she used the device of a brooch lost because its pin has caught in a shawl. Though she ended the incident happily in *Anne of Green Gables* and Elizabeth Gaskell ended it sadly in *A Manchester Marriage* it was the same literary device and Montgomery was almost certainly familiar with Gaskell's writing.

To make the charge of plagiarism stick this is the first essential: that a writer could and did have access to the work in question.   But the second essential—that she consciously and deliberately copied—is fraught with difficulties.   Lawyers may walk round with neatly pigeon-holed minds (and dreams of expensive litigation) but I suspect most writers have rag-bags for minds into which have been tossed snippets, patches, unused remnants from a lifetime of avid reading, listening, eavesdropping, dreaming, watching, wondering …

Of course McCullough's *The Ladies of Missalonghi* does share a number of similarities with Montgomery's *The Blue Castle*. It would be surprising if it didn't—given the very similar lives middle-class Church of England spinsters lived round the turn of the century in small Dominion towns, sharing fashions, moral attitudes, aspirations, daily routines. Unfortunately, though, McCullough also uses a similar plot device, if more clumsily, and it was this which had her publishers worried for a while. Yet I suspect the furore had as much to do with the fact that McCullough has made millions from her writing—and Montgomery still has many loyal fans more than fifty years after her death. When two unknown American writers, using the pseudonym "Pauline Dunn", pinched much of Dean R. Koontz's horror novel *Phantoms* it went unnoticed for more than a year and caused little stir.

The German playwright, Bertolt Brecht, claimed without reticence that he needed someone else's characters to get his own inspiration flowing but I think most fiction writers would rather face hungry lions than admit they are not bursting with unique and memorable ideas.

Biographers often talk kindly of their subjects as having a derivative phase but when does derivation, imitation, admiration, idealisation become plagiarism? T. S. Eliot had his own succinct definition: 'Immature poets imitate, mature poets steal.'

Those who pioneer a new style, a new genre, a new fashion, tend to be hardest hit by the copyists. Georgette Heyer took an author to court for blatant copying of her work. Yet she had made the Regency Romance so remarkably her own that the writers who tried to enter her field were invariably compared with her and almost invariably had to suffer having "in the style of Georgette

Heyer", "a worthy successor to Heyer", "another romance in the Heyer tradition" on their publishers' blurbs. Is it any wonder some of them felt they might as well borrow if they were not to be allowed their own identity and their own fame?

It has been said, 'Borrowing from one writer is plagiarism, borrowing from many is research.' But surely the key word is borrowing. How do you return what you have "borrowed"? Through fulsome expressions of gratitude in your introduction? If plagiarism is borrowing rather than taking then it seems to undermine the protection writers are seeking for the uniqueness of their work.

Yet I think we all plagiarise; a turn of phrase here, a style of dialogue there, a favourite relationship, a setting, a period—and often unwittingly. I had the strange experience of writing a novel and several months later reading Elizabeth Jolley's *Palomino* in which she'd used almost identical names for her heroines. I felt vaguely that my manuscript had become "second-hand" and feverish accusations of plagiarism, should I find a publisher, rushed through my mind. Yet my choices were based on those little things that inspire—a wedding notice, a snippet of news in a friend's letter—and voila, there were my elusive "right" names for my heroines.

It is sometimes said that autobiographical novels provide many writers with their breakthrough. Simply because—your life is uniquely yours. But, thinking back, I remember the children who shared my background and grew up on nearby farms, who attended the same school and the same local functions, who heard the same gossip and looked out on the same landscape. And might they too be tapping away trying to distil that essence of childhood into their big breakthrough?

AUTHOR BIOGRAPHIES

GRAEME BOURKE

In 1985 Graeme took up fly fishing in Tasmania and during this journey he kept a diary which was used to produce his first non-fiction book *Come Fly Fish With Me*, which has now been put up as an ebook. This book received wide acclaim from the fly fishing fraternity. He then completed a correspondence course on writing and began writing articles for sporting and travel magazines. In 2008 he published his second book on fishing *If Only The World Would Go Fishing*.

His main ambition was to write fiction, so in 2010 he published *Hawkins' Grove* which has also been converted to an ebook. These three books are available in hard copy from "Window on the World" bookshop in Ulverstone, Tasmania. *Mountain Pride, The Ghost Ship, The Gates of Hell* and *The House of Dreams* are available only as ebooks.

In June of 2014 Graeme uploaded the first book in his trilogy *The Orphan and the Shadow Walker: The Awakening.* The feedback has been very positive. Sales from the second and third book have been encouraging. *An Ancient Warrior* is his most recent fiction novel.

Graeme writes book reviews for a local newsletter and from these he has compiled the best of these reviews; if you are looking for a book to read he guarantees you will find something here. He has just published a new book called *A Fortunate Destiny*, a love story set in the early seventies. *Tears in Thailand* has now been published as well; this is a true story telling of Graeme's journey in Thailand, his experiences and emotions as he finds happiness in the land of smiles.

ANT DRY

ANT DRY moved from Zimbabwe to Tasmania in 2007. He has lived in the Burnie area since then with his wife, Yvonne. Their four children live on the mainland. He sees himself as the most contented person on the planet, after all, who could ask for more from life than living in Tasmania and having the world's most wonderful family?

ELISHA GOSS

Ellie A, lives and works nestled between the Tarkine Forest and Cradle Mt National Park. Her debut, 2016 children's folklore story, *The Bunyip's Bath* was followed by *Mermaid Spell* in 2020. Ellie has a growing number of contributions in various publications, including; indie books, ezines, magazines and anthologies across genres, including publishers Enchanted Conversations, Scary Snippets- Family & Siblings Editions, Stinkwaves 2019, 518 Publishing - A Guide to Useless Sidekicks and upcoming 42 Short Stories Anthology.

Join others in following her here:
https://facebook.com/EllieAGoss
https://eligoss76.wixsite.com/elishagoss

JENNIE HERRERA

Jennie Herrera was born in Toowoomba but has lived in Hobart for 36 years. She is President of FAW TAS and some of her novels, short stories, and poems can be read at https://jlherrera.com Her work has also appeared in a number of anthologies.

She works on issues such as West Papua and the Sue Neill-Fraser case and loves reading.

GRAEME HETHERINGTON

Born in Tasmania's Latrobe in 1937, my first thirteen years were spent on the island's West Coast where I attended the Rosebery and Zeehan state schools before going to boarding school in Launceston for five years and then on to the University of Tasmania. As a teacher in the Classics Department there for over a quarter of a century I fell in love with European culture and have lived much of my life in that part of the world trying to flesh out what I taught which was nowhere to be found in Australia.

In 2013, I returned to Tasmania in the interests of regaining what after all are roots deeper than even my European ones.

[Image courtesy of Australian Book Review]

My story of restlessness arising to a large extent out of a search for my "true home", with its attendant sense of dislocation and disorientation is to be found in my nine books of poetry: *Remote Corners* (Twelvetrees Press); *In The Shadow Of Van Diemen's Land* (Cornford Press); *Life Given* (Ginninderra Press); *A Tasmanian Paradise Lost* (Walleah Press); *A Post-Colonial Boy* (Fullers Publishing); *At Large* (Ginninderra Press); *An Inherited Epic Of Gilgamesh* (Ginninderra Press); *Another Love, Another Life* (Ginninderra Press); and *The Divided Self: A Tasmanian Odyssey* (Ginninderra Press), the latter due out early in 2022.

An unfinished epic poem awaits my attention if I can summon up the necessary in my 84th year.

ALLAN JAMIESON

Allan Jamieson retired in 1999 after a long working life as a chemical engineer in the pulp and paper industry, living on four continents and visiting 21 countries for business purposes. He has resided in Burnie since 1981. Currently Allan is President and Secretary of FAWNW.

He began writing books in the early 2000's. So far, he has published nine books. The titles for which copies remain for purchase are:

. *Surviving is Dead Easy* (a novel about 'the island' in 2150)
. *Voyage through the "Big Empty"* (his experience as a passenger on a container ship from Melbourne to Philadelphia)
. *Meandering Mind* (a collection of short stories)
. *Honto Henro* (his 88 Temple Buddhist Pilgrimage in Japan)
. *Service Above Self* (75-year History of Burnie Rotary Club 1942—2017)
. *Enthusiastic Amateurs* (a cautionary tale for golf and sporting clubs)
. *No Return* (a novella of Rachel Newton's life 1803-1855)

For more information, see
<https://fawwritersnorthwesttasmania.blogspot.com/>
For copies of Allan's books, email Allan at jamtin79@gmail.com

ANNE LAYTON-BENNETT

Anne is a published writer both in Australia and overseas in both print and online publications. For several years she juggled writing commitments with a part-time job in a school library, and running a commercial flower growing business with her partner. She now writes regularly for specialist magazine *The Veterinarian*, and occasionally writes features for www.tasmaniantimes.com, an online journal.

Anne co-edited: *An Inspired Pursuit*: 40 years of writing by women in northern Tasmania, (Karuda Press) 2002, and has essays included in *An Inspired Pursuit*: Volume 2, (Tatlers) 2012; *Breaking the boundaries*: Australian activists tell their stories (Wakefield Press) 2016, and *The Fabric of Launceston* (Launceston Historical Society) 2016.

Challenged several years ago to try her hand at writing poetry, Anne also has a growing portfolio of poems – some of which have been published. She still writes letters.

MEG McLAREN

Meg was born on the island of Trinidad, in the West Indies. She had a happy and colourful childhood and her writing is influenced by these experiences. Over the years she has travelled extensively and has come into contact with many different lifestyles. She is now retired and lives in Tasmania where she is able to pursue her love of writing.

DAWN MEREDITH

Born in a small town beside the English Channel, Dawn later lived in the hot suburb of Perth, Western Australia and still later on an island in Norway in a pre-WWII house with a toilet in the barn. She now lives on a 100 acre farm in Northwest Tasmania with her family and a collection of animals. Before committing to writing fulltime, Dawn was a teacher for many years, trained in Art, English and Special Education. Dealing with quirky kids has definitely influenced her work.

To date, Dawn has authored 11 books, in fiction & non-fiction and written pieces for curriculum based publishers such as Hodder Headline, Rigby Heinemann and Blake Education. Her most successful book to date is *12 Annoying Monsters* - Self Talk for Kids with Anxiety, reaching children all over the world. Dawn has produced a wide variety of work, including the five year project with WWII veteran Jim Haynes to produce his memoir *The Boy Who Went to War*.

In 2016 Dawn won the 2016 SCBWI Andrea Davis Pinkney Writer Award for her then incomplete manuscript *Letters From the Dead* which was published in 2017. In 2020 her young adult fantasy novel *Rebel* was published by Shooting Star Press. It is book one of her FLIGHT trilogy.

In 2021 her young adult Urban Science Fiction novel *Elkwood* will be released. Currently she is working on book 2 in the FLIGHT trilogy, *Runaway*.
WEBSITE: dawnmeredith.com.au
BLOG: dawnmeredithauthor.blogspot.com

JAKE O'MARA

Jake grew up on a farm in regional South Australia. He tried several occupations in widely separated parts of Australia before graduating as a registered nurse in 1987. He later completed a Graduate Diploma in Tropical Medicine at James Cook University, Townsville and worked in Indigenous communities in many remote areas. These included the Torres Straits and Cape York, the Gibson Desert, the Kimberley and Arctic Canada. Since then he has worked in both inpatient and community mental health in Queensland and Tasmania.

LESLEY PODMORE

For Lesley, writing has always been a latent talent, waiting to be noticed. Since moving to Stanley fifteen years ago, inspiration has taken over, and she now writes poetry and children's stories. Her childhood was spent in a small town on the north-west coast of Tasmania, surrounded by a very arty family, with many organic fruit and veggies growing in the back yard. Her father had a natural talent for writing poetry, her mother taught both piano and art, her aunt drew exquisite pictures of birds, and her grandmother was multi-talented in a great variety of arts and crafts. Lesley inherited the lot. She is passionate about our environment, plays harp with a group called Harpeggio, paints landscapes, practises yoga and meditation and has taught Tai Chi and Mindfulness.

BRENDA SLAVOFF

Brenda has written poetry, plays, short stories and novels. Many of them were based on the author's vivid dreams. One of her novels has been read in serial form on radio, two of her plays have been performed and she has published many short stories and poems - and all this between gardening, theatre, composing music, playing the harp and dancing the tango.

EDITH SPEERS

Edith Speers was born in Canada, grew up in Vancouver, and completed a B.Sc. (Hon. Biochem) at Simon Fraser University then emigrated to Australia where her poetry and short stories have won many literary awards and publications. Her work has been published in all the major Australian literary magazines and many anthologies, as well as several, Canadian and American journals. She is the author of three published collections of poetry. She has also published other Australian writers as proprietor of Esperance Press.

ADAM STOKELL

Adam Stokell's poems have appeared in various journals, including Cordite, Plumwood Mountain, Meanjin and Communion. His first poetry collection, *Peopling The Dirt Patch* (A Published Event, 2018), formed part of The People's Library exhibit at the Long Gallery, Salamanca. He lives in Hobart, Tasmania.

PETE STRATFORD

Born in New Zealand, I lived there until well into adulthood, and being in a rural community farming life has a significant influence on what I write. Later in life a change to working for over a decade as night care worker and counsellor at a shelter for homeless people, which along with interests in photography and the world of nature in general, gives me a rich source of material to draw from.

Mentally composing poems while working at repetitive activities, such as shearing sheep or fruit picking, kept my brain cells active, but was rarely recorded. However while on "grey nomad" trips around Australia, my wife made brief notes for me as we drove along so that I could expand on the ideas of an evening. Thus was the gestation of my first book of verses. Now with the self-publication of my third book of poems I continue writing for the pleasure of it.